AS FAR AS THE WEST
BLOOMS OF THE BITTERBRUSH
BOOK TWO

BARBARA A. CURTIS

Copyright © 2025 by Barbara A. Curtis

All rights reserved. No portion of this book may be reproduced or transmitted in any form or by any means—photocopied, shared electronically, scanned, stored in a retrieval system, or other—without the express permission of the publisher. Exceptions will be made for brief quotations used in critical reviews or articles promoting this work.

The characters and events in this fictional work are the product of the author's imagination. Any resemblance to actual people, living or dead, is coincidental.

All Scripture quotations are taken from the Holy Bible, King James Version.

Cover design by Wild Heart Books

ISBN: 978-1-963212-39-6

O magnify the Lord with me, and let us exalt his name together.

— PSALM 34:3

As far as the east is from the west, so far hath He removed our transgressions from us.

— PSALM 103:12

CHAPTER 1

CALDWELL, IDAHO
MAY 1920

Lizzie Morgan dumped the slop into the pig trough and jumped back as brown droplets splattered her apron.

"Come and get it!" She dodged the critters lumbering toward their last meal from her. Let her four younger brothers vie for this position. Once she got to Irma's Roadhouse in Boise, she'd be feeding patrons who possessed some manners and appreciated fine cooking. "You're safe from me, you nuisances. At least you won't be the ones sizzling in my skillet."

She tossed her braid that tamed her curls over her shoulder and spotted her father. People said she was a replica of him with her dark-brown hair, dark-brown eyes. Sturdy and plain were probably what they meant, nothing notable. A jab of homesickness clogged her throat already as her father limped to the barn to harness Jasper and Stardust for the trip to the depot. Was being saddled with that limp really worth trying to beat the truth out of a scoundrel twenty-three years ago? And on top of that, Papa even forgave the man. She shook her head.

"Papa—" But he'd already entered the barn. Now she wouldn't have a few minutes alone with him before she left the Double E, because...she couldn't follow him in there. Her feet were rooted in the mire along with the pigs. Even they grunted out their disgust for her.

Please... She rubbed the scar over her right eye. *Please help me to walk inside there. One last time.*

Lizzie left the pigs and managed a few steps toward the barn. Stopped. Listened. All was quiet inside—no kicking against the slats of the stalls, no shrieks from unbroken horses. Hopefully, every last one of them was out in the back field.

Kep Two, named after the original ranch dog, came up beside her and licked her hand. He always seemed to sense when someone in the family needed encouragement.

A few more steps and she stood at the threshold. The sharp smell of polished leather and even a low groan coming from inside the barn couldn't coax her farther into the darkness.

"Papa?" Lizzie dared to stick her head around the doorframe. And there he was, bent over, clinging to his saddle-making table. Kep looked from her to Papa, as if deciding who needed him most at the moment. But when Jasper nickered softly from his stall in a comforting sound for Papa, Kep remained by her side. "Papa."

He straightened and looked her way. Lizzie couldn't identify the expression that flitted through his dark eyes. Surprise? No, something more than that. Probably just shock that she actually stood at the entrance to the building.

"Sorry, Lizzie girl. I didn't hear you come out here." He walked slowly over to her at the doorway.

"Is your leg bothering you?"

"No worse than usual. But I expect a storm is brewing somewhere." He rubbed his knee.

"Don't you ever wish you could get your hands on the man who caused your injury, who did that to you?" Every time she heard the story, her emotions anchored deeper into her heart. Anger. Sadness.

"No, Lizzie girl. I did once, and it came to no good, I'll tell you that. Bitterness does no one any good. I had to learn to forgive as God has forgiven me. 'As far as the east is from the west, so far hath He removed our transgressions from us.'"

Words he often quoted from Great-grandmother Roberts's big black Bible that he read from to the family every night.

He drew her close. While she could smell the pig slop on her apron, he smelled like fresh air and leather. "I'll sure miss you, Lizzie. And if you ever find yourself lonesome there in the big city, step outside and listen. When you hear the birds singing in the sun and the frogs croaking on a moonlit night, think of us here. And know you're loved." He released his hug and ran a hand over her cheek, then cleared his throat. "How about you pick some bitterbrush flowers for your mama? Eliza will need a reminder of your smile once you're gone."

Lizzie clenched her teeth, nodded. Even managed to scrounge up a smile. That old bitterbrush out back—always a reminder of what she wasn't. The generations of women in Mama's line were known for being long like a white pine with bitterbrush blooming on top. She'd never be like Mama—the legendary Eliza Morgan, tall and stately, her hair as yellow as the spring blossoms. Lizzie resembled the bitterbrush in its other seasons—drab, sagebrush-like. She couldn't even redeem herself by following in her mother's footsteps as the Angel from the East, the renowned lady horse trainer. The horses didn't respond to Lizzie—except with thrashing hooves and razor teeth. There was only one chore she could do well with the Double E animals. Feeding the pigs.

"Sure, Papa." She left him in the barn and went to the edge of the yard behind the house and broke off an armful of bitterbrush branches. Though she'd never be courageous like Mama, if she could be like Papa, wise and kind, even forgiving, that should be enough.

The blooms wound their sweet aroma down to her soul. A scent of something floral and spicy and lemony and cinnamony all mingled together. The beauty of the blossoms did seem to offer a promise of hope, of God's provision, as Mama always said. A reminder of His goodness and faithfulness. That's what she'd need in Boise—her own bitterbrush of sorts. Something to remind her that God would go with her.

She headed into the house, and just as she finished arranging the bouquet, Mama entered the kitchen, her sky-blue eyes widening.

"Goodness!" Mama gathered Lizzie into her arms. "I'm going to miss you so much, sweet girl. Are you sure you want to go off and work in Boise?"

Nestled against her mother, no, she wasn't sure. It'd be so much easier staying with her family, even feeding those old pigs. But working in Boise meant she could contribute money —albeit from safely afar—to help keep the Double E in horses for Mama to train and Papa to make saddles for.

"I'm sure."

"Well—" Her mother freed Lizzie and crossed her arms. "If not for living above the roadhouse with Mrs. Farber, I doubt I could bear to let you go."

"Oh, Mama." Lizzie smiled. "You were twenty-one when you left New York and headed far out West for adventure—so I'm old enough. Almost."

"Adventure." Mama shook her head. "I never should have told you those stories."

"Then I wouldn't know how you and Papa met."

Mama laughed. "I don't wish any of those frightful times upon you. But you're right. How would I have met my dear Caleb otherwise?"

"Or saved the Double E."

"Lizzie..." Mama ran a hand along Lizzie's cheek. "This time it's different. It's simply a matter of sales being down. They'll pick up again, and we'll be fine."

"But it's both the horses and Papa's saddles. When I get to Boise, I can send back some mo—"

"No, dear. Thank you. But the ranch is not your responsibility."

"But Mama—"

"No. We're letting you go to Boise—under Mrs. Farber's watchful eye, mind you—so you can try your cooking out on city folk. Leave the Double E to your papa and me. This is our life. Now go get ready."

Within minutes, Lizzie donned her green chiffon dress with the flounce and wide rouched waistband. Even if she was overdressed for the roadhouse, she would arrive in confidence and style. Her Sunday lace-up walking boots would be easy on her feet as she served customers all day, and keeping her hair in its long braid down her back would be professional. With a smile, she set her brown cloche hat with a dark-green ribbon on her head.

She lugged her carpetbag down the stairs and headed for the kitchen, about to swing open the door when an almost inaudible sound stopped her. Not the loud jabbering of her brothers—but the hushed tone of secrets. And then—

"...warn Lizzie?" Mama's voice cracked.

Lizzie halted. Listening in on others was rude. Just plain rude. Wasn't that what Mama had taught her?

Still, she edged closer to the door and pressed her ear next to the casing.

"No, Eliza." Papa's voice carried better. "I don't think we should even mention it to her. She's too adventurous as it is. I don't want her anywhere near that man."

"But he lives in Boise. What if he discovers she's there? What if—"

"He won't. It's a big place with so many people. He couldn't possibly know she'd be there, much less where. For now, I think we should leave things alone. We don't know for sure that Benton Calloway even has anything to do with this."

Benton Calloway? Lizzie inhaled, almost too loudly. Did her parents really suspect that he might be the cause of the Double E's troubles again? Twenty-three years later? Could be... Because of Papa, Mr. Calloway had landed in prison. What if Benton Calloway, now apparently a free man, still wanted revenge? What if crippling Papa wasn't enough, or he was set to come after Mama again?

"Let's—" The outside door banged, and Papa's voice came through the crack in his normal volume. "Yes, Isaac?"

Oh, if Lizzie could grab the oldest of her brothers and shake him. Though at sixteen, he surely wouldn't stand for that. She pushed the kitchen door open and stepped inside, ignoring the consternation in her mother's stare.

"Well." Mama clapped her hands like the schoolmarm she used to be. "Let's get going before Lizzie misses her train. Isaac, please round up Winston and Zephaniah and tell them to head out to the wagon. And where's Sammy? Find him and make sure he stays in the wagon too."

Now they probably would be late, as the little five-year-old had more hiding places than Kep had for bones.

"Come now, Caleb, Lizzie."

A truck was what this ranch needed, something modern and fast. Something easier on Papa's leg than climbing in and out of the old wagon. And Lizzie aimed to make sure he got one.

She followed her parents as they headed outdoors but turned back for a final look at the kitchen where she'd learned to cook and bake. Of what was familiar to her. Mama wasn't the only one who'd be needing a smile in a few hours. Or a reminder of God's hope and provision.

Lizzie snatched a twig of yellow flowers from the bitterbrush bouquet and tucked it under the ribbon on her hat. She was ready to embark on an adventure in Boise, all right. And not just in her new position at Irma's Roadhouse.

If Papa wouldn't track down Benton Calloway to get the truth out of him and to save the Double E, then she would.

~

Josiah Calloway laid down his pencil and rubbed his calf. Without looking out the second-story Boise office window, he knew rain was coming, sure as the cramp creeping up his left leg. The only good thing about being an accountant was the salary that covered the meals and rent on his small room at Mrs. McPhearson's boardinghouse. And the solitude, as the owner rarely came into this office, preferring to work from the larger main office across town. And sometimes the drudgery even kept his memories at bay.

The numbers jumbled on the page about as well as the accounting of his life balanced. He hadn't been able to protect the children and their families in a little French village in the Great War, couldn't earn enough to repay everyone his father had cheated, and couldn't run a ranch, let alone afford one. Of course, the Good Book was right. *Pride goeth before destruction, and an haughty spirit before a fall.* He again rubbed the leg that proved it.

He poised his pencil over the ledger columns. Two years since the war, and yet these numbers had no end.

Bullets whizzing past each head

The poem started in his head, then flowed into the ledger's margins.

> Leave with all a sense of dread.
> But what pierced my heart, my soul

He turned his pencil upside down and erased the words. He couldn't write the next line. If Victoria's screams turned into words, they'd no longer be just a memory. But it was too late. Josiah clamped his hands over his ears as the child's cries echoed as loudly as the moment the soldiers had burst into her village square, the shrieks piercing his very soul. He coughed as memories, heavy like smoke, sucked the air out of the office. This time, he even smelled the burning shack. The screams were so close, he was sure he could look out the window and see Victoria running.

Josiah walked to the window to clear his head from this living nightmare. But it was right down there on the street. Had war come to Boise? Flames shot like arrows from the roof of Irma's Roadhouse up into the sky. As fast as he could, he hobbled down the stairs, his war injury noticeable usually only on steps or when he was exhausted.

Out on the street, people shoved him aside as they fled. Josiah ducked into an alcove, but even there, the heat of the flames seeped through his suit coat. He took a step deeper into the recess and bumped against something. Someone. A woman huddled in the corner, head bowed. Sobbing.

"Ma'am?" Josiah placed a hand on the woman's shoulder. She raised her head. "Mrs. Farber!" He barely recognized the German woman beneath the soot striping her face. "What happened?"

Irma Farber stared at him, as if horror didn't translate into English.

"Can you tell me what happened?" He shed his jacket and wrapped it around her.

Though her lips moved, no words emerged. Josiah took one of her hands in his, rubbing it until her eyes focused on him.

"The helper man––he smoke in kitchen––burn my place down!"

Josiah breathed in a lungful of smoke. "Where will you go?"

She held out empty hands. "I have no place. No money. No anything."

Surely, she must have friends she could stay with. Or family. She'd been feeding people in the neighborhood for years, long before people knew or even cared that she was German. And she was still well loved now. "Let me help you get somewhere safe and with people you know."

She shook her head. "*Nein.*" She said some more words in German, then shook her head again. "Nein."

"Do you have friends you can stay with?"

"No. In Nampa, I have friends I visit. A family. But not my family."

"How about your family, then?" Though he'd eaten occasionally at Irma's Roadhouse, he'd never stopped to ask her about her life, her own family.

"Far away. My sister only."

"Where does she live?"

"She live in California."

"Then I'll take you to the depot and buy you a ticket so you can get to Nampa, and your friends there can help you get on a train to California. Would you like that?" He tugged his grocery money from his pocket and handed it to her for necessities on her journey. "We'll stop by my room to pack you some food and get you a coat." And more money from his envelope so he could pay his father's debt to her in full now, though it would delay his repayments to the others. Plus, train ticket money out to California.

Mrs. Farber cupped his cheeks in her hands. "May the good Lord bless you, Josiah Calloway. You are good man."

Her words seeped into his soul like a balm over the accusation already embedded there.

"You're about as valuable as a pig wallowing in its mire."

Twenty minutes later, minus his overcoat and the apple and cinnamon roll he'd saved from this morning, Josiah hurried Mrs. Farber through the Boise streets. She was a refugee now, like those he'd boarded trains with during the Great War. His coat swallowed her frail frame, his scarf swathing her head like a shield against further pain.

As they approached the depot, the inbound train on the Caldwell–Boise interurban loop was rolling to a stop. Mrs. Farber pulled against him, heading to the bench alongside the depot.

She shook his arm. "I need sit here."

"Mrs. Farber, please come inside with me." Josiah urged her along gently. "We must purchase your ticket."

She looked at the bench one more time, then tightened her grip on his arm and resumed shuffling, head down, alongside him. By the time they returned outside, one final passenger was disembarking the train. The young lady's hat splashed a yellow spray of hope into the sooty air with a jaunty bitterbrush sticking out on top. Yet her countenance contradicted her hat's joy, as did her worn brown coat and button-up walking boots. She clutched her carpetbag as if fearful someone would snatch it from her while she stood staring at a scrap of paper in her hand.

The conductor approached her, and with a grasp of her elbow, propelled her out of the way of approaching passengers. "All aboard!"

Josiah drew Mrs. Farber toward the short line of people waiting to board the train, but he checked over his shoulder. The lady had moved beneath the wide eaves of the depot and taken a seat on the bench. With her back against the sandstone wall, she glanced around as if searching for someone. Yet no one stepped toward her.

If she needed aid or directions, perhaps he might offer assistance.

"Mrs. Farber, I'll be right back. You stay here in line." He released her arm and took a step toward the young lady with the chocolate-colored braid. Her eyes, as dark as his childhood seal-brown horse—Brownie—met his, then she looked down at her lap.

"All aboard!"

Josiah turned back to Mrs. Farber and took hold of her arm again. She was his priority, but once she was safely on the train, he could help the younger traveler.

"May I help her on board?" Josiah asked the conductor.

"Hurry up." He waved his pocket watch in the air.

Josiah assisted Mrs. Farber onto the train and situated her into a window seat. "May God go with you and grant you safety and peace."

She cupped Josiah's face once more. "Yes, you very good man, Josiah Calloway."

The conductor glared at him. "Now go, if you don't have your own ticket."

Josiah clambered down from the train and headed to the bench where the girl with the yellow bloom had been seated. Not seeing her, he poked his head inside the station. She was gone. Maybe someone had come to meet her, after all.

He stepped back outside as the interurban lurched forward into the billowing smoke from the roadhouse.

"God bless you, Mrs. Farber!" He waved until he could no longer see the train windows. "Lord, please be with both of these women—Mrs. Farber and that lady traveling alone." Surely, she was safe. Anyone who would stick a wild desert-like flower in her hat must have spunk and her wits about her.

Once the car was gone, Josiah turned to head back to the accounting office. As he stepped across the tracks, he spotted a splash of yellow covered in dirt.

He bent over and picked up a stick of bitterbrush, its flowers now crushed.

CHAPTER 2

*L*izzie gritted her teeth as she trudged in the direction she and her parents had walked three weeks ago with Mrs. Farber. That day, the city had been alive, people everywhere, horses and automobiles vying for space on the roads, pedestrians and bicyclists trying to stay out of the way. She had tried to memorize the route they took but soon gave up as she forgot to pay attention whenever a new sight caught her eye.

And now, after only a block from the depot, she'd already lost her bearings. But she couldn't—wouldn't—crumple alongside the street and weep. Even though she was as downhearted as that poor bent-over lady being escorted onto the train—by her grandson, perhaps?—looked.

Looking up at the smoke clouds, she bumped into someone. "Watch it." A man in a patched-up coat all but snarled at her.

"I beg your pardon, sir. I'm so sorry."

"Keep your eyes on the road. There's no pie up there in them clouds."

"Yes. No, of course." She scurried past the man, glad to be out of his way.

Lizzie adjusted her hat. Surely, she looked as wilted as her bitterbrush must be by now. Where had she even lost it? It was supposed to have been a reminder that God was watching over her, maybe even willing to instill some courage into her. But now it was gone, along with her hope of ever being as brave as her mother.

What kind of legacy would she leave to her family? Nothing to match that of Great-grandmother Elizabeth Rose Roberts, who had founded the Double E along with Great-grandfather Elliott. Most certainly not like Mama, Elizabeth Rose Roberts Morgan, who had saved the ranch from ruin by becoming a horse trainer. No. She, the third Elizabeth Rose of the family, would be the one to cause the Double E to fold up. For she was not the assistant horse trainer that Mama needed, preferring to stay in the kitchen and even feeding the pigs over the horses. And the boys were still too young to take on that responsibility, though Isaac was yammering to try. So too much fell to Mama and Papa.

But now that she was here, what could she do other than strike out on her own and hunt for Mrs. Farber? She'd promised to be waiting at the depot. Surely, she hadn't forgotten Lizzie. Maybe the roadhouse had gotten busy or a server hadn't shown up and now Mrs. Farber couldn't get away. So if Lizzie could find her way back to Irma's Roadhouse, she'd save Mrs. Farber the trip altogether.

Even the air of three weeks ago—then a mix of perfume, sweat, and baking bread—was snuffed out by this terrible smoke that seemed to consume the city. This stench that lodged in Lizzie's lungs made even the smell of pig slop preferable.

A churning pillar loomed over the street in the direction she reckoned the roadhouse to be. She put a handkerchief over her nose as a barrier to the smoldering wood. Something horrible must have happened. Perhaps there were now neighbors who were homeless. That must be why Mrs. Farber hadn't come to the depot—she was cooking for these families, offering baths to cleanse their skin and to soak some peace into their souls.

Lizzie quickened her pace, eager to assist with supper preparations. And hopefully be offered some of it to eat as well.

"Miss!"

Lizzie looked up. A burly policeman, arms crossed, blocked her path.

"You can't go any farther. This area is closed."

"I'm on my way to work, sir."

"Where?"

"Irma's Roadhouse."

The officer uncrossed his arms. "Haven't you heard?"

"Heard what? I'm new to town."

"Irma Farber's roadhouse is gone. And so is she."

"No!" Lizzie covered her face with her hands. Not kind, God-fearing Mrs. Farber. "How can she be gone?" Just three weeks ago on her family's visit to Boise, Mrs. Farber had been bustling about, singing, smiling. Sneaking shortbread cookies to Lizzie's brothers with a wink at Mama.

A woman standing nearby with a group of ladies stepped over and encircled an arm around Lizzie's shoulders. "No, no, dear, not deceased." She glared at the policeman. "She escaped the fire. Heard tell she's headed out West to her sister's to be with her only family. There's nothing here to stay for." She gestured at the charcoaled ruins and smoke-filled sky with her free hand.

"You mean…she's alive? Thank You, Lord!"

The women stared at Lizzie—probably at her too-loud praise of God's goodness—and moved their huddle away from her.

Lizzie stared at the smoldering rubble, all that was left of

15

Mrs. Farber's life in Boise. Had she been injured or had time to grab anything from her rooms upstairs? Sentimental trinkets or even her pocketbook? Clothes? Money? Thank the Lord indeed that her new friend was safe.

But in the midst of her thanksgiving, Lizzie's own problems crashed down on her. She no longer had a job. And no place to live. But returning to Caldwell was not an option. She had come to Boise to not only get away from the ranch but also to help Mama and Papa save it. So she'd find a way to stay in Boise and fulfill her purpose. The last thing she was about to do was go running home as a failure on her first day on her own.

Mrs. Farber had been the only person she knew in the whole city, and without her, Lizzie was forsaken in Boise. Homeless. Maybe like that gruff-speaking man. If she didn't come up with a plan, was that what would become of her too?

Perhaps that policeman could help her figure out what to do. She took a step toward him.

"Everyone!" The officer waved his arms at the crowd of onlookers. "Disperse. Let the firefighters do their job. Off with all of you." As the crowd slowly disbanded in all directions, Lizzie took another step toward him. His eyes riveted on her. "Miss, I said everyone."

"But—"

He crossed his arms again. "That includes you."

"Yes, officer." She could feel his eyes still on her as she turned and walked away, each step taking her farther away from Mrs. Farber's roadhouse, the only establishment in the city she knew.

Oh, why had she been so determined to leave home? Even the thought of feeding those old pigs in the safety and comfort of the Double E was better than wandering these streets alone. And once nighttime approached—

That was enough to make her turn around. Maybe with the crowd gone the policeman would help her now. But he was still standing there, arms crossed, eyes on her. A frown anchored on his face.

She turned back and continued on, on this unknown road to an unknown destination. And when she finally looked around her, she was alone on the sidewalk, with no one else headed this direction. And though the shadows of evening hadn't yet started creeping in, she had to find shelter for the night.

Maybe she needed to start over again back at Mrs. Farber's burnt roadhouse and try a different direction. As so far, she hadn't passed a single inn.

~

Josiah was tempted to work longer this evening than necessary. Even the hot meal provided by Mrs. McPhearson at the boardinghouse wasn't enough to entice him to hurry home. Because to get there, he'd have to push away from his desk and climb down the stairs. Again. That extra trip down earlier had ensured there'd be no relief for his leg for the rest of the day, probably even the night.

But if he didn't leave soon, he'd miss supper altogether, if he hadn't already. He took a deep breath, then scooted back his chair and stood. Thankfully, no one was around to hear his muffled groan. Maybe if on the way down he thought about something he'd like to do, the trek would be more bearable. The only topic that came to mind, though, was the old longing to own a ranch. The dream lodged in his thoughts like a burr that wouldn't let loose. But each stair step was a reminder that he'd probably not even be able to swing up onto a horse, much less get down. And how was he to run a ranch from the ground?

Maybe he could raise something other than cows or horses, like sheep. Or pigs. They were decent animals, though outcasts. Maybe he had more in common with them than he'd thought.

But of course, finances were a problem. Paying back those his father had cheated—at least the ones he knew about after finding a few names and amounts among his father's possessions the last time he'd been arrested—had quickly depleted his savings. And though he was glad to pay for a train ticket for Mrs. Farber to get to her sister's, it had wiped out a chunk of the largest debt he'd been working to repay in full.

But with pigs, he wouldn't need much acreage, nor as much money to start a farm.

Thinking about the pigs got him down the stairs without dwelling too much on the pain. He leaned against the doorframe at the bottom to catch his breath. The smoke from the fire still covered the street—perhaps the entire city—like a canopy. Not an evening to be out and about, even though the sun wouldn't set until close to nine. But vandals were likely already lurking in the shadows, waiting to visit the rubble of the roadhouse in the dark. Hoping to glean some treasures from poor Mrs. Farber's misfortune.

A man stumbling along the sidewalk bumped into Josiah.

"'Scuze me." The man clutched an open bottle against his chest, and the smell of whiskey saturated him. "You got some money to spare for a poor soul? I be needin' somethin' to eat." He waved a hand at the remains of the roadhouse. "Ain't nowhere to go anymore in this neighborhood to get good scraps."

Josiah shook his head. "It'd be best if you go on home for the night."

The man stared at him. "Home. Ain't got no home. Where's your home?"

"I just live in a boardinghouse. I'm sorry I can't help you." Perhaps if he'd had his own place, he could find something for the man to eat, but he couldn't very well bring him to Mrs. McPhearson's doorstep and expect her to feed him.

But the man wasn't waiting around for Josiah to offer a solution. He staggered down the street toward a lone figure out walking, a dark braid swinging across her back.

Foolish woman. What respectable lady would be strolling alone on this street in this part of the city?

Out of the shadow of a store, another man stepped in front of the drunk. Even from here, Josiah could see tangled hair and an unshaven face. This man looked between the drunk and the woman, appearing to weigh who to bother first.

"Be on your way, man." The long-haired man glared at the drunk until he ambled down the road, bottle still in hand. Then the newcomer hurried toward the woman. "Ma'am, hold up!"

Don't turn around! But before Josiah could turn the thought into a shout, she turned.

The lady from the depot.

"No," he whispered into the smoky air. Was she in trouble? What other reason could she be out here alone on these streets after every business was closed for the night?

In another two strides, the man reached her, his tangled hair fluffing in the evening wind. "Good evening, miss."

Josiah hurried to catch up, gritting his teeth with each landing on his left leg.

The woman backed away, but the man gripped her around her upper arm, stopping her retreat.

"I said, 'good evening.' Where's your manners?"

"I—"

"It's not safe for a purty young lass like you to be out alone with night comin' on. Where you going?" He slid his hand down to her wrist. "I'll escort you."

The girl jerked her arm, but the man seemed to clasp it harder.

"You've got spunk." His laugh pulsated into the air.

Finally, Josiah reached them. "Leave the lady alone." He grabbed the rowdy's shoulder and spun him around. That was enough to loosen the man's grip. The woman stumbled against a building and scraped her hand down the bricks as she caught herself, then took off running down an alley.

The ruffian swung, throwing Josiah off balance. Josiah wasn't a fighter—he'd learned early on from his mother about his father's fights and that it didn't pay. But she'd also taught him to protect women and anyone being accosted.

He held up his hands. "Easy, sir. Let's just go our separate ways before a constable on patrol strolls this block, shall we?"

The man glared at Josiah, then grunted. "I was just offerin' to escort the lady home."

"I think she'll manage without either of us, don't you?"

He looked in the direction of the alley. "S'pose so." He finally turned and headed in the direction the drunk had gone.

At least that hooligan had been distracted long enough that the young lady was able to escape. But was she safe? The silent street was foreboding in its emptiness. Didn't the lady know better than to roam a city of over twenty thousand people after business hours? And unescorted? Or what if she had no place to go?

A young woman arriving alone in Boise, clutching her carpetbag as though she wasn't used to traveling, and sporting a bright yellow flower did not speak of a woman accustomed to strolling deserted streets. Whatever she was doing out here alone, if she needed help, he'd gladly miss supper.

Once the man was out of sight, Josiah stepped into the alley himself. "Miss?" he called softly, as he'd learned to do with Brownie. Gentle, easy, no sudden moves, and a quiet voice. "It's safe. You can come out now if you're hiding."

But why should she come out for another stranger?

"My name's Josiah. I want to see if you need any help."

The silence of the gloomy alley was all that answered him. He went farther into the alleyway, checking behind garbage cans and in each doorway. But all was still. He exited at the other end and looked out on the street from there. A few closed businesses were all he saw. No homes with lights on that she could have gone to for help. Had she kept going past here?

"Miss?" he called out again. She had to be hiding. "Do you need help?"

He listened closely for any movement, for any sound of breathing. "Please, miss. I mean you no harm. I just want to make sure you're safe for the night."

Josiah's leg hurt more now that the rain must be getting closer. Overhead, the smoke-filled sky turned angry with storm clouds, and thunder sounded in the distance. But he kept going, kept calling. And still, there was no sign or sound of her. She had completely disappeared.

Lord, please keep her safe.

He could hardly blame her for not coming out even if she could hear him. Because due to his own actions, she most likely pegged him a ruffian as well.

Josiah finally gave up his search and with a prayer for her still in his heart, headed to the boardinghouse. The men were scraping their plates of the last bites of apple pie when he walked in.

"Well, there you are." Mrs. McPhearson set down a pile of dirty dishes and placed her hands on her generous hips and looked him up and down, certainly noticing his disheveled clothes. "You're a sight. But you're lucky I saved you a plate of food in the oven. And"—she winked—"a piece of pie." She reloaded her arms with the dishes and bustled into the kitchen.

"Looks to me like Straight and Narrow's been fighting." Hugh Griffin nudged the man next to him with his muscled arm. Tall, blond, impeccably dressed, Hugh had everything—except manners. "Did you forget to turn the other cheek?"

"He probably ducked." Markos, the slim man next to Hugh, laughed.

"Let's leave him to his apple pie. Though he shouldn't go

21

expecting a reward for his sinning." Hugh guffawed and stood, motioning for the lingering men to follow him from the dining room.

One of these days—

"Never you mind them, Josiah." Mrs. McPhearson, returning to the room with a plate of food and a slice of pie, had apparently heard every word. "My guess is that you were protecting or defending someone else. Is that right?"

Josiah shrugged. How he'd love to be as gallant as Mrs. McPhearson always made him out to be. But he had no idea if the young lady was safe. All he'd done was given her a moment to run.

"Thank you for saving supper for me."

"Pshaw. That's what you're paying your rent every month for, isn't it?" But she winked at him as she made another trip out to the kitchen with a stack of dishes.

After Josiah finished his supper and pie, he trudged up to his room and locked the door. He extracted two books from his secret hiding spot. First, he looked at the ledger. After giving money to Mrs. Farber, there was nothing left to put against the debt. And wouldn't be for a while. He closed the ledger and opened his poetry book.

He closed his eyes a few moments in thought before taking pen to paper.

> Gone
> One gone from town, from hopes and dreams
> Destruction left behind amid the screams.
> One gone down the street, lost in the night
> Away from men too prone to fight.
> Both gone.
> Just a bitterbrush bloom left behind,
> Crushed underfoot.

*L*izzie remained hidden behind the back of one of the shops, still not daring to move. Or scream, not even when a rat scurried by on its way to feed on garbage just feet from her. The minutes ticked by—twenty? An hour?

"'The Lord is my light and my salvation; whom shall I fear? The Lord is the strength of my life; of whom shall I be afraid?'" Barely a sound came out as she recited the psalm in a whisper. Who had known back when she'd memorized it that she'd need it as she did tonight?

She hadn't waited to find out who won the fight, just grabbed her chance to run down the shadowed alley. Little light had seeped between the buildings, barely illuminating the trash she had to dodge. She'd come out to a side street where the few shops were dark, and the longer she waited, the closer nightfall would be. And then the man who had miraculously appeared was calling for her. Checking if she was safe. Asking if she needed help.

Yes, she needed so much. But not from a stranger at night when she was alone in this city.

"Oh, Lord." She added the prayer in that faint whisper, but maybe even that was too loud. *Please help. Please provide.*

Who else was looking for her? The drunk? The tangled-hair man? Anyone else who might come along at this hour?

She stayed put until the night wind picked up, swirling debris and dirt around her and its tendrils of icy cold down her neck. Surely, it was going to pour any moment. She needed some kind of shelter. And something to eat.

Lord, please show Your faithfulness.

Slowly, she stood and edged out to the front of the shop. Lizzie looked up and down the street for someplace she could go for help. Like a sweet elderly couple or a kindly woman who might harbor her for the night. Maybe if she just went a little farther. But even as the businesses thinned out, she came to no houses with inviting lights shining in the windows. Only neighs and snorts coming from a stable punctured the darkness.

Please, no, Lord!

But what could she do? Stay alone, unprotected all night long on the street in the cold? Or go into the horse barn out of the wind and coming rain?

Familiar smells and sounds of horses wafted onto the street, reminding her of home. Of Papa working out in the barn, settling the horses. Maybe these also would sleep for the night and she could find a safe corner or a hay loft away from them.

Footsteps slapped along the road, coming closer, and there remained no choice. With a deep breath and a prayer, Lizzie tried the door. Oh, thankfully, it was unlocked. She inched it open to lessen any creaks, but all was quiet. She slipped through and closed it just as quietly.

She stood with her back against the door, letting her eyes adjust to the dark interior. Where could she go now that she was inside?

Horses rustled against the boards of their stalls, on alert at the entrance of a stranger. From a shaft of light coming from a streetlight, she could make out the closest stall. Lizzie took a step closer and read the nameplate. *Rebel.* Only a wooden door separated the big dark horse from her. He thrust his head over the barrier, and Lizzie jumped back. Surely, he was aptly named.

Then he emitted a low, soft nicker, much like Jasper's murmur of compassion for her father. He stared at her with large eyes and bobbed his head.

"Rebel. How did you get that name?" She raised a hand, then lowered it as she realized she'd almost petted the animal. "Are you in the wrong place too?"

Lizzie took a deep breath of horse sweat and polished leather. It smelled almost of home, of Papa.

She pictured him as he came out of the barn last week whistling a tune. She'd been sitting outside the double doors, waiting for him.

"Have you ever been afraid, Papa?"

His eyes had softened as though he understood her fear of leaving the Double E, of living in Boise away from everyone and everything she knew, even her fear of horses.

"Fear's brought me down way too many times. But now when I'm afraid, I recall what God told Isaiah the prophet. 'For I the Lord thy God will hold thy right hand, saying unto thee, Fear not; I will help thee.' If God Himself is holding onto me and promising His help, what more do I need?" He'd pulled her up by the hand and hugged her. "He'll hold you, too, Lizzie girl."

Lizzie stared down at her hand now. "Are you really holding me, God? Do You see me?"

Rebel gave another low nicker. Yes, even though she was standing in a smelly stable filled with huge horses, no one had followed her in here. None of them were making a ruckus, kicking at their stalls. She was out of the wind, and there surely were horse blankets she could wrap up in. And there was a gentleness about Rebel so that her heart had quit thudding so loudly in terror.

If she hid in the loft, she'd be safe for the night. She found two thick blankets, and as she scrambled up the ladder into the loft, Rebel neighed after her. Like a good night call.

Just as Lizzie settled into a mound of hay, the skies opened and rain pelted the roof. But she was safe and dry inside.

"Thank You, God." She closed her fingers against her palm. Not in a fist, but like she was holding hands. With God.

She could do this. For one night.

CHAPTER 3

*I*nstead of waking up to the smell of bacon grease and Mama's scrambled eggs, Lizzie woke up to the smell of horse barn. Sweat, hay, and manure. Not the sweet aromas from Mama's kitchen she loved, but still a pleasant reminder of home. Of Papa and the boys, who were probably already outdoors taking care of the ranch animals.

She peeked over the edge of the loft down at the horses. All was quiet in the stable. Apparently, no one had been in yet to feed them. So she'd better hurry and get out of here before someone did. Lizzie climbed down from the loft and plucked stray pieces of hay from her wrinkled dress. And even standing in the stable with two rows of horses quietly watching her from their stalls, she was grateful for this safe haven through the night.

A soft nicker turned her to the dark-brown horse staring at her.

"Rebel, good morning." He stuck his big head toward her, his eyes gentle, belying his size.

"Who are you, and what are you doing here?" A booming

voice at the door broke the solitude and peacefulness of the morning.

Lizzie whirled and shrunk at the sight of a brawny man in overalls staring at her, pitchfork in hand.

"I-I needed a place to sleep, and I...I can pay you." She opened her carpetbag and dug out some coins.

The man continued to hold the pitchfork upraised.

"I was supposed to work at Irma's Roadhouse—Mrs. Farber's roadhouse..." Lizzie babbled on when the man still said nothing. But maybe he'd take heart and not send her running with him waving the pitchfork behind her. "But it's gone—burned down—and I didn't have a place to go, and then three men—"

The man leaned the pitchfork against a wall. "Naw," he said, gesturing to her outstretched hand holding the coins, "no need. Come up to the house, and the missus will feed you."

Lizzie stared at him now.

"Don't dally—get a move on before someone else eats all the eggs up." He grinned and held out an apple to Rebel. "On second thought, here, miss, you take it. I don't think Rebel will mind sharing."

"Thank you, sir." Lizzie stuck the shiny apple in the pocket of her dress. Maybe one day, she could replace the apple Rebel didn't seem to mind surrendering to her.

The man held out a hand. "Name's O'Shannon. Conor O'Shannon."

Lizzie grabbed his hand and shook it. "Thank you, Mr. O'Shannon. I'm Lizzie. Lizzie Morgan."

"Glad to meet you, Lizzie Morgan. Now follow me." He led the way to the house next door.

"Glory be, Conor O'Shannon, who do you have here?" A smiling red-haired woman ushered them inside.

"Molly, dear, this here is Miz Lizzie Morgan. She was sleeping in the barn overnight."

"In the barn?" Molly exchanged a look with her husband, then grabbed Lizzie by both arms. "Look at ye, child. Come in and sit down. You must need something to eat. Ain't nothing in the barn to feed you. The eggs are still steaming."

And oh the heavenly scent of them. And toast and jam already sitting on the table.

Lizzie didn't have the willpower to even try to refuse their kindness. "I don't have anything to offer you, though." Unless Mrs. O'Shannon would be willing to accept her coins.

"Oh, nonsense. You wash up right over there while I set out another plate. And would ye like a cup of coffee?"

"Yes, thank you." Not that Lizzie often drank it, but the smell of perked coffee in the air was another reminder of home. Perhaps Mama was taking a cup out to Papa at the barn even now. And anything hot would be welcomed to warm her insides. "I would love a cup, Mrs. O'Shannon."

"None of that, now. It's Molly and Conor."

"Thank you, Molly."

Just washing the grime of traveling off and the smoke that surely clung to her hair and clothes revived Lizzie for the day ahead. A day where she must find a job and proper lodging.

After all three of them were seated, Conor said a prayer for the hearty bounty they were about to eat. And Lizzie certainly did enjoy the food he'd just prayed over.

"So what brings you to our barn overnight, if I might be askin'?" Molly poured Lizzie a glass of milk in addition to the coffee as she talked. "Straight from our cow," she said with a wink.

"Our Lizzie here came to work at Irma's Roadhouse." Conor took over before Lizzie could form an answer.

"Oh, sweet girl! So, of course, you're jobless as well as homeless. Did you see Mrs. Farber? Do you know what happened?"

"No," Lizzie said. "When I arrived at the depot, the air was already filled with smoke and soot, and Mrs. Farber wasn't there to greet me. I found my way to her roadhouse, but—"

"'Twas gone." Molly shook her head. "Such a shame. Such a good woman Mrs. Farber is."

"Someone in the crowd by the roadhouse told me she had escaped the fire and was heading farther out West to be with her sister. But she was already gone when I got there."

"I'm mighty glad she has someone. And how about you? Do you have family?"

"Yes, ma'am. I'm from Caldwell and came to Boise to work and earn money to send home. Up until now, I lived with my parents and four younger brothers."

"So will you be returning to Caldwell now that you have no job?"

Returning? Not until she'd done her part in helping to save the Double E. And finding the man responsible for its troubles —Benton Calloway. "No. I intend to find a job—and a place to live. Hopefully today. Might you know of another roadhouse or someone looking for help?"

Conor and Molly looked at each other, then shook their heads.

"I'm sorry, lass," Conor said, "but Irma's was the only one we know of. I could use some help at the livery if you want to muck out the stalls and—"

Molly swatted at him. "Conor O'Shannon, that's no task for Lizzie here." She grinned at Lizzie. "But we'll keep our eyes out for a proper job for you."

Lizzie held in her sigh of relief that Molly had rescued her from working around the horses. "Thank you so much for your hospitality this morning, Molly. And for the lodging last night, Conor."

"'Tis our pleasure." Molly spoke, and Conor echoed her words simply with a nod. "Now, we have no proper room to offer, but we will always have food and a welcome for you.

29

Always. And anytime you need help, you just find yourself back over here."

"And should you lose your way," Conor added, "just ask for Conor O'Shannon. Everyone knows where my livery stable is."

"I cannot thank you both enough." Lizzie looked from one to the other. "You indeed are angels unawares, just like Mama and Papa talk about."

"Why, we're the ones blessed." Molly placed her hands over her chest. "You've brought sunlight right into our hearts."

"I'll say goodbye to Rebel for ye, lass." Conor winked. "Seems to me ye've made a friend of him."

"Please tell him I'll repay him his apple one day." But if that was a promise she was going to be able to keep, she'd better get started looking for a job. She gulped the last of her milk and stood. As was her chore at home, she stacked the plates and started on the cups.

"Gracious, girl." Molly took the cups from Lizzie's hands. "You're quick as a wink. Thank ye, but I'll finish up and walk you to the door. Oh, wait. Mrs. Farmdale over at the market a few blocks from here is always complaining how busy she is and how she needs someone with younger legs. You might try her. She's a mite crotchety, though, so you'd have to not mind listening to her aches and pains. And then there's always the Owyhee Hotel. Surely, they'd be a-looking for help."

"Oh, thank you." Lizzie placed her hat atop her head and stepped into the morning sunshine. She didn't even need the reminder of her bitterbrush bloom to know God was watching out for her.

She headed down the street in the direction the O'Shannons pointed her to for Mrs. Farmdale's market. In the daylight, this neighborhood she'd run through last night was so different from the part of Boise she'd seen when visiting Mrs. Farber's roadhouse. Carriages still shared the road here with motor cars, and people walking were few and far between on the sidewalks.

She found the market with no problem—at least, the faded sign over the door said *Farmdale Market*. But with a crack in the front window and more white paint missing than on the clapboards, was it still in business? Mrs. Farmdale certainly must need help desperately. Well, Lizzie knew how to wield a paintbrush and could climb a ladder if items needed to be stocked up high.

She opened the door. Inside, a single lightbulb lit the drab room.

A voice came from the shadows in the direction of the counter. "Can I help you?"

"Yes. I'm looking for Mrs. Farmdale."

"What do ya want?"

"Might that be you?"

"Yeah. What do you want?"

"I-I—Conor and Molly O'Shannon said you might need some help."

"Help with what? I've been running this place for forty years and ain't had no help."

"Oh. My name is Lizzie Morgan, and I'm looking for a job and wondered if there was something I could do here—"

"Look around you. Does it look like I have money to hire anyone?"

"No, ma'am. I just thought—"

"I ain't hiring."

"Yes." Lizzie took a step backward. "Thank you, ma'am." She turned and scurried back out, thankful that Mrs. Farmdale wasn't hiring.

But the six-story Owyhee Hotel, her next stop, was a different story. Its opulence and roof garden with a view of the foothills was known even in Caldwell.

When she stepped inside, she gawked at the columns reaching from the lobby all the way up to the second floor, above the the ornate balcony. The plush furniture was the most elegant she'd ever seen. How she'd love to sit on one of the upholstered sofas. But she dared not with her rumpled dress from sleeping in the hay.

She approached the front desk where the man behind the counter eyed her up and down over his spectacles. "How may I help you?"

"My name is Elizabeth Rose Morgan, and I'd like to apply for a job." Surely, a place like this had the money to hire workers. "I have experience in the kitchen and in cleaning and would be happy in either position."

"I'm sorry. We have no openings currently. We do, however, have quite a long waiting list for people wanting to work here. Would you care to add your name to it?"

"Oh. I was hoping for something where I could start right away."

"I'm sorry. There is nothing."

"Thank you." Now what? Maybe she'd have better success back closer to the roadhouse, where people knew Mrs. Farber and might be willing to give Lizzie a chance based on the fact that Mrs. Farber had wanted her.

She worked her way closer to the area of Mrs. Farber's restaurant, easily found by following the lingering smoke like a guiding star. Or the pillar of cloud the Israelites had followed on their exodus, led by God.

Up and down the streets she went, inquiring as to open positions. But no one was hiring today. No one was looking for her set of skills—cooking, cleaning, watching young children. Feeding pigs.

She sank onto a bench just vacated by a homeless-looking man. If she didn't find something by nighttime, she'd be just like him. Or back in the stable again.

Lizzie looked up once more at her pillar of cloud. If only God could use it to lead her. But it hadn't moved beyond this bench. And what a preposterous thought that was—that God would want her right here.

~

*J*osiah made another entry into the ledger and erased it. The same as he'd done with the last two. Why couldn't he keep his mind on his work today?

He knew exactly why. Walking past Mrs. Farber's burned-down roadhouse, smelling the scent of destruction still in the air… Wondering about the bitterbrush girl. All he had were the lines from his poem, words he'd made up.

> Just a bitterbrush bloom left behind,
> Crushed underfoot.

But what had happened to her last night when she took off down the alley? Did she find a place to sleep for the night, out of the cold, off the streets? And food.

The thought of food reminded him it was getting toward noon, time to stop and eat. If he took a quick stroll down the street, maybe he'd spot the young lady with the worn brown coat and long brown braid. But if she was hungry and needed a place to stay and a job, maybe she'd be out on the streets searching. If she had come to Boise by herself, she must have some spunk.

Unless she had come to Boise to hide.

Not that he should be the one looking for her to offer help. Except a kindly woman had helped him and his mother when he was a boy. When they were hungry and Mother needed a job. *"Always keep an eye out for who you can help, Josiah,"* Mother had taught him. *"'For unto whomsoever much is given, of him shall be much required.'"* So he needed to at least try.

Josiah made it out to the sidewalk and spotted a group of

ladies huddled outside Mrs. Farber's burned home and roadhouse.

"Such a shame it is." A tall lady's voice carried loud and clear, and those with her bobbed their heads.

"Yes." Another crossed her arms. "Now we have no decent place in our neighborhood to eat anymore."

"Well, I heard..."

Josiah couldn't catch what the woman said, nor did he care, as he walked past.

"Excuse me—sir!"

Josiah turned. Was someone calling to him?

The tall lady motioned for him to come back. "Aren't you the fellow who escorted Irma Farber to the train depot yesterday?"

"Yes."

The ladies gathered around him, all eager-eyed and throwing questions at him.

"Is she coming back?"

"Where did she go?"

"What's she going to do?"

"Is she going to open another roadhouse?"

"Ladies." Josiah held up a hand. "I don't know her long-term plans. She was too upset to think beyond losing her livelihood. Her home, her clothes. All her worldly belongings. But I have her sister's address, if you'd like to write to her to offer encouragement."

They each quieted down. "We just thought you might be able to tell us, that's all," the tall lady said, and the others backed away, dismissing him.

"I'm sure she'd appreciate your prayers."

"Of course."

But from the woman's tone, Josiah doubted any prayers would be going up on behalf of Mrs. Farber from these women. If these ladies who knew Mrs. Farber didn't care enough to write to her, to reach out to her themselves, or even to pray for her, who would care enough to help an unknown girl?

"Always keep an eye out for who you can help, Josiah."

How could he even do that? He didn't know her name, why she was in Boise. Or even where to find her. And now it was time he got back to work. He continued down the street.

He could do something—pray for her. Keep looking for her after his work hours were over, just in case.

Or be like the women he'd left behind and do nothing.

CHAPTER 4

At what should have been lunchtime, Lizzie crossed the street into a new block. With a heavy sigh, she set her carpetbag down and leaned against the brick building on the corner. Her feet hurt. Her legs were tired. Even her heart ached after so many rejections.

She just needed a moment of rest. A bit of encouragement. And—she fingered Rebel's apple in her pocket—something to eat. Because that apple apparently was going to be her dinner. If she didn't find something soon, she wouldn't have time to also hunt for a place to stay. And who would rent to her without a source of income?

Lizzie picked up her bag, ready to resume her search, and walked to the front of the building. In the wide display window was an oasis of candy. Boxes of DeMet's Turtles. Whitman's Samplers. Cadbury's. Jars of wrapped candy. Life Savers and Brach's caramel squares. Necco wafers and butterscotch Reed's Rolls. This was the haven of hope she needed. Each name was familiar, flooding her with memories. Standing in front of jars with her brothers, each one picking a favorite and then swapping for a taste of another's.

Was this the answer to her prayer? A simple sign over the window proclaimed it to be Brighton's Candy Shop.

With a smile, Lizzie entered. And oh, the aroma of chocolate—even its warmth flavoring the air. In the middle of the room was a marble slab for making fudge—with a fresh batch of chocolate sitting right on it. And along one side of the space was the counter. From the other side, a boy with a mop of red hair, who didn't look any older than her eleven-year-old brother, Winston, watched her with piercing green eyes.

"Are you a customer or just come in to gawk? We don't give out no free samples."

If she spent just one cent, would that make her official enough to get some information? At least she'd get something to eat. "I'm a real customer."

"Good. Then, welcome to Brighton's Candy Shop. How may I help you?"

Lizzie stepped up to the counter, where jars of penny candy left barely any wood visible underneath. "Let me see." She perused various choices—Tootsie Rolls, Hershey's Milk Chocolate Kisses, Mary Janes. And the gums—Clark's Teaberry and Wriggley's Juicy Fruit. No need to choose too quickly. She looked at the boy. "What's your favorite?"

His face almost exploded in a grin. "I like them all. Anytime I work here, my grandma lets me choose something. Today I'm waiting for the fudge to cool. That's the best there is."

"Does your grandmother own the store?"

"Yes, ma'am."

"Is her name Brighton?"

He puffed up a bit more. "Yes, ma'am. Mine too. And one day, this whole place will be mine, and I'll get to live upstairs just like she does."

Lizzie grinned at him. "That's wonderful. Is she here that I may speak with her?"

"Hey, you said you was a customer."

"Oh, I am." She looked at the candy jars again, longing for more than one piece. "But I also have a question for her."

"Well, she ain't here. I'm in charge. So first, which one do you want?"

Lizzie eyed the little imp, a bargainer just like Winston. "All right. I've made my choice. I'll have a Mary Jane. Thick, chewy, and peanut buttery." That should satisfy her stomach the longest. She looked up at him. "And sweetened with molasses, right?"

He grinned as if pleased at her choice, even if only one candy. "That'll be one cent, please."

She handed over a coin.

"Thank you. Would you like a bag?" He said the words stiffly, as if reciting phrases he'd been drilled on.

"No, thank you. I plan on eating it right away." She folded her hand around her prize.

"Hey, you wanted to know something?"

"Yes. I had wanted to ask if the candy shop was hiring. But I see your grandmother already has a good employee." She winked at him like she would have her brothers.

"Aw, I don't really work here. Just when she has to go somewhere and doesn't have anyone to watch the store. And she doesn't pay me 'cept in candy."

"Then that works out well for both of you, I'd say."

He shrugged and grinned. "It works for me. But she's always saying she can't afford to hire nobody except someone who'll work for candy."

"She's blessed to have you, then. Thank you for your good service today." She walked to the door.

"Hey, ma'am, wait."

She turned around.

"What kind of job are you looking for if you can't work in a candy shop?"

"I'm willing to do just about anything. Even work on a pig farm."

"There's no pigs round here. Can you sew?"

"Yes, I know how. Do you need a button put on or a rip fixed before your grandma gets back?"

"No, not me." He pointed across the street to a window display featuring a woman's stylish tailored suit with a dark-green cloche hat. "I saw the man from there put a sign in his window this morning when I came in. I think he's looking for help."

Oh, she could hug this boy.

"Thank you so very much—what's your name?"

"Gideon Brighton."

"I'm Lizzie Morgan. I thank you ever so much, Gideon Brighton. And if I come in again and have the pleasure of meeting your grandmother, I'll be sure to tell her what a help you've been."

"Thanks. Hey, I think the fudge is probably cool now. I'll share my piece with you if you want."

What a dear boy. "You're so kind, but if I'm going over there to ask about a job, I'd better not have chocolate on my fingers, right?"

He grinned. "Nope. Good luck."

Oh, she had more than any old luck—she had God going before her.

Now her feet wanted to skip across the street. But she managed to walk sedately until she was close enough to read the small sign in the window corner. *Seamstress Wanted.*

Gideon certainly was right.

Lizzie set down her carpetbag and peered through the glass. Spools of thread like a rainbow lined the windowsill, and a treadle sewing machine sat off to the side of the main room, though no one worked it at the moment.

She moved to the door and looked up at the sign over it. *Boise Tailor Shop.*

The door opened and out stepped a lady in an elegant red ensemble who nearly ran into her. "Oh, excuse me. I'm so sorry. I didn't see you there."

"I'm quite fine, ma'am." Lizzie did some quick thinking, hoping to detain the woman before she moved on. "Ma'am, I see you do business at this shop. Are you happy with their work?"

She smiled. "I certainly am. I have found their custom-made dresses exquisite and their turn-around time beyond compare."

"That's wonderful." Lizzie's heart pounded faster and faster. "And, uh, what about the owner?" If she were to work here, that would be of utmost importance.

"Oh, he's very charming. Very easy to deal with—even when I'm undecided on what style or even what color to order a dress in."

"Have you ordered here often, then?"

"For a few months now. If you use this tailor, I'm sure you'll find yourself very happy. My husband doesn't mind paying the price here for what he says makes me beautiful. And your husband will be happy with the results too." She gave Lizzie an impish grin.

"Oh, I'm not—"

"There he is now." An automobile pulled to the sidewalk, and the woman waved at the man inside. "I have to go, but I'm sure you'll find the perfect dress and style here, dear." She smiled at her husband as he got out and assisted her into the conveyance.

That sounded like as good of an endorsement as she'd find in an employer. Lizzie picked up her carpetbag and opened the door, enjoying the jingle of an overhead bell as she stepped inside. A man about her father's age looked up from behind the counter lining a side wall. His tall frame seemed out of place in the confined space, as though he'd be more comfortable out on an open range on a galloping horse. His hair was so dark, it was almost black, and his pale blue eyes looked her up and down. With her dress still bedraggled from her travels and smelling of smoke and the carpetbag in hand, he certainly wouldn't peg her as a customer of his fine shop.

"May I help you?"

"Yes, sir." *Be brave. Be confident.* Lizzie drew up a smile and walked to the counter. "I saw your sign in the window seeking a seamstress. I'd like to apply for the position."

The man raised his chin. "Would you, now?"

"Yes, sir. What are the requirements?"

"The requirements? I require skill and attention to the finest details. Hand sewing. Tailoring. Machine sewing complete garments. Alterations." He ticked them off one by one. "And superb skills with my clientele. Are you adept at all of that?"

Lizzie swallowed. Some of them she could manage. And she could be pleasant to customers, especially if they were like the lady she'd just spoken with. "I have had experience in both hand sewing and machine sewing, mending, and cutting patterns." She unbuttoned her coat to show her green dress. "I helped my mother construct this dress. In addition to following a pattern, we added pockets and extra rouching. And"—she twirled to demonstrate—"extra flounce. I'm a fast learner and work hard."

"Where have you had this experience?"

"At my family's ranch."

He scoffed. "A ranch? I'm afraid that's hardly comparable to sewing high society fashion, which I deal with here."

Another establishment that didn't need her skills. Or her. "I understand. Thank you." She turned to leave.

"Wait. What's your name?"

"I'm sorry. I should have introduced myself. I'm Elizabeth Rose Morgan." Had she imagined the slackening of his jaw? "I go by Lizzie."

"Lizzie Morgan." He studied her intently. "Where are you from?"

"Caldwell, sir." She refused to shift from one foot to the other as he stared at her in silence—and before she started babbling.

"When can you start?"

"Start?" He was hiring her just like that? "Why, right away, if you'd like, sir."

"Fine. Right now is ideal."

Glory be, she had a job!

"Should I inquire as to my hours? And...and the pay?"

He laughed. Maybe mocking her ignorance? Or hopefully just chuckling over her zeal. "Yes, you should. The hours will be every day except Sunday and from the time I open to the time I close. When I'm not here, you are to be. And you will also tend to the desk in my absence. And the pay? I'll decide once I see your work."

Oh. Well, of course, he couldn't offer her a wage until he knew if she met his standards. She'd just prove to him that she did. And she had just told him she worked hard, so the long hours would prove that too. But *thank You, Lord!* She had a job now. And after work, she could look for a place to rent.

She pointed to the empty chair at the sewing machine. "Is that where I'm to sit?"

"Yes. And your first project is waiting." He led her to the jade-green fabric on top of the sewing machine. "Finish the seams and then hem the garment."

"Yes. Yes, thank you." She took off her coat and hung it on the back of the chair. "Oh, excuse me, sir. What is your name?"

"Pardon my lack of manners, Miss Morgan." He smiled, and

his blue eyes glinted oddly. "I'm Mr. Calloway. Benton Calloway."

Benton Calloway? This was the man who had lamed Papa? Who'd threatened and frightened Mama? Who might be sabotaging the Double E yet again?

Papa's words were as clear to her now as they'd been when he'd whispered them on the other side of the kitchen door just yesterday. *"I don't want her anywhere near that man."*

Lizzie stuck out her hand. "I'm glad to meet you, Mr. Calloway. Thank you for the job, and I'll get started right now."

This was her perfect opportunity to find out how he was targeting Mama and Papa and to help save the Double E. Oh, yes, God was leading her step by step.

~

Finally, the end of the workday came, and Josiah could line up his pencils in the drawer, close the books, and head for the comfort of his room at the boardinghouse. He had a new poem he was itching to compose after supper tonight.

> After the stars fade...

Once he reached the bottom of the stairs, he locked the door behind him and started his trek along the street.

> After the stars fade and the break between night
> and day appears...

Today, he headed the long way home. Occasionally, he went this way to pass his father's shop. Never to go inside or say hello. Just to make sure the tailor shop was still in business, that his father hadn't been hauled off to prison again and left Josiah with more problems to handle and debts to make good on.

Before he reached the corner the shop was on, he crossed the street as usual so as not to be noticed passing by. Though it wouldn't surprise Josiah if his father still saw him, eagle-eyed as he was.

The door opened and out came— The young lady from the train depot? From the street last night?

Surely not. Josiah stopped in front of the candy store window. Pulling his hat brim down, he took a discreet peek across the street. Dark-brown hair plaited into a braid, the same worn coat from yesterday, and the hat minus the bitterbrush bloom. Yes, it was her.

He didn't dare cross the street while she remained in front of the tailor shop door. Yet she just stood in place, looking up and down the sidewalk, as if not sure which direction to take.

He half turned in case his father came to give her assistance —which was unlikely, but perhaps his prison terms had changed him. Josiah was more than thankful he'd been raised by his mother, God rest her soul. And that he'd inherited her features—her plain brown hair, plain brown eyes—rather than have a daily reminder of his father whenever he looked in the mirror.

Benton Calloway's lifestyle had killed her as surely as if the man had taken his own hands to her—deserting them for months at a time, leaving Mother to work her fingers to the bone while struggling to survive and raise their son alone. A man who'd had no use for his only child then. And certainly not now as Josiah's limp, slight as it was, stood as a sign of weakness to his tall, well-built, muscular father.

At last, the lady moved away from the door and headed toward the next street corner. Josiah walked parallel for a bit, then crossed over, making sure there were other people nearby before he approached her. For if she recognized him from the brawl last night, she'd no doubt take off running.

"Miss?" Josiah spoke as softly as he would have to one of the horses he wished he could've someday raised. She looked ready to bolt, so he doffed his hat as he approached. "Excuse me, miss, but I just wanted to check that you are safe. I spotted you at the train depot yesterday and then again...in the evening."

Her eyes were wide, like a frightened yearling's. "I'm fine."

"My name is Josiah."

She eyed him as if debating whether she should identify herself. Then, "I'm Lizzie Morgan."

Morgan. The same name of the man his father had stolen the most from. It was a common enough name, though. "I saw you at the train depot yesterday." Maybe if he reminded her again of that fact, she'd recall he'd been helping someone. If she'd noticed him at all.

"Yes." A flash of recognition seemed to lodge in her eyes, that he was telling the truth. "I'd come to Boise to work and live at a roadhouse—Mrs. Farber's. Do you know her?"

"Ah, yes. I was taking her to the train station after her roadhouse burned down. She went to be with her sister in California."

"She was there? At the train station when I arrived?"

"Yes. I was buying her a ticket and then helped her board."

"That was her? Then that's why she didn't meet me as she'd planned. So it's true, she lost everything she had?"

"Yes. Everything she owned." He shivered against the crisp air, hoping Mrs. Farber was warm within his coat. "So that put you out of a job and a place to live." It wasn't so much a question as what he saw as obvious. And the reason she was out on the street alone last night.

She nodded. "I did find work today, though." She looked back at the tailor shop.

No. Caleb's stomach clenched. No, she mustn't work there.

45

Maybe she had just stopped in to inquire about alterations or something.

"The boy from the candy store told me about the sign in the window advertising a position for a seamstress. And I got hired."

Oh no, no, no. But what could he do to stop her from working there? While she seemed happy to have a job, there was a tiredness in her eyes, and she was looking at him as though she was waiting for him to say something. But he could not congratulate her. "Where did you spend the night?"

She looked at her feet. "I found a place."

"What kind of a place?"

She met his eyes, her cheeks reddening. "A stable."

The only one he knew of in the direction she had run was Conor O'Shannon's livery. Probably as good a place as any if she had to spend the night among horses. He closed his eyes a fraction of a second and drew a deep breath. *Dear Lord, what can I even do to help?* Maybe that was his problem, always wanting to help when...maybe he couldn't. But as soon as he thought that, an idea centered in his heart.

"Mrs. McPhearson, the owner of the boardinghouse where I room, will help, if you'll come with me."

"What? No, I—"

"She's honorable. She runs a respectable boardinghouse."

"But I don't have money yet. Mrs. Farber was going to provide me with room and board and a small wage in exchange for helping her."

"Mrs. McPhearson will help" was all Josiah could think to say again. And prayed that she would.

They walked in silence the few blocks to the boardinghouse, which Josiah took as agreement. But he needed to speak with Mrs. McPhearson privately and before Hugh and Markos spotted Miss Morgan.

"Should I wait out here?" Lizzie Morgan asked when they approached the steps to the boardinghouse.

"If it's not too cold for you." Josiah led her to a rocking chair on the porch. "I'll be but a few minutes."

He hurried inside just as Hugh and Markos and a few of the others descended the staircase into the dining room. Mrs. McPhearson bustled to the table with a steaming pot of something.

"Hey, Straight and Narrow." Only Hugh could camouflage his sneer as a laugh around their landlady. "Did you do your good deed for the day?"

Surely, Hugh couldn't have spotted the lady on the porch yet or known what she was here for, if he had. Josiah ignored him and followed Mrs. McPhearson back into the kitchen, where the boarders weren't even supposed to be ever since...

She tucked strands of hair back from her flushed face and filled a basket with rolls. "Josiah—"

Whether she was about to reprimand him, enlist his help, or send him out of here, he couldn't wait to find out. "Mrs. McPhearson—a young lady whom Mrs. Farber was going to hire arrived yesterday right after the fire and has no place to stay. Please, is there a room here for her?"

"Josiah, I cannot think right now. No, I have no extra room. And this is a men's boardinghouse."

"But she has no place to go. She slept in a horse barn last night."

"Josiah Calloway, take these rolls into the dining room." She thrust the basket into his hands and turned to another task.

He obeyed but hurried back. "She's..."

Mrs. McPhearson planted her hands on her hips. "She's what, Josiah?"

"On the front porch."

"Then mercy me! Bring her into the kitchen and I'll feed her."

"Thank you, ma'am."

He hurried out the back door and walked around to the front porch. Bringing her through the dining room past Hugh and Markos would serve no good. So he brought her to the back entrance.

Mrs. McPhearson was headed toward the dining room door with a second bread basket. At their entrance into the kitchen, she backtracked.

"Good heavens, child. Sit. Both of you. I'll be right back to feed you, then we'll figure something out. In the meantime, here." She set four steaming rolls from her basket on a plate and shoved it in front of Josiah, then hurried on her way.

When Mrs. McPhearson returned, she joined them at the table.

"Mrs. McPhearson," Josiah said, "this is Miss Lizzie Morgan. Miss Morgan, Mrs. McPhearson, the owner of this boardinghouse."

"I'm glad to meet you, ma'am. Thank you for these rolls." Miss Morgan eyed the last two on the plate but looked too polite to take a second one.

"I'm glad to make your acquaintance as well." Mrs. McPhearson studied Miss Morgan a moment. "Josiah here tells me you're in need of a place to stay."

"Yes, ma'am. But I don't mean to cause a problem. I'll be on my way, and—"

"Nonsense. We'll come up with a solution." She went to the stove and ladled up two bowls of stew and set them in front of Josiah and Miss Morgan, then took her own seat again.

"Thank you, ma'am." Miss Morgan took a deep whiff of the stew. "This smells so much like my mother's. It's like a little bit of home."

Mrs. McPhearson beamed. "Now, Lizzie, if I could, I'd be glad to rent to you, but I'm full up. And this is a men's rooming house."

Before Josiah even thought it through, he blurted out the solution that landed in his brain. "She can have my room, and I'll move in at the accounting office."

"Oh no, you can't do that!" Lizzie's eyes widened, and she shook her head, her braid swinging.

"The boss used it as an office and tiny living quarters until he expanded to a bigger space across town and turned this one solely into an office. It'll work fine."

Mrs. McPhearson raised a brow at him, and he nodded. "All right, then," she said.

"But I just started my job today, and I don't even know how much I'll earn."

"If you help me prepare breakfast and serve supper each day, your rent will be covered. And it'd be a blessing to me, as I can barely keep up with all these men. My room and yours are the only ones in that wing, and you can use the back stairs that come down right into the kitchen here. Also, I have a private bath you can share, so you'll be safe there. It's a perfect solution."

Lizzie glanced at Josiah as if seeking permission or his approval.

He smiled at her. "The room is yours. I'll move my belongings out immediately."

Lizzie looked between them, tears in her dark-brown eyes. "Thank you, both of you."

"Josiah, you will still take your evening meals here," Mrs. McPhearson added.

"Thank you, ma'am." And with that, Josiah finished off his stew and two rolls and headed upstairs to pack. Even having to spend more time in that office was a small price to pay if it kept Miss Lizzie Morgan safe.

And until she could leave employment with his father at the Boise Tailor Shop.

Within minutes, someone rapped softly on his door. "Josi-

49

ah." He opened the door to find Mrs. McPhearson. "I'm sorry to rush you, but the men will be finishing up soon. It'd be best if you left before they see you and ask you questions tonight. I'll let them know you've left and Lizzie will be taking your room and give them orders on how she's to be treated. Then tomorrow I'll introduce her. But come now—down the back stairs. I want to get her up here quick, but I still need to sweep and change the sheets."

"Of course." He dumped his clothes from the last drawer into his duffel and followed her down the back staircase.

"Thank you so much, Josiah." Lizzie already stood at the sink, washing the dishes the two of them had used.

"Leave those be for tonight. You can start tomorrow." Mrs. McPhearson grabbed the broom by the kitchen door. "Josiah, you go out the back. Lizzie, come with me. Quickly, now."

Lizzie took the broom from Mrs. McPhearson. "Let me do that. You take care of your men, and I'll be fine."

Mrs. McPhearson looked her over and nodded. "Yes, you're a blessing here for sure." She turned back to Josiah. "Why are you still standing there?"

"I'm going." He hiked his duffel bag higher on his shoulder and headed out the back door.

With his quick offer, he hadn't given any thought to the ramifications. Though one problem was solved in that Lizzie Morgan had a safe place to stay, he needed to ask his boss for permission to live at the office. A yes might be just as bad as a no, for then he'd get no relief after a dreary day at work.

And if the answer was unfavorable? Then he'd be the one out on the street with no place to sleep. And the only money he had was—

How had he been so stupid? In his haste, he'd forgotten to pack not only his envelope of money but also his ledger and poetry book. All hopefully hidden well enough that Lizzie Morgan would not find them. For if she did...

CHAPTER 5

How blessed she was.

Lizzie swept the floor, though it was practically spotless, and settled into the small room containing a bed, a desk and straight-backed chair under the window, a multicolored rag rug, and a wardrobe. Josiah had hurriedly vacated with his one stuffed-full duffel bag. From the looks of the room, that represented all he owned in life.

After a bit, Mrs. McPhearson came up with fresh sheets—which she insisted on changing herself.

"Are you sure Josiah really meant his offer?" Why would a stranger do this for her?

"My goodness, yes, dear. That's the kind of man he is. Generous. Honest. Helpful. One you can trust. Now some of the others downstairs…" She shrugged. "I gave them a firm lecture about their speech and actions in your presence and treating you like a lady. If any of them ever gives you one speck of trouble, you let me know. Most are gentlemen, but a couple of them I have my doubts about."

Lizzie had yet to meet any of the men, but she trusted Mrs.

McPhearson that she'd be perfectly safe in this little room just down the hall from her own living quarters.

After a good night's rest in a real bed, Lizzie showed up in the kitchen early, ready to help serve breakfast. Dressed in her navy gored skirt, ruffled cream-colored blouse, and black pumps, she was ready for her first day of work, both here and at the tailor shop.

"Good morning." Mrs. McPhearson looked Lizzie over. "You look nice."

"Thank you. I'm ready to get started. What should I do?"

"First, sit and eat."

"Oh, no, ma'am. I'm here to work."

"Not yet." Mrs. McPhearson pointed to a chair and handed her a plate filled with ham and eggs. "You can start helping me this evening, once you're a bit acclimated."

"Thank you, ma'am. This smells wonderful."

"I like to make sure everyone in my house starts their day with a good hearty meal. Oh, and this is for you." Mrs. McPhearson pulled a square of paper with a map drawn on it from her pocket. "I sketched this for you until you learn the route to and from the shop by yourself. It won't take you long to walk, but make sure you always leave work when the streets are well populated and in the daylight. That's important. Do you understand? Always."

"Yes." If Mr. Calloway allowed her to do that. The day before, she was surprised at the late hour to which he kept the shop open. Had it not been for the kindness of Josiah showing up and bringing her to the boardinghouse, she didn't know what she would have done, as it had been too late to inquire around for a place to rent. But God had sent Josiah right when she needed help, just as He had provided a job—all within one day. "And I'll try to be here on time tonight to help you serve supper."

"I know you will, dear. Now, off with you. God bless you, and I'll see you this evening."

Lizzie followed the map and arrived back at the tailor shop, all set for her first full day of work. The welcoming bell jingled as she pushed open the door.

"Good morning, Mr. Calloway." She'd never envisioned the man in Mama's stories as such a handsome, dapper man. His navy pinstriped suit brought out his blue eyes, and not a strand of his brilliantined black hair was out of place.

"Miss Morgan." He didn't bother to stand at her entrance but stayed seated on his stool behind the counter. He checked his watch and frowned. "I've been open five minutes and have already accepted a mending job from a customer. I expect you to be here on time. Before I open."

On time? Lizzie had thought she was early. She should have asked exactly when he opened up. "Yes, Mr. Calloway. I'm sorry, I didn't realize—"

"Set to work. I'll be in the back. You can handle anyone who comes in with mending. If they would like to order a custom garment, then you may call me. But do not come behind the curtains."

So many rules. "Yes, Mr. Calloway."

With that, he ducked behind the black curtains separating the main room from...his office, she guessed.

She took her seat at the latest model Singer sewing machine and threaded the bobbin. It was similar enough to Mama's older model that she could get started without having to ask for help. What a luxury this piece of equipment was. And the joy the work environment offered with the rays of the morning sun dancing across the colorful spools of thread beneath the front window, truly like her very own rainbow. The ray of hope she'd needed. A symbol of her answered prayers.

After she'd completed three more hems on garments

stacked on the shelf to be finished and secured buttons on another, the bell tinkled, and in walked a most regal woman. Maybe in her early thirties.

Lizzie stood and walked to her. "Good morning, ma'am. May I help you?"

"Hello. Are you new here?"

"I am. I'm Lizzie, the new seamstress."

The woman held out a gloved hand. "It's nice to meet you, Lizzie. I'm Mrs. Donaldson, and—"

"Ah, good morning, Mrs. Donaldson." Mr. Calloway appeared from behind the curtains. "How are you today?"

"Very well, thank you."

"That's delightful to hear. I see you've already met my new seamstress, Lizzie."

Mrs. Donaldson smiled at Lizzie. "Yes, I have."

"She just started with me yesterday, but I expect you'll be very pleased with her work. Speaking of which, how might I assist you today?"

"I need a new suit for an event I'm attending with my husband, but I haven't quite decided on the style or color."

"Of course. That's no problem. Come over to the counter, and let's see what we can come up with. Lizzie, will you join us?"

She was delighted to be included already. She stood beside Mrs. Donaldson, taking in her auburn hair, hazel-green eyes, and tall, slim size, as Mr. Calloway discussed styles with her. Once they decided on the style, Mr. Calloway turned to Lizzie.

"I'll leave you to measure Mrs. Donaldson, and perhaps the two of you can pick out a color and fabric. I'll be in the back, but please call me if you need any further input from me."

"Of course." Surely, she must be beaming on the outside as she was on the inside. Already Mr. Calloway trusted her with a customer—not only to make the suit but to work with Mrs.

Donaldson all the way from measuring to helping her choose a fabric and color.

"Your blouse and gored skirt are lovely," Mrs. Donaldson said once they were alone. "And the short row of buttons along the sides are so stylish."

"Thank you."

"Did you sew these yourself?"

"Yes, my mother and I did. She's a wonderful seamstress, and I learned from her. We like designing clothes, so we added the buttons for a bit of flare." She grinned, then retrieved a tape measure from the sewing machine. "May I?"

"Yes, please, dear." She lowered her voice. "I'm so glad you're here to do the measuring. As I need to tell you that I'm with child. So you can make the necessary provisions."

"Of course." Lizzie kept her voice down also. "I have four younger brothers, and my mother showed me how she made pleated skirts which allow for the needed growth." She jotted down Mrs. Donaldson's measurements as she took each one. "I don't have an exact pattern here, but I'm sure I can adjust the one you picked out."

"Wonderful. That sets my mind at ease."

Lizzie gave her a conspiratorial smile. "An extra nice thing is that you can wear it after the birth of your child as well, as it looks like an everyday skirt. The secret is in using hooks and eyes to let it out or take it in, so even the hang remains the same."

"You're a true godsend to me, dear."

"Thank you. And I've been thinking about just what color will look lovely on you, if you don't mind my suggestion?"

"I'd welcome it."

"See the emerald green on the second shelf on the left?" Lizzie nodded in the direction as she continued to take measurements, noting where to add for the growing child. "The fabric is sturdy but still soft for a suit, and the color will be beautiful with your eyes and hair. And, if you don't mind me saying, with your glow."

Mrs. Donaldson's gaze went to the fabric, and she gave a little gasp. "That indeed is the perfect one. It's elegant and yet with the style of the suit still sedate enough for the event."

"And I believe we have just the buttons that will add an extra bit of enhancement to your ensemble."

"Mr. Calloway made a wise choice in hiring you, Lizzie."

"Thank you, ma'am." And Lizzie couldn't agree more—for a reason Mr. Calloway would have no idea of.

When the details of the garment were taken care of, Mr. Calloway reappeared in the main room. "Thank you for stopping by today, Mrs. Donaldson. Good day to you." After she left, he turned to Lizzie. "Miss Morgan, have you found living accommodations in Boise yet?"

"I have. At Mrs. McPhearson's boardinghouse within walking distance from here."

"Hmm. Mrs. McPhearson's. Isn't that a men's boardinghouse?"

"It is. But a kind gentleman offered his room while he'll sleep at the accounting office where he works, and my room is right next to Mrs. McPhearson's in a private hall. I'm to help prepare breakfast and serve supper in exchange for rent."

"I see." He looked thoughtful, and a gleam skimmed across his pale eyes, deepening the blue momentarily. Pleased at the generosity of Mrs. McPhearson and the kindness of a boarder, perhaps? "That works out very well, indeed."

"It does. I'm both grateful and blessed."

"But you shall not let your duties there interfere with your job here."

"Oh, no, sir. I won't."

"Very good. I'm stepping out now for my midday meal. I'll

bring back something for you to eat if you'd be so good as to start on Mrs. Donaldson's order."

"Of course. And thank you so much." She'd forgotten all about eating after the hearty breakfast this morning. And regretfully, she'd also forgotten to bring along Mrs. McPhearson's wrapped rolls with her.

He turned and walked out the front door, and Lizzie settled in to work. She had to prove herself on this job, no matter what.

After Mr. Calloway returned with the promised food, she took a few minutes to eat, then got right back to work. The afternoon passed quietly as Lizzie sewed, enjoying each time she got to select a new thread from the rainbow of spools.

As the day pressed toward five o'clock, the bell over the Boise Tailor Shop door once more jingled. The tinkling was so cheerful, like a welcoming song to their clients.

"What now?" Mr. Calloway grumbled as he stalked out from the back room where he—well, did the books, she supposed. "Oh, Mr. Donaldson." Mr. Calloway flashed a grin and held out a hand. "It's a pleasure to see you. A pleasure, indeed."

"Hello." Mr. Donaldson stopped mid-step near the door and looked over at Lizzie seated in front of the Singer. She smiled at the kind-looking, dark-haired man whose wife she was apparently sewing for. "I'm sorry to stop in so near closing time, but I was passing on my way home."

"No, don't concern yourself at all with the time. That's no problem. I always make myself available to my customers. Come right in." Mr. Calloway led him over to the counter. "It's a delight as always to see you. We're expecting Mrs. Donaldson in a few days for her fitting. I do hope all is well?"

"Certainly. But I wanted to see if you could add a hat to my wife's suit to surprise her when she comes in."

"Of course. What would you like?"

"Something stylish. I'll leave that up to you."

"Indeed, she'll be pleased. I'll let my new seamstress, Miss Morgan, handle the details. She and your wife seemed to work well together this morning."

"Fine, then. Shall I pay now?"

"Yes, as usual. And if with the fabric chosen it comes to more, I'll let you know, and we can settle up upon its completion." As soon as he accepted and recorded the payment, he took hold of Mr. Donaldson's arm, discreetly edging him toward the door. "We'll see you soon, then."

"Good day." Mr. Donaldson tipped his hat to Lizzie on his way out.

Once the door closed and the bell hadn't yet finished its last jangle, Mr. Calloway turned to Lizzie. "Stop what you're doing and make a hat. And don't leave until it's completed." He opened the door and tossed a single key to her across the room. "Lock up when you leave."

"But what should—"

He pulled the door shut after him.

Lizzie stared through the window as he blended into the crowd on the sidewalk, brushing past people.

"I don't want her anywhere near that man."

Maybe Papa had been right, after all.

But if she didn't hurry and get to work, she'd be late helping serve supper at the boardinghouse. And the street would be emptying out of people getting off work before she could leave. Surely, Mrs. McPhearson's warning about leaving before the area became deserted, much less before darkness settled in, had a reason behind it. What if she ran into unruly neighborhood men again, as she had on her first night?

~

Thankfully, Mrs. McPhearson had insisted Josiah still take his evening meals at her table. But she had served the men herself, with no sign of Miss Lizzie Morgan keeping her end of the bargain. The last one to finish his meal, he pushed back his chair and carried his plate to the kitchen door, rather than leaving it for Mrs. McPhearson to pick up. If Miss Morgan wasn't here, though, would Mrs. McPhearson let him back upstairs to retrieve his books and envelope?

She swung open the door and took his plate, a deep frown on her face. And Josiah couldn't blame her. What must she think with her new employee apparently already spurning her kindness?

"The streets are thinning out with traffic. I think you should go check on Lizzie."

"But—" He'd gotten a glimpse of the sink full of dishes before the door had swung closed. Dishes that Lizzie Morgan should be standing over with her hands in the soap suds.

"Hurry, Josiah. Perhaps something happened to her."

The image of the drunk and the improper man from two nights ago was still vivid. But where would he even start? His father's shop closed at five and not one minute past. Miss Morgan could be anywhere. But one thing was sure—she wasn't here fulfilling her duties.

"Of course, I'll look for her. But first, I was wondering if I could—"

"Go now. You can talk later."

"Yes, ma'am." He headed out the back door to avoid any men lingering in the parlor. He'd start at his father's shop. Perhaps Mrs. Brighton at the candy store would have seen which direction Lizzie had taken when she left. Even after hours, Mrs. Brighton watched the neighborhood from her living quarters above her store. Yes, she'd probably be likely to notice a pretty newcomer in town.

Josiah walked the few blocks to the tailor shop—and stopped when he saw the light bulb shining in the front room. Had Lizzie left it on? His father would have a conniption at the waste—

And then he saw her. Lizzie Morgan hunched over the Singer sewing machine as the all-but-empty street settled in for the evening. Why was she still here? Surely, his father wasn't in the back—he always left at five o'clock.

Josiah stepped up to the door and knocked. Hopefully, she'd locked the door—but he wouldn't scare her unnecessarily by trying the knob. Even at the soft knock, she jumped up, knocking her chair over.

"Miss Morgan?" Could she hear him through the door? "Mrs. McPhearson sent me to look for you. Are you all right?"

She nodded but made no move to let him in.

"May I escort you back to the boardinghouse?"

She shook her head but walked to the door. Unlocked it. Cracked it open.

"I didn't mean to frighten you." Josiah softened his voice. "Mrs. McPhearson was worried about you. Why are you still here?"

She swiped at her eyes. Red-rimmed, he now saw. Had she been crying?

"I can't leave yet. Mr. Calloway said I have to stay and finish this hat before I can leave."

Anger balled in Josiah's stomach. He took a deep breath and kept his voice low, calm. "I don't doubt those were your instructions, but perhaps he didn't realize the street would be empty or it might even get dark before you finished. Why don't you close up, and I'll walk you back to Mrs. McPhearson's? He should understand that your safety is more important, when you explain it to him tomorrow."

"Do you really think so? He was quite adamant."

Of course, he was. That's how he ran things. Charming at

first, and if that didn't work, ordering and bullying people to do his bidding.

No, his father wouldn't understand or be lenient—but "I'll speak to him myself if there's a problem. However, I do know he wouldn't want the lights burning too long. Gather your belongings, and we can lock up."

"I'm almost finished. I could come in early, perhaps—after I help Mrs. McPhearson prepare breakfast, that is."

"I'm sure that would be fine."

Once Lizzie gathered her bag, Josiah ushered her to the door, turned off the light, and locked the door behind them with the key she produced. That in itself was odd, his father trusting anyone with a key to the premises. But if he'd wanted to leave and yet have Miss Morgan stay, he wouldn't have had a choice.

"I guess I should properly introduce myself." She'd find out eventually who he was, anyway.

She cocked her head. "You said you're Josiah. You're not?"

"I am. But I didn't tell you my last name. Josiah Calloway."

"Calloway?" She stiffened, as if processing the name. "Is he—"

"He's my father."

She stepped away from him, her mouth open.

"I don't wish to get you in trouble, since he can be...rather forthright...in his manner. But since Mrs. McPhearson did send me to find you, if you'll still allow me to, I'll escort you to the boardinghouse."

She still stared at him. Then looked up and down the street, hopefully realizing how desolate it was and that he was her best option. "All right. Thank you. I hope she's not upset with me as well, as I also missed my duties with her tonight."

"Not at all. She was worried about you with evening setting in. You'll find that she enjoys having someone to mother."

"Does she have family?"

"Yes. Her son and his wife. Her hope is always that they'll move to Boise one day. But they live in New York City, where his wife is from."

"Really? That's where my grandmother and grandfather live. Though I never met them. And my great-aunt Belinda and her daughter too. I've never met them either." She shrugged, and Josiah couldn't determine if that didn't bother her or if she simply didn't want to divulge family history. He certainly understood that, as his own family had its mountain of secrets. "But"—her thoughtful brown eyes lit up with a hint of mischief—"Mrs. McPhearson will be a wonderful grandmother while I'm here."

"I'm not sure she's quite that old." He couldn't help but laugh, thinking of Mrs. McPhearson's reaction if she knew they were discussing her age.

"Maybe an aunt, then?"

"Yes, I think that would please her." He'd never met any of his grandparents either. He didn't even know if he had any living ones—or aunts or uncles, or even cousins. But he had Mrs. McPhearson too. "She's a wise woman no matter how you think of her."

He reached for Lizzie's elbow to guide her across an intersection, thankful he'd found her yesterday. Beyond grateful she had a room and a job. Together they walked the remaining blocks all the way up onto Mrs. McPhearson's back porch before Josiah realized he still held her elbow. And that Lizzie Morgan had never once pulled her arm away.

As if she trusted him in spite of who his father was.

She gave him a smile as she reached for the doorknob right as Mrs. McPhearson flung the door open.

"There you are, child!" She wrapped Lizzie in a hug. "I was worried about you. Thank you, Josiah, for finding her." She smiled at him. "You can always count on Josiah if you need anything, Lizzie. Right, Josiah?"

"I will always try, ma'am."

"You two come in here and sit. I saved you a plate for supper, Lizzie, and an extra piece of apple pie for you, Josiah. I'll put on the teakettle while you eat. Tea may not be the solution to everything, but it's a good start—after prayer, of course." She bustled about, waving them down in their chairs if they tried to get up to help.

Josiah finally accepted Mrs. McPhearson's attempts for what they were—treating him like family. The way his father never would. Short of a miracle.

CHAPTER 6

*L*izzie finished her pie and sipped her tea, looking over the cup at Josiah as he and Mrs. McPhearson talked.

"A spot more of tea, Lizzie?" Mrs. McPhearson asked.

"Yes, thank you. But I'll get it." She wasn't ready to leave the table yet, wanting to linger as long as Mrs. McPhearson kept Josiah engaged. Perhaps she could learn something of importance. Wasn't that what the Bible said? Be slow to speak, swift to listen? She poured more tea for each of them and settled back in to listen. And think.

So Josiah Calloway was Benton Calloway's son. How perfect was that for Lizzie's investigation? And she was now staying in the room his son had vacated.

Though it was hard to imagine Josiah and Mr. Calloway were related at all. Josiah must be at least two inches shorter than his father and with brown hair, brown eyes. Eyes that seemed to look deep into her soul. Eyes that turned a dark chocolatey color with concern about her and reflected kindness. Eyes that she shouldn't be noticing even now. Or how he'd held her elbow so securely the entire way home, as if he were her protector. In contrast, Benton Calloway was so tall, black-haired, his eyes pale and watery blue. With a calculating slyness at times in his gaze.

"Thank you again," Josiah was saying to Mrs. McPhearson, "for your kindness in allowing me to continue taking my supper here. It's such a welcome change to leave the accounting office for this respite with"—he looked from Mrs. McPhearson to Lizzie and grinned—"such fine company."

While his words were those of charm, like his father's, his tone was sincere, his voice calming. When no customers were within the shop, Mr. Calloway's speech was rough and edged with arrogance, quickly casting off any charm he exuded with his clientele.

But the two men shared the same last name. And that was a start to helping Papa. Surely, a father would divulge his business dealings with his son. So until Lizzie could get into Benton Calloway's office at the tailor shop, her next best option was to search his son's room for anything he might have left behind. She'd just have to ignore the little whispering voice that hoped she'd find nothing.

Lizzie finished her tea, then stood and gathered the plates and cups. Enough talk for the night. She'd do the dishes quickly, then be on to her mission upstairs.

"Josiah." Mrs. McPhearson apparently wasn't done talking yet, though. "What was it you wanted to ask me earlier?"

Or maybe Lizzie needed to linger a few moments more to hear this. She set the dishes in the sink and ran the water.

"Oh, just leave the dishes, Lizzie." Mrs. McPhearson waved her hand at the stack. "I'll do them in a jiff. You just head on up to your room, as you've had a long day." She turned back to Josiah. "Now, go ahead. You wanted to know if you could... what?"

"I..."

Josiah's eyes shifted from Lizzie to the back stairs. And what was that on his face? Maybe not guilt, exactly—but anxiousness?

"Could I help you with the dishes in exchange for meals?"

"Oh, goodness, no!" Mrs. McPhearson patted Josiah's hand. "Thank you, though, dear boy. But that's something I enjoy doing at day's end. Now why don't you get on home also after your long day?"

Josiah stood. "Thank you again for everything. Good night, then, Mrs. McPhearson." He nodded at Lizzie. "I'll see myself out."

"Wait, take this with you. Perhaps it'll be your breakfast tomorrow." She wrapped the last piece of apple pie and handed it to him. Then he was gone out the back door.

When Lizzie lingered, her landlady waved her hand. "Dear, go on upstairs."

"But I haven't helped you yet today, and—"

"No, there'll be plenty days ahead for you to help me. Starting tomorrow will be just fine. Off with you, now, and I'll be up shortly as well."

With a yawn that Lizzie could barely restrain, she acquiesced...but she wouldn't be able to sleep until she'd at least checked the room.

Once inside the small bedroom, she slipped her shoes off and stood in the middle of the floor and looked around. All Josiah had taken with him had been one canvas bag. But maybe not everything he owned had fit inside. Lizzie looked again in each drawer. Still as empty as they'd been when she had moved in last night and put her belongings in the top one. Underneath the bed there was nothing, as she'd swept it herself last night.

What about under the mattress? Wasn't that where people hid things? But no, when she lifted the covers and peeked under the mattress, there was nothing.

Perhaps the wardrobe? She carried the chair over to the wardrobe and stood on it and ran her hand along the top, under the woven runner, and behind the planter. Likely hiding spots, but nothing was there either.

Desperately, she needed to gain access to the back room behind those curtains where Benton Calloway was likely to keep his private records and correspondence.

She put the chair back and sat on the bed. Everything about this tiny room was neat and precise. Except for the rag rug of browns and reds and golds—off center and not even next to the bed, where it was most needed for cold feet in the mornings.

She walked over to the rug and used her foot to slide it to a more suitable spot. And right through the thin, twisted fabrics, she stubbed her toe on something. Maybe that was why the rug was positioned oddly—to cover up a damaged floorboard to prevent such a stubbing. With the rug moved, Lizzie bent down to investigate the floor.

And there was her answer. The edge of one board stuck up just enough that she could pry it loose.

Two books and a bulging white envelope were hidden underneath.

She tugged them out. The first book was some accounting ledger, which made sense, as that's what Josiah did. Perhaps he had brought work home with him. The straight columns of numbers had neatly inked words weaving along the margins.

> But sobs of sorrow pierce my heart.

What was that? She followed the winding words back along the side toward the bottom.

> As the day fades and the stars appear
> When the mist rolls away and the view is clear
> Firing and explosions echo as villagers hide
>   and dart
> But sobs of sorrow pierce my heart.

Josiah was a poet? What happened that he'd write something like this? Maybe—

She closed the ledger. No, she certainly should not be reading his private thoughts.

Except the last words—*pierce my heart*—had ended right beside a name in the ledger.

Mrs. Farber.

Maybe if she just kept her eyes on the numbers, didn't read the words from his heart, it'd be fine to look again, as this might be the information she needed. Lizzie opened it back up and found the entry again.

Mrs. Farber. And in the column by her name—$25.00.

And under that, deductions of three dollars per week. Then an entry from two days ago showing the amount paid in full, another figure designated *train ticket*, and a California address penciled in.

What was that about?

Lizzie turned the page and read the next entry. Mrs. Brighton, candy store—$23.00. And again, payments carefully recorded week by week with a balance showing of $5.00.

And the next page—Bea McPhearson—balance $35.00. He owed Mrs. McPhearson money? For what—unpaid rent? Again, small deductions were shown for several weeks prior.

Some other names showed a zero balance.

Lizzie flipped to the last page. And her heart thudded as she stared at the entry.

Caleb and Eliza Morgan—$300.00.

What in the world?

Beside their names was no week-by-week payment. No deduction at all. She picked up the white envelope, now suspicious at its thickness, and peeked inside. Sure enough, it was bulging with bills of various denominations, but not three hundred dollars. Another stack, thin and tied with a string, held only a few bank notes. Enough for what—rent, maybe?

She held the proof she needed in her hands—a debt owed her parents that was not being repaid while a stack of money accompanied it. But there was no elation of victory. For not only was Benton Calloway involved somehow in sabotaging the Double E, did this not prove that Josiah was too? Even if he was trying to repay some of the people—a change of heart on his part, perhaps? a guilty conscience?—it was clear no effort had been made at all to repay her parents.

"Thank You, Lord, for bringing me to Boise at just the right time. For giving me a job working for Benton Calloway and a home right in this room." If that wasn't God's clear guidance to bring the father and son to justice, she didn't know what was. Maybe she was like Queen Esther, placed here for such a time as this.

And her own parents would be proud of her for putting a stop to the Calloways. Helping to save the ranch. Yes, she was braver and more capable than they thought. She didn't need to be kept safely away from Benton Calloway, for with God's help, she was the one who would bring the Calloway family to justice once and for all.

Now what?

The entire walk from the boardinghouse back to the accounting office, Josiah berated himself. Maybe if he'd spoken up sooner tonight—or insisted that he must go upstairs and retrieve his belongings before he went on his search for Lizzie Morgan—then he wouldn't be in such a fix.

How would he get his books back now, let alone the money to repay people?

What if Lizzie had somehow found them? For if she read either book, she'd be looking straight into his soul.

But he'd hidden them well—mostly out of caution from

the prying eyes of Hugh and Markos should they ever try to sneak into his room. So surely, they'd be safe until he could recover them. But how could he even do that? Mrs. McPhearson wouldn't let him into a lady's room—and he couldn't very well ask her to do it for him. She would most certainly respect her new boarder's privacy—as she did everyone's.

And he wasn't about to ask Lizzie to return them. He couldn't take a chance on her glancing through either book. Which would be worse—her seeing into his heart through his poetry or spotting her parents' names in the ledger? For by now, there was no doubt that Caleb and Eliza Morgan from Caldwell were her parents.

How had she even stumbled upon his father's advertisement for an employee out of all the positions that must be available in Boise? He refused to entertain the thought that she had somehow known. No, he was an expert at spotting untrustworthiness. And her eyes had been clear from all ill intent when she'd told him about the boy at Brighton's—who had to be Mrs. Brighton's grandson—spotting the job sign in the window.

Just yards from the accounting office, a voice called out. "Sir? You got a coin? I ain't had no food all day." A man stepped out from the shadows of an alcove. The same drunk from the other night, just in a new location? Possibly, though the voice wasn't slurred. But Josiah had no extra money to give the man even if he'd wanted to.

"I'm afraid not. But here." He thrust the wrapped pie toward him. "A piece of nice home-baked apple pie."

"Pie?" Both interest and hunger surged in the man's voice. "I ain't had a piece of real pie in...a long while, at least. Thank ye." He took the package and unwrapped it right there and took a bite. "Mm, mm. May God bless you." Then he shuffled on down the street.

Though Josiah would have to go hungry in the morning, at least the man had something enjoyable to end his day on.

Josiah unlocked the door of the accounting firm, and currently his abode as well, and trudged up the steps to the second-floor office. On every stair, his fingers—his very heart—yearned to continue the poem he'd started about little Victoria. The village girl who'd won his troops' hearts with her smile and big, innocent brown eyes. The little girl who with her family and neighbors had become numbers on the tally of casualties in France.

The only chair was at the desk where he sat all day, but he sat again, pencil in hand. Then words poured from his lips even as he placed them one by one onto paper.

>"But sobs of sorrow pierce my heart.
>How is there justice for some? But not for all.
>'Victoria! Victoria!' I still hear her mother's call."

Josiah put his pencil down as that dark day came back. The smell of sulfur. Thick smoke in the air. Gunfire and screams. Oh, the screams. And he was unable to do anything to protect Victoria and her mother and those who had edged near the Americans in the village square to hear the harmonica playing. That wound—one he'd carry forever—was worse than the shrapnel in his leg. The shrapnel that prevented him from lunging for the girl to cover her, that prohibited him from ranching, which tied him to this desk with unending numbers staring at him until he could pay his father's debts. The physical weakness which made his father despise him even more. Yes, he'd gladly carry the shrapnel wound if only it'd been in exchange for protecting at least one innocent child.

Oh, Lord, please make me useful...

He added the words to the paper, then stared at them. Were they a line of his poem—or the desperate prayer of his heart?

Josiah sat still and doodled until his heart ceased pounding hard. His head stopped spinning. And then really looked at what he'd drawn. A pig.

And the idea of a pig farm rooted itself a bit deeper into his thoughts. He started a new page, one he could transfer into his ledger book later as he calculated the actual cost of starting a pig farm. But until he got his father's debts repaid and could start saving money for his future, this was at least the seed of an idea. A plan. A hope.

"You're about as valuable as a pig wallowing in its mire."

Maybe one day, his father's words would cease to haunt him. Because a pig farm was honorable. And valuable to a family, to the community, to the nation.

Yes, if the Lord allowed it, he just might be able to one day still see his dream fulfilled. Not owning a horse ranch, but a new possibility. One that could be considered a type of ranch as well, he supposed. A pig farm.

And running it together with a wife who loved the creatures as much as he did would be perfect.

CHAPTER 7

At breakfast, once the boarders were seated at the dining table, Mrs. McPhearson handed Lizzie a platter of eggs off the stove and grabbed the pot of oatmeal. "Come, dear, it's time to introduce you to the men."

"Yes, ma'am." Lizzie followed her into the dining room and stood close to her. This was the first she'd even seen any of them, and they all stared at her. Some expressions were curious. Others—one in particular—all but shouted who she needed to avoid.

"Gentlemen." Mrs. McPhearson looked at each one. "This is my new helper, Lizzie. Now, as I've already advised you, she will be treated with utmost respect. She will be assisting me with serving breakfast and supper. I'll make the introductions before you start eating. Walter is at the head of the table." He nodded. "Around on the other side are Peter, Frederick, Melvin, then Markos and Hugh."

Lizzie nodded, not daring to smile or give any encouraging sign that she sought interaction with them other than in the dining room. Especially to the one named Hugh, as along with his nod, he added a wink. One Mrs. McPhearson apparently didn't see. Lizzie looked away and set the eggs in the middle of the table and scooted back to the kitchen.

"Most of them are a fine lot," Mrs. McPhearson said behind her. "But if any of them give you the slightest problem, you let me know, and I'll take care of them."

"Thank you." She knew exactly which one to watch.

After practically running to the tailor shop, Lizzie managed to arrive early. If she could get a head start on the hat this morning, perhaps Mr. Calloway would be forgiving about her leaving it uncompleted yesterday. At the door, she stopped to catch her breath. But Mr. Calloway stood inside, a glower on his face and the hat in hand as he pulled the door open.

"Did I not give clear instructions that this hat was to be finished before you left last night?"

"Y-yes, sir, you did. But—"

He thrust the hat at her, and Lizzie scrambled to catch it before it fell to the floor.

"I don't want any excuses. If you want this job, you'll do as you're told."

"Yes, sir." Lizzie hurried to the sewing machine, yanking her coat off on the way, and sat down to work.

"It will be finished today, or your wages will be docked."

Lizzie kept her head down so he wouldn't see the tears she could barely hold back. "Yes, sir."

"I'm stepping out for some breakfast. You'll show me your progress when I return."

"Y—" But he was gone.

What was she going to do? It was impossible to work for this man who—

Who'd lamed Papa, threatened Mama, and was set to destroy the Double E. *Dear Lord, please give me the strength to continue.*

She finished the stitching on the hat and added the adornments which matched in color with the buttons, tying the outfit nicely together. There. Done. She glanced at the front window. And before Mr. Calloway returned.

When he reentered the shop, he walked straight to the back without a greeting or even a nod in her direction. Which was fine with her.

A few minutes later, the door jangled, and a woman in a stylish gray suit entered. "Excuse me, is Mr. Calloway available?"

"He—"

"Ah, Mrs. Redding." All of a sudden, Benton Calloway was standing in front of the woman. "You made good time in stopping by."

"You had a hat you wished to show me?"

"Indeed. It's a new creation." He stepped over to the sewing area and picked up Mrs. Donaldson's hat that Lizzie had placed on the shelf of completed items. "My young seamstress here has designed this one-of-a-kind hat and just completed it this morning. What do you think?"

She accepted the proffered hat and turned it around, fingering the embellishments and then the inside. "It's quite exquisite." She turned to Lizzie. "And you came up with this yourself?"

"Yes, ma'am." What was Mr. Calloway doing? Did he want her to make another one for this lady? Or—

"No one else has anything like it?"

"No, ma'am. Perhaps similar, as it is a popular style, but I added my own touches to it for—"

"This was created with someone of your tastefulness in mind, Mrs. Redding." Mr. Calloway clasped his hands and nodded. "The color will complement several of your outfits from my shop."

"Yes, I'll take it. Thank you so much for thinking of me." She turned and headed to the counter with the hat. Mrs. Donaldson's hat.

"Mr. Calloway," Lizzie whispered, "this was for—"

"Back to work now, Miss Morgan. As you have a suit and a hat to still finish for Mrs. Donaldson, I believe? But this is now Mrs. Redding's signature style, so the next one cannot be in any way similar." He caught up with the new owner of the green hat. "Now, Mrs. Redding, I trust you're glad you did stop in."

"Most certainly." She looked over at Lizzie. "And I'll be sure to tell all my friends about your talents, dear."

"Thank you, ma'am," Lizzie murmured.

As soon as the door clicked behind Mrs. Redding, Mr. Calloway turned to Lizzie. "Back to work, dear. You still have a hat to make. And you need to come up with another idea for Mrs. Donaldson. She wouldn't want to be wearing a hat identical to someone else in her circle of friends, now, would she?"

With a whistle, he walked into his secret back room.

Once Lizzie had the ideal opportunity to sneak back there and find the evidence against him, she could quit working for that horrid man.

∽

Of all days for the boss to come visit the smaller office on this side of town. But Josiah needed to get going very soon if he had any hopes of meeting Lizzie after she got off work and escorting her back to the boardinghouse.

Mr. Henry worked silently, seated in the lone chair, while Josiah stood next to the desk. As tedious as it had been for Josiah to enter the numbers, Mr. Henry took at least that long to study each one. All while the minutes closer to five o'clock ticked by.

Finally, Mr. Henry pushed his spectacles up on his nose and closed the book under his hand. "Everything looks to be in order, a job well done. You do good work for my firm, Josiah, and it's much appreciated."

"Thank you, sir."

Mr. Henry's gaze roamed around the room, then landed on the doorway to the adjoining room. And visible from the entry was the blanket spread on the floor where Josiah now slept. The blanket Mr. Henry must recognize as the one he'd left in the office for when the days got cold.

His boss said not a word, but his eyes asked a myriad of questions.

"Um, Mr. Henry, I should have asked your permission first. But I, well, in light of some circumstances, gave up my room at Mrs. McPhearson's boardinghouse a couple days ago and have been sleeping here."

"I see. Have you met on hard times and found, perhaps"—he cleared his throat—"that I'm not paying you enough?"

"No, no. Your wage is above fair."

Mr. Henry studied him a moment. "I lived here myself when I first started out. I believe I have told you that."

"Yes, sir."

"This space is meant to accommodate living quarters, small as they may be."

"So is this arrangement agreeable with you then, sir? It's only temporary, I assure you."

"Of course. But I might be able to provide you a proper cot. And some more bedding."

"Thank you, sir."

Mr. Henry nodded, assessing Josiah under his stare. "Knowing your character, am I safe in assuming you're here because you're helping someone?"

"I—"

"Of course, you can't say. But know this, Josiah. I admire your character and am proud to call you an employee."

Since Josiah would never hear praise from his father, this was the next best person to receive it from. And it landed like a warm blanket, wrapping right around his heart. "Thank you, Mr. Henry."

"Yes. Now, I'm consulting with a possible new client tomorrow evening and would like to ask you to meet with us over supper near the main office. This is very important." He sat forward. "Can I count on you to attend?"

It would mean not walking Lizzie home after work. But Mr. Henry rarely asked for anything outside of regular work hours. "Yes, of course. I'll be there as soon as I close here tomorrow."

"Very good." His boss stood and shook Josiah's hand. "Tomorrow, then. I'll show myself out."

"Thank you for coming." Josiah let the man leave first, unwilling to hold him up by walking out together while he took the stairs at a slower pace. But if he didn't hurry now, he'd miss Lizzie. Unless his father kept her after hours again. And in that case, he'd wait across the street until she came out the door.

Josiah stayed on the other side of the street from the shop, arriving just in time to see his father open the door and step outside whistling. That was most unusual. Odd, even. Josiah quickly turned and peered into the candy store. He hadn't even gotten a glance into the tailor shop's front window to tell if Lizzie was still at the sewing machine or had left.

In the reflection of the glass, he watched his father pull the door closed behind him, but he didn't stop to lock it. Did that mean Lizzie was still inside? His father headed to the right and walked briskly down the sidewalk, with the determination of a man with a destination.

Josiah crossed the street. But how not to scare Lizzie, as she must still be inside? He made out her form at the sewing machine, so perhaps the best thing to do was knock. That's how any customer would get her attention if they found the door locked—which though it wasn't, she might have assumed his father had done so.

Did the man have so little regard for others that he wouldn't take a moment to make sure his female employee, left alone in his shop, was secure within? Josiah tapped on the door with what he hoped sounded like a friendly knock.

Lizzie's head bobbed up. He could tell the moment she realized it was he, as she smiled and came immediately to the door.

"Josiah! What brings you by?"

"After last night, I wanted to make sure you got home safely."

A softness lit her eyes. "That's very kind of you. But since Mr. Calloway didn't instruct me to stay, I was just about ready to pack up."

"Did you finish your hat this morning with no problem?"

The light immediately left her eyes, and she looked down. "I did finish it, yes. But..."

Her heavy sigh sounded as though a burden weighed on her. "But...?"

She waved a hand in dismissal. "Yes, that one got finished. It's already been sold, so I'm currently making another."

"Oh. I guess that's good?" Odd. It seemed like a good thing. Yet her eyes indicated otherwise.

She didn't answer, just quickly cleared the sewing machine of fabric and loose threads and put her coat on. "If I'm to be on time this evening to help Mrs. McPhearson with supper, we need to be going. Come, and I'll lock up."

He trailed beside her and waited while she secured the door.

She took a couple of steps, then stopped. "You don't need to escort me back to the boardinghouse."

"I know. But I'm headed there, anyway, for my own supper, remember?" He smiled at her, and was that a blush across her cheeks?

"Of course."

"But tomorrow I won't be able to come, nor be at supper, as

my boss has asked me to join him and a possible new client for a meeting and a meal together afterward."

"Your boss sounds nice."

"He is. And fair." Lizzie's single nod highlighted the unspoken truth between them—that hers was not. "But on Saturday, I promise, I'll be here waiting."

And oh, the sweet, shy smile she gave him. "Then I'll look forward to Saturday."

They didn't speak the rest of the trip, nor did he take her elbow this evening. But words weren't needed, as each step to the back entrance of the boardinghouse was filled with wonder and brightness with her next to him.

Once she was inside, he walked around the house and entered through the front door. Apparently, Lizzie had made it in time to help Mrs. McPhearson, as he could hear the two women talking behind the kitchen door, and not all of the men had assembled at the table yet. Except, of course, Hugh and Markos were already in their seats.

"Well, well." Hugh poked Markos in the ribs. "Our Mr. Goody Two-Shoes has honored us with his presence." He gave a mock bow, and Markos saluted.

Sometimes an unholy rage burned in Josiah's chest, scaring him that he was like his father. *Oh Lord, please forgive me.*

"Good evening." Somehow, Josiah managed to sound civil.

"Are you going to turn the other cheek?" goaded Hugh. "Isn't that what you're supposed to do?"

Josiah looked him in the eye and let silence hang in the dining room as Peter and Melvin entered with Walter and Frederick right behind them. "Yes, Hugh, that's exactly what I'm going to do."

Melvin gave Josiah a clap on the back as he passed by. "Good for you, Josiah."

"Yeah," Peter added with a frown at Hugh as the men took their seats.

"Oh dear, oh dear." Hugh directed his mocking back at Josiah. "What are you going to do? Tell Mrs. McPhearson on me, *Snitch*?" Hugh aimed a daggered glare at him. Then just as quickly, he laughed, and Markos joined in rather half-heartedly.

"There's no need." Mrs. McPhearson stood in the dining room doorway, a bowl of what smelled like beef stew in her hands. "Gentlemen—if I may even use that term this evening—in my home, there will be civility. Is that understood?" She held each one's gaze until he nodded, lingering a bit longer on Hugh. She plunked the serving bowl down on the table and nodded for Lizzie, who was right behind her, to set the basket of rolls next to it.

"*Snitch.*" The venom in the word had left no doubt of what Hugh believed about Josiah. But telling Hugh the truth wouldn't solve things either.

Josiah kept his eyes on his plate, not daring to even glance at Lizzie. What must she think of him? That he was just like his father to get involved in such an exchange in the first place? Or weak for not standing up to Hugh?

Either way, he couldn't tell her why Hugh hated him. Nor of his vow to never be like his father.

CHAPTER 8

Lizzie set off to the tailor shop at a brisk pace as soon as her breakfast duties at the boardinghouse were complete. Her first Saturday at work. Her first payday. And a promised day of rest coming up. And how she needed that.

Benton Calloway was becoming an increasingly harder man to work for. And what if he and Josiah were in cahoots together? Though the very fact that she'd missed him yesterday told her something.

As Lizzie approached the shop door, Gideon Brighton waved to her from across the street where he was washing the candy store window. "Hey, Miss Lizzie."

"Good morning, Gideon. Your window is looking good."

"Thanks. I have to do this 'cuz Grandma says too many handprints land on it every day. People pointing to their favorite candy, you know, wishing they could buy it. But they don't all come in. Grandma says they're not all little fingers either."

Lizzie laughed. "No, I suspect not." She could picture Isaac, Winston, Zephaniah, and Sammy pressing up against the window, wanting a sample from each jar. Maybe when she returned home for a visit, she'd buy them a bag of candies to share. "I'd better get to work."

"Yeah, you'd better. He's a mean one, I hear."

"You do?"

He looked up at the open window above the store—maybe worried his grandmother had overheard him. "Forget I said that. One businessman should not speak ill of another businessman. That's what Grandma says. But you'd better get in there, anyway. And if you want some more Mary Janes, you know where to find them."

"I do. Thank you." She unlocked the shop, glad Mr. Calloway wasn't again waiting at the door to berate her. She took her seat and set to work. But did Gideon say that about Mr. Calloway from personal experience? It was doubtful he'd heard it from Mrs. Brighton. Or actual tailor shop customers. So how did he know?

Ten minutes later, Mr. Calloway came through the door with his usual scowl.

"Good morning, Mr. Calloway." Mama insisted on pleasant words being the first to be spoken in a day.

His eyes perused the completed projects shelf beside her head. "I see Mrs. Donaldson's new hat must still be unfinished as it's not up there."

"No, sir." She kept her words light, sweet. Though if he looked, he'd see it on the sewing machine as they spoke. Or maybe he had seen it. "But it will be done in ten minutes." Before the shop officially opened.

"Then get to work." He strode behind his curious curtains, leaving Lizzie to work in solitude and peace.

She finished hand sewing the final embellishments to Mrs. Donaldson's hat that had required much inspiration. With this new design and even the complementing color instead of a perfect match to the suit, it was superior to the one Mrs.

Redding had purchased. She added it to the completed projects with what seemed like a hundred other little repairs and alterations.

Then she returned to working on Mrs. Donaldson's suit, pleased with the pleats she'd added in the skirt to accommodate the growth of the baby.

Most of the day, she worked alone in the front of the shop while Mr. Calloway stayed behind his curtains. And whatever he did back there, it was done in silence. When Lizzie stopped the sewing machine to change bobbins and the top thread colors, she would listen. Nothing. When customers came in and the front bell jingled, she would wait to see if he would appear. Which he didn't.

So she would stop her work again and smile and see how she could help them. Only if a customer requested him would he appear. As if he was listening. And he would greet them exuberantly with a wide smile. And pile more work on her before he returned behind the curtains.

But in a few hours, she would receive her wages, money she could send home. And then rest. After this first partial week at the tailor shop, she was exhausted.

At five o'clock, Mr. Calloway stepped out from the back. "Though I'm closed tomorrow for the Lord's day, I expect you back early Monday morning, ready to work hard. Good night. Lock up when you've cleaned your area and swept." He strode to the door.

Was he not going to pay her? "Mr. Calloway..."

His hand was on the knob, and he turned back with a frown. "What?"

The irritation in his voice didn't bode well for asking him anything. And now she'd be calling from across the room. She rose and walked toward him. "Did you— Are you—"

"Spit it out, girl. I have business to attend to."

She swallowed. "I thought I was to be paid today. The end of the week."

His brows rose, and he scowled more deeply. "Did I tell you that Saturday is payday?"

"N-no, sir. But..."

Without a word, he marched to her workstation and grabbed the skirt right off the sewing machine bed where she'd set it down. "Who is this for?"

"Mrs. Donaldson."

He inspected the stitching, fingered the pleats she'd added in. "This is not the style you were supposed to make. What are these doing in here?"

Oh, Lizzie's face had to be beet red by now. How could she tell him the reason for the pleats?

He tossed the skirt over the arm of the Singer, not waiting for an answer, then tromped behind his curtains and returned with some bills. Held them out. "Here. Of course, I deducted for the breakfast I brought you and for being late and for not completing Mrs. Donaldson's hat in a timely manner. Now good night." He stalked to the door and exited. And thankfully, didn't look back.

Lizzie stared at the few bills in her hand. That man! After her hard work, there was barely anything to show for it. And definitely not enough to send anything home to Caldwell. Was he trying to get her to quit? Just as she knew who he was, he must know she was the daughter of his enemies.

She stuffed the money into her pocket and returned to the sewing machine. After folding Mrs. Donaldson's lovely skirt, she put it on a shelf and straightened the area. Then she swept the floor and locked up just as she'd been requested to do.

Because she was not giving up until this man was again in jail.

Out on the street, she leaned her back against the door with a deep sigh. Alone. And empty. That's what she was. But she shouldn't be.

"*On Saturday, I promise, I'll be here waiting.*" Where was Josiah? He wasn't standing in front of the candy store peering into the window.

And what was she even doing, starting to look forward to being with him? Especially since he was a Calloway. Though he was nothing like his father. And if he was, he had sure fooled Mrs. McPhearson too.

"Okay, think, Lizzie." Now that her anger over her pay had calmed some, she needed a plan. One thing was sure—she could not tell Mama or Papa about any of this, not who she was working for, and definitely not how he was treating her. For they'd never allow her to stay.

"Lord, help me to..." To what, she wasn't even sure. But if there was anything she'd learned on the ranch, it was determination and tenacity. And she had plenty of both. She could not afford to quit or get fired, for then she'd lose all chance of stopping this man from ruining the Double E.

She'd grit her teeth and bear his unpleasantness. For Mama and Papa. By concentrating on the pleasant aspects of the job—the sewing itself and helping the customers and learning about the fashions Boise women wore to events—she'd show Benton Calloway just what the Morgan women were made of.

"Good evening, miss." A matter-of-fact voice spoke next to her.

Lizzie looked at the lady who had crossed the street. "Ma'am."

The tiny woman with a tight black bun stuck out a hand. "I'm Mrs. Brighton, owner of Brighton's Candy Shop right there. And you must be the Miss Lizzie my grandson speaks of."

Lizzie shook her hand. "Yes. Lizzie Morgan. I'm pleased to meet you. Gideon's a very fine worker and a nice young man."

Mrs. Brighton beamed. "Glad to hear that. I just wanted to come over and introduce myself, seeing that you lasted longer than the last seamstress. You must have pluck."

"Ma'am?"

Mrs. Brighton chuckled. "You must have spunk or grit to work here more than two days. All the others quit within the week. Or are you locking up for the final time yourself?"

Oh, wouldn't she love to be doing just that. But Lizzie called up some of that spunk and grit. "No. Just for the night. I shall be back on Monday."

"Good for you." Mrs. Brighton's eyes lit with approval...or mischief.

"So have there been very many others?" If Lizzie could find out more about what went on at the tailor shop...

"Oh yes. That man can't keep a girl more than a few days at most."

"Is he...dissatisfied with their work?"

Mrs. Brighton shrugged. "Who knows. Probably, as nothing would satisfy that man. But when the girls go stomping out of here, leaving unmade garments right on the sewing machine mid-stitch, mark my words, I hear a thing or two. Though I shouldn't be repeating them."

"Of course. Have they ever spoken about his treatment? As an employer."

"Not directly to me. But I do know he's a hard taskmaster who pays little."

Lizzie fisted her hand around the meager bills in her pocket. "I see. Have they reported his conduct to anyone who could perhaps help?"

"No one stands up to Benton Calloway and walks away unscathed. And"—Mrs. Brighton waved a finger at Lizzie—"don't let your spunk get the best of you. If I could afford help—more than the candy I pay Gideon—I'd be offering you a job myself. But I do keep an eye on what goes on in the neighbor-

87

hood. So just know you're not alone. I see Josiah escorting you in the evenings." She looked around. "Some nights, anyway. I didn't see him last night either."

"Yesterday he had a meeting and supper with his boss, so he wasn't able to be here." But tonight? Maybe he'd simply been detained. If she stood here talking for just a few minutes more, perhaps he'd show up.

"A good man, he is. But if you ever need help when he's not around, missy, I'm in the store all day and right above it after hours. Ring the bell if you ever need me."

"Thank you. I certainly appreciate that."

Mrs. Brighton returned to her side of the street, and if Lizzie didn't leave right now, she'd be late in helping serve supper. But where was Josiah? He wasn't among the people scurrying along the sidewalk. Was he not coming tonight as he'd promised? Of course, he wasn't obligated to see her home each evening—even though the times spent together had been pleasant.

Mrs. Brighton waved from the candy store door. "Remember, ring my bell if you ever need to." Then she stepped inside and closed the door behind her.

So maybe Lizzie wasn't alone and was safe staying in Boise, surrounded with protection as she was—Mrs. Brighton, Mrs. McPhearson. And Josiah?

No matter how kind and caring he'd shown himself to be in spite of being a Calloway, he wasn't here as he'd promised.

~

Josiah slid into his seat at the dining table just moments before Mrs. McPhearson swung open the door and brought supper in. If only he'd gotten here early enough to go around back and explain to Lizzie why he hadn't been on time to walk her home tonight.

"Thank you for joining us this evening." Hugh smiled, and

he somehow made it look almost genuine. "We missed your presence last night. I do hope no ill will has befallen you." All proper, civil words, but each one dug deeper into Josiah's certainty that Hugh was up to something.

"Thank you. All was fine." He needn't detail his business. He gave each of the other men a nod in greeting. But where was Lizzie? Had she made it home safely? Or should he go out looking for her?

Just as Josiah had been about to leave work, his employer had tromped up the stairs. While Mr. Henry brought good news—that the client from last night wished to hire the firm— he was so joyful that he stayed to talk. And give each detail of what the client had liked. And laid out possible future plans. By the time Josiah left and stopped by the tailor shop, half hoping Lizzie was still working, she'd been gone. But he had yet to see her here.

Mrs. McPhearson made a second trip into the dining room with her nightly basket of hot rolls and a bowl of potatoes. Josiah tried to grab a quick glimpse into the kitchen before the door swung closed behind her. And now his heart was beating faster when he didn't see Lizzie in the kitchen. Where was she if she wasn't helping Mrs. McPhearson with serving?

Since the men weren't permitted to wander beyond the doorway anymore, he'd have to wait until supper was over. Then he'd go around the house and knock properly on the back door, as Mrs. McPhearson seemed to allow that.

He choked down what food he could. Not eating would rouse questions he didn't welcome nor want to answer. Finally, Mrs. McPhearson came to clear the dishes for Saturday night dessert. Waiting even longer was becoming tortuous. He wouldn't be able to eat a bite of whatever the dessert was, and yet he'd have to sit here until everyone was finished and—

The door swung open once more, and there was Lizzie, carrying a tray filled with plates of white cake.

Lizzie with her long braid. Looking out of breath, a bit disheveled...and upset.

With quick steps, she reached the table, Hugh eyeing her the entire way. "Ah, there you are. Your beauty has been sorely missed this evening, miss." He smiled at her as if expecting her to succumb to what he probably considered his winsome charm with ladies.

She stuck a plate in front of Hugh without a word, then Markos. Moved to Walter at the head of the table. Around to Peter, Frederick, and Melvin. Then she was beside Josiah. He looked up at her, smiling to put her at ease. To tell her with his eyes that he was sorry, that he needed to talk with her. To—

His plate landed solidly in front of him, and she walked off without another glance in his direction.

"Well, well." Hugh roared with laughter. "I guess the little lady had a message for you. Perhaps you've been seeing her elsewhere? Maybe tried to steal a kiss?"

"Shut up." Josiah fisted his hands under the table. If they got anywhere close to Hugh's face, he'd—

He'd be just like his father.

He unclenched his hands and put his napkin on the table. Rose. "Excuse me." He exited the front door and stood on the porch. Where should he go? Not back to the accounting office, his home now. Not roaming the streets.

The back steps.

What? There was no reason to go there now. Lizzie was safe, and she'd made it very clear she wasn't wanting to talk with him.

He took a step to the stairs. He'd just go on back to the office, where he belonged. Maybe a poem would come to him, though it'd be a sad one if he wrote from his heart.

The back steps.

The urging nudged him again.

Maybe Mrs. McPhearson would send Lizzie out so he could

explain. With a look back at the dining table through the front window, he could see the other fellows digging into their dessert. Hugh, of course, being the only one talking. But at least Hugh wasn't following him outside.

Josiah walked around the big house and onto the rear steps. What was he thinking? Should he knock on the door and hope Lizzie opened it? He plopped onto the top step to think.

And the door opened. "Oh, Josiah!" Mrs. McPhearson stood over him, a smile replacing her shock. "Come into my kitchen. I saved your cake." She winked and pulled him up by his arm and inside. "Hurry now, we're letting the heat out."

He stumbled along beside her, let her push him into a chair at the round table in the corner. And within seconds, a plate of cake appeared in front of him.

"Thank you. You didn't need to do that, especially since I left so rudely."

"I have ears, Josiah. I know what goes on in my house. And who doesn't abide by the rules. A certain somebody is going to have a good talking to. And an ultimatum is coming soon."

"Please, not on my account. I'm trying to obey the Good Book, is all."

"I know." She patted his hand. "You're a good man, Josiah Calloway."

Calloway.

And that was the problem right there. To Lizzie, he was a Calloway, the son of her boss, who undoubtedly was not treating her properly. And what must she think of Josiah when he hadn't been at the shop on time?

He looked toward the dining room door. Where was Lizzie, anyway?

"I sent Lizzie off to her room."

Oh, surely, he hadn't spoken his question out loud. Now how could he talk with her? "She did look a little…"

"Weary. She had a hard day—and week—at the tailor shop.

She just needs a bit of rest, and I'm sure she'll be back down here in the morning, ready to help in the kitchen. Rest, Josiah. That's what weary bodies need. And souls as well." Mrs. McPhearson pinned him with one of her looks that said he'd better not deny it.

And yes, he was weary. In both body and soul.

"'But they that wait upon the Lord shall renew their strength; they shall mount up with wings as eagles; they shall run, and not be weary; and they shall walk, and not faint.' You know that verse, yes?" Now her eyes held gentleness, compassion.

He nodded, letting the words find their way down into his soul. "Yes. From Isaiah."

"That's God's promise, Josiah. Just wait upon the Lord."

She rested her hand on his arm like his mother used to when she wanted to comfort him. Callie Brownington Calloway had known what it was to be bone and soul weary, married to his father. But she had learned through the years to cling to God, to trust in Him. Had taught Josiah not only this verse but the ones preceding it.

Hast thou not known? hast thou not heard, that the everlasting God, the Lord, the Creator of the ends of the earth, fainteth not, neither is weary? there is no searching of his understanding.

"God sustains us, Josiah. Always remember that."

"But I'm tired."

How many times had he said that in complaint? And each time, Mother had simply pulled him close. *"He giveth power to the faint; and to them that have no might he increaseth strength. Even the youths shall faint and be weary, and the young men shall utterly fall.'* Say it with me, Josiah."

"'But they that wait upon the Lord shall renew their strength...'"

They'd recited the verse together over and over until it became part of him. And now that he was no longer a child, he looked back and was amazed at his mother's resilience amid the hardships of her life. Of raising him basically alone. Thankfully, raising him alone. Teaching him love and goodness and trust in God. That was his heritage, a godly mother.

Mrs. McPhearson stood. "Eat your cake now for physical strength. And you know what to do for the strength of your soul." She winked and bustled out to the dining room. By the time she returned with a load of empty dessert plates and placed them in the sink, he added his to the stack.

"Thank you—" What was he doing, getting all choked up? He cleared his throat. "Thank you for the cake and the advice." And, though it was doubtful she was old enough, for being like a godly grandmother to him. Maybe an aunt, like Lizzie had suggested. He gave her a hug and walked out the back door.

On the porch step, he looked up into the night sky lit with twinkles of hope.

He would always be a Calloway in name, but what could he do to make Lizzie Morgan see him as more?

CHAPTER 9

Sunday morning after helping serve a bountiful breakfast and a fast cleanup in the kitchen, Lizzie attended a delightful small church with Mrs. McPhearson. Or maybe not so delightful, once the reverend stood up and preached from the Bible.

Words that convicted Lizzie for being mad last night. Mad at Mr. Calloway. Mad that she'd worked hard and yet at the end of the week, she'd been paid nothing but a pittance. Mad at Josiah for... Not even so much for failing to escort her to the boardinghouse last night—for that was not his duty—but for simply being a Calloway. And she knew that was wrong. So wrong.

So the next time she saw him, she'd do what was right. She'd apologize for her unkind treatment toward him. But even now she cringed in the pew, thinking how she'd plunked his cake plate down without so much as looking at him. Well, Hugh's, too, but he sort of deserved it as an acknowledgment of his ill manners. Not that hers had been any better. But still, that was not how she should treat anyone.

And should Josiah forgive her and even offer to again meet

her after work and escort her back to the boardinghouse, she would not turn him down. For the truth was, she had enjoyed her walks with him. Had looked forward to them as a balm after her days' work.

Once the service ended, Mrs. McPhearson guided Lizzie to the back to meet the reverend, who stood greeting people as they departed.

"Reverend Matthews, this is my new boarder, Miss Lizzie Morgan. From Caldwell."

He stuck out a hand, which Lizzie shook. "It's nice to meet you, Miss Morgan. But"—he turned back to Mrs. McPhearson—"new boarder, hmm? I thought you rented only to men."

"I do. Lizzie isn't an actual boarder, I guess." She patted Lizzie's hand. "She's helping me in the kitchen in exchange for a room and meals. And her room is in my wing."

"Then I'm sure this works out well for both of you. Again"—he smiled at Lizzie—"it's a pleasure meeting you. I hope you'll enjoy your time in Boise as well as at our church."

"Thank you, Reverend." Lizzie let Mrs. McPhearson tug her outside to meet yet more parishioners. And there, standing in the churchyard, was Josiah Calloway. Had he attended the service here as well, maybe sat in the back and been one of the first to exit? Perhaps to avoid her?

When she'd told herself she'd apologize to him the next time she saw him, well, she wasn't expecting him to be at this church.

Mrs. McPhearson also spotted him and waved him over. "Josiah. I'm sorry—I didn't see you come into the service."

There, see how easy it was to say the words *I'm sorry*?

He smiled, though it mostly was aimed at Mrs. McPhearson. "I arrived as the singing was starting, so I sat in the back." He looked at Lizzie and opened his mouth.

But before he could utter a word, she jumped in while she had the nerve. "Josiah." She scuffed the toe of her boot in the grass. Something Mama would say was unladylike. "I'm sorry that last night when serving dessert I was..."

He looked at her, brows raised.

"Rude to everyone. Especially you." And though Mrs. McPhearson hadn't witnessed her actions firsthand, now she certainly knew what an unpleasant employee she had.

"Thank you. But I wanted to tell you why I was late getting to the tailor shop last night and couldn't walk you to Mrs. McPhearson's since you'd already left and that I was sorry."

"You came?"

"Yes, of course. I promised. I..." He looked down as though he was shy, then met her eyes. "I've enjoyed our walks. And knowing that you were safe, of course." He smiled, and this time, it lit his eyes as they looked straight into hers.

Lizzie took a quick intake of breath. Or lost a heartbeat. Or something—she didn't even know what that little flutter in her pulse meant. But, oh, it was there. As warm and delicious as Josiah's brown eyes on her. Making her feel as secure as she had the night he held her elbow.

"Yesterday, as I was getting ready to leave to meet you, my boss showed up, and I couldn't very well walk out on him." The glitter in his eyes suggested that maybe he had wanted to, though. "But tomorrow, I'd like to walk you to the boardinghouse again. If you don't mind?" His eyes turned from mischievous to hopeful.

And there it went again. That odd, yet wonderful, pulse-hastening sensation. And because of that, words slipped out before any old niggles of doubt could burst in. "Thank you. Yes, I'd like that."

Oh the smile that bloomed—what better word for it than that?—on his face. And that was all the confirmation she needed that he was indeed the good man that Mrs. McPhearson and Mrs. Brighton claimed.

"Mrs. McPhearson, Lizzie." Josiah nodded at both of them,

his smile resting on Lizzie a tad longer. "I'll see you tomorrow, then." With that, he left the churchyard.

Did he take his noon meal with his father on Sundays? Though she had not seen them together even once. Or perhaps he had friends to eat and visit with? While Mrs. McPhearson invited Lizzie to eat leftovers with her at the boardinghouse, she provided no meal for the men on Sundays except a substantial breakfast. And Josiah, of course, had not been present for that.

So while Lizzie wouldn't see Josiah again today, what a promise he'd left her with. A reason for her to return to the tailor shop tomorrow, to keep her hands busy throughout the day until time to lock up. *Tomorrow.*

After they returned to the boardinghouse, Mrs. McPhearson and Lizzie shared a meal in the kitchen.

"Well, dear." Mrs. McPhearson yawned. "I'm going to take a nap. Nothing revives me for the next week like my Sunday nap. It's a nice day out, so perhaps you would like to explore Boise a bit? Or maybe you're like me, needing that nap?"

"Exploring sounds lovely. And actually, I know right where I'd like to go if you could direct me. Mr. and Mrs. Conor O'Shannon's house. They told me to come visit any time. And Conor said everybody knows how to get there."

"Mercy, that'd be a right good place to go. And he's right. Everybody knows where his livery is. I'll draw you a map, so you won't get lost going or coming." She grabbed a pencil and paper and set to work.

With the map in hand and after several twists and turns, Lizzie arrived at the O'Shannon house. From the stable next door, Conor's deep voice rang out in song as he crooned to someone. Molly? Papa sang like that to Mama when they worked in the barn together.

Lizzie walked over to the barn and poked her head into the

doorway. No one other than Conor was in sight. But he stood grooming—and singing to—Rebel.

The horses she could see in the double row of stalls perked their ears forward at Lizzie, and Rebel tossed his head. Conor turned and stopped mid-note.

"Aye, Miz Lizzie. Come on in and greet the horses. They're delighted to see you. Look at that." He nodded in pleasure at the welcome he deemed the horses gave her as they stuck their heads over their doors.

Except a black horse. He tossed his head and pinned his ears back, and Lizzie froze in the doorway. Ears back like that was her warning sign of a horse's unrest.

"Never mind ole Mud Puddle here. He's an ornery one, aren't you?" Conor stepped over to the horse and rubbed between his ears, now flicked forward at his touch. "He's been like that ever since the missus gave him his name. I think he's protesting." He winked at Lizzie.

"Now take Rebel. He's also misnamed. He's a fierce-looking horse but gentle as a lamb, he is. The only thing he takes a dislike to is a saddle. Then he tends to live up to his name. Don't you, fella?" He patted the horse on the head. "But he's a good strong carriage horse. Though with it lookin' like my carriage horses will be out of their jobs with the automobile taking over, he might just have to learn to be a riding horse, won't you, boy?"

Lizzie laughed.

"Step over and pet him if you like."

"Oh, no, thank you."

"He loves attention and a good petting on the neck or muzzle, don't you, ole boy?"

Lizzie didn't move.

"You do like horses, don't you?"

"Not to hurt their feelings—or yours—but no."

"But the day I found you, you'd gone and spent the night

out here with them."

"That was out of necessity. Though they were all well behaved. Especially Rebel."

Conor clapped Rebel on his sleek neck. "He has quite a sense for people—for a horse, that is."

Rebel nickered softly and stuck his head toward Lizzie, his dark eyes soulful.

She stepped back from the doorway.

Conor chuckled. "He's saying hullo. Are you sure you don't want to pet him? Just step on in a mite. He'll be your faithful friend forever if you do."

Could she? There was no need to get any closer to him today. But just a quick pat on the head—and with Rebel inside his stall and Conor standing right beside her, his hand on the horse—maybe she could.

And she had to try. With his and his wife's kindness to her, he was harder to refuse than Mama or Papa.

She took a deep breath. Closed her eyes just long enough for a quick prayer. *Strength and courage.* Then took slow steps to reach the stall.

"That's it, exactly how these horses like it." Conor practically beamed at her. And in his eyes, approval shone. "Nice and slow. Nothing to spook them. No sudden movements. See, you already have an instinct about them."

Not instinct. Just hearing Mama say it over and over. *"Slow and quiet. Gentleness. Don't spook them."*

Tentatively, she held out her hand. *"Move your hand slowly toward the bridge of the nose so the horse isn't startled."* And she was touching Rebel's face. He leaned into her touch, just as Jasper did with Papa, with his ears forward.

Conor laughed. "There, you did it! Now you'll be his friend for life. And of course, now Rebel is expecting a treat." He reached into his pocket.

"Wait. I have something for him." Lizzie pulled an apple

from her own pocket. "Mrs. McPhearson said I could bring this for him. In repayment of the one you gave me when we met that was supposed to be his."

"Well, well. He'll be mighty pleased. Won't you, boy?" Conor patted Rebel's head. "Would you like to feed it to him?"

"Oh, no. I couldn't do that." She handed the apple over to Conor.

"I don't blame you. He'd pester you from here on out if you did." Conor laid the apple on his palm, and Rebel chomped it in one bite.

"Now that I have a job and have been paid, I can bring him another next time."

Conor winked. "Now that he's heard that, he'll hold you to it. But come, let's go inside and see what my Molly can rustle up for *us* to eat. She'll be delighted to see you again."

The horses nickered after them as they left the stable and headed to the house.

"Molly!" Conor bellowed as soon as he opened the door into the kitchen. "Lookee who I found."

"Glory be." Molly, her red curls springing out from underneath her scarf, rushed to Lizzie and enveloped her in a tight hug.

"Good afternoon, Molly."

"Now sit, sit. I'll pour some coffee and set out scones—"

"With jam and cream?" Conor winked at his wife.

"Of course. That'll tide you over until the evening meal. So tell us, Lizzie—have you found yourself a job and a place to stay? You've been in our prayers daily."

"Thank you. I have. I'm staying at Mrs. McPhearson's boardinghouse—"

"Hmm." Molly assembled a plate of scones and pulled out lemon curd and clotted cream. "Has she changed it over to women now? I hadn't heard."

Lizzie now expected that to be the first question people

asked and gave her short answer. "No, but she's letting me stay in a room in her wing of the house in exchange for helping prepare breakfast and serve supper." Not once had she needed to go into more detail.

"Ah." Molly nodded. "That sounds like Bea McPhearson. She's one of the finest women you'll meet. She'll take good care of you."

"Oh, she does. She's lovely." Lizzie set the scones on the table as Molly scooped coffee into the percolator on the stove.

"Good, good."

"And I found a job as a seamstress."

"Indeed, that's wonderful." Molly reached for plates, cups, and saucers from a shelf. "Who for, if I may ask?"

"The Boise Tailor Shop. For Mr. Benton Calloway."

Molly stopped with her hand midair and exchanged a look with Conor, some unspoken message passing between them.

"And are you being treated well there?" Molly asked as she set the table. Did she know something?

"Well, I've only been there a few days. And I'm very busy." All true. "Mr. Calloway keeps mostly to himself, but he's very pleasant with his customers when he steps out front." Also true. Oh, that neither Molly nor Conor would pursue an answer to the actual question.

Lizzie set out napkins but didn't miss the look Molly gave Conor again before she spoke. "I'm glad you found a job and a room so quickly."

"Is there anything I should know about working there?" Other than she'd discovered Mr. Calloway's charm was just that —charm with no substance. And only displayed to his customers to their faces. His mumblings under his breath about them—well, she tried not to listen to those.

"People talk—that's all." Molly smiled and checked the coffee. "His business seems to be quite established, and I hear his society customers are very pleased with his creations as well as alterations. I'm sure you do fine work yourself and will help him out greatly."

By now, the coffee aroma was filling the air, and Molly motioned for them to be seated.

"I do like the sewing. The fabrics are so beautiful and fine—and oh the threads. They're a rainbow of color."

"Well then, it sounds as though you're in just the right place. But if you ever have any trouble, just come get us. We're almost always around—Conor out in the barn or me in the house. Unless it's my shopping day."

"Thank you. You're my first friends in Boise, and I'll always be grateful."

"And we'll always be grateful to have you come visit us." Molly looked at Conor again as she poured the coffee with its wisps of steam rising into the air.

He cleared his throat. "Remember, any trouble from *anyone*, you come a'running."

∽

Sunday was supposed to be a day of rest, but for Josiah, it was also the loneliest day of the week. Usually after church, he'd go to his room at the boardinghouse, sit on the porch with Peter and Melvin for a bit, then hole up the rest of the day with his book of poems. This week he had neither—his room nor his book. Books, as he was also missing the ledger. And the money envelope. So he'd been wandering the streets of Boise all afternoon.

The bright point of the day, after the sermon, of course, had been sweet Lizzie and her apology. And the way her eyes had lit up at his offer to meet her after work tomorrow to walk with her to the boardinghouse.

"*Yes, I'd like that.*" Her words set him to whistling every time he replayed them. Along with her smile. Her lilting voice. The sparkle in her brown eyes.

A lone dog barked as he retraced his route back to the accounting office. The building loomed in the distance, dark and closed up, most unwelcoming. Nothing to urge his steps to quicken as they did on the way to the tailor shop to meet Lizzie. Or rounding the boardinghouse for supper after walking her to the back porch with the hope of seeing her again in the dining room.

She served with grace, as if it came naturally to her. Her movements were quick and sure, as though she'd had experience in a kitchen. And her smile was sweet. So sweet. He really couldn't blame Hugh for noticing her too.

As Josiah neared the door leading to the upstairs accounting office, he spotted a hulking figure in the alcove. A vagabond? Thief?

At Josiah got closer, he saw exactly who it was.

No.

The man smirked. "Well, well, you finally decided to show up."

"Hello, Father." He'd never stepped foot in the office before, so what could possibly bring him today when it was closed?

His father straightened to his impressive, towering height. The stance was probably meant to intimidate. "Where've you been? I'm tired of waiting for you."

"What do you want?" There was always some catch.

"What do I want? Is that any way to greet your pa after I went to the trouble of tracking you down?"

"How did you find me here?"

"Well now, that's interesting. My newest employee told me her sad little story about needing a place to stay and how Mrs. McPhearson took her in because someone gave up his room for her. Someone who moved to the accounting office where he worked. And seeing as I'm pretty good at numbers myself, I put two and two together." He held out his hands, as though he was quite witty.

"All right, you found me. What do you want?"

"I want you to get information for me."

"No." No matter what it was. He refused to be a part of any of his schemes.

His father patted him on the back. "I see the army tried to instill some backbone into you." He laughed.

"Whatever it is, I won't do it."

"Ah, but see, there's where you're wrong. You will do it. If you don't want to see my new employee, Miss Lizzie Morgan, hurt."

"Leave her out of whatever this is about!"

"As you'll see, I can't do that. She's the perfect piece I need to exact revenge on my enemy, Caleb Morgan. And she walked right into my shop, asking me for a job."

Josiah reached for his father's collar—with any luck, his throat—but his father batted his arm away as if he were nothing.

"Temper, temper. Now listen." He grabbed Josiah's tie and lifted him up on his toes. "I can't keep an eye on her after she leaves work. But you can. I want to know when she contacts Caleb or Eliza, her parents. I know you meet her after work, so you just continue that each day and escort her back to the boardinghouse. Show some interest in her. Talk with her. Find out if she writes to them." He shoved Josiah away. "And report back to me."

He walked away as if the matter were settled, then stopped mid-step and turned around. Standing on the otherwise empty sidewalk, he gave Josiah a big grin that gleamed in the late afternoon sun.

"Or else." He turned back around and sauntered down the street, whistling a tune.

Meanwhile, Josiah clung to the office door to keep his legs from buckling under him.

CHAPTER 10

Only two things made Lizzie return to the tailor shop on Monday morning, her second week of work. Her need for money—more so now with the shortage in her pay—and the hope of finding out what Mr. Calloway was up to.

And as of yet, she still had had no chance to get into the curtained-off back room. For one thing, Mr. Calloway stayed in the back except to come out front to greet the richest customers and to load her with more work. And when he did leave the premises, he varied how long he was gone for lunch or appointments, so she dared not be caught back there upon his return.

Even when he'd left her alone in the shop after hours, she'd been too upset to have thought of going back there. But would the evenings be more dangerous? What if someone in the neighborhood reported a light shining from that part of the building when he was gone?

Mrs. Donaldson came in shortly after opening for her fitting, towing a handsome lad—maybe three or four years old and dark-haired, dark-eyed like his father, in contrast to her upswept auburn hair and hazel-green eyes. She preened in front of the cheval floor mirror in the green suit.

"I love it. The color. The style. I've never seen such a stylish skirt to wear in my condition. Your workmanship is beautiful."

Lizzie adjusted the jacket sleeves. "It looks lovely with your hair and brings out the green in your eyes. An excellent choice in color. And"—she set the newly created hat on Mrs. Donaldson's head—"this is the crowning touch."

"The hat's lovely, but I didn't order one."

"Your husband stopped in one evening last week and requested it to surprise you."

"He did? Oh, he's a dear. It's beautiful. I love how the color complements rather than matches the suit. And the simple lines let the ribbons be the focal point with their splash of matching color to the suit."

The anvil sitting on Lizzie lifted. Mr. Calloway had hated the hat, declaring it too plain for the elegant suit and high-paying clientele. But Lizzie was not a hatmaker and hadn't had enough time to do anything else. "Thank you. And—"

"Yes, indeed." Mr. Calloway stepped from the back room and strode over to Mrs. Donaldson. "This hat certainly will set you apart among your peers. The ribbons, as you observed, are the bold statement of sophistication, and they enhance the light in your eyes. I'm glad you approve of my creation."

His creation? Lizzie's glare all but bounced off his thick smile.

"Might I also suggest a suit for young Master Donaldson?"

"Oh yes. He does need a new black one." Mrs. Donaldson clapped her hands. "Edward, please come here to get measured."

"Miss Morgan here"—Mr. Calloway motioned to Lizzie—"will take care of the measuring. It was nice seeing you again, Mrs. Donaldson. As always, it's a pleasure doing business with you. If you can return in"—he checked his watch—"an hour, Miss Morgan will have the final touches to your suit completed, and you can pick it up then."

"Why, that'd be lovely." She turned to Lizzie. "Is that enough time for you, dear?"

With Mr. Calloway's eyes boring into her, she dared not hesitate or issue so much as a sigh. "Yes. Hemming the skirt and the sleeves will be simple, so an hour it is. May I take Master Edward's measurements first while you select the material?"

At that, Mr. Calloway reversed his exit to the back room and returned to the front counter, no doubt to listen better.

"Oh, yes." Mrs. Donaldson turned to the boy. "Edward, you stand still like a gentleman while Miss Lizzie measures you, and then we'll go across the street to the candy store. Yes?"

The boy's eyes lit up and he nodded. He stood still as a statue while Lizzie measured and his mother picked out the fabric she wanted.

Once Lizzie jotted down the last measurement, she smiled at Edward. "You did a wonderful job. Now, I believe you and your mother have a fun trip planned across the street while I finish up her suit."

"Let's go!" he all but shouted.

"Edward?" Mrs. Donaldson raised a brow at him.

"Thank you, Miz Lizzie."

"You're welcome. Now enjoy your visit to the candy store."

Lizzie put away her measuring tape and headed to the sewing machine as the two Donaldsons walked out the door hand in hand.

With a smirk, Mr. Calloway stepped behind his curtains, leaving Lizzie with a growing pile of work to do and even less time now to complete it.

An hour later, Lizzie snipped the final thread on the skirt as Mrs. Donaldson and Edward returned. The little boy held out a paper bag to her. "This is for you, Miz Lizzie."

"Edward, how thoughtful." She peeked in the bag. A whole box of Turtles and packs of gum and handfuls of penny candy. "All for me?"

"I putted lotsa Mary Janes in." He held out his hands. "As much as I could hold."

"Thank you, Edward. Mary Janes are my very favorites. And I love Turtles and Tootsie Rolls and gum too." She smiled at Mrs. Donaldson. "Thank you. This is most kind."

"You're very welcome, dear. It's the least I can do for you. You've been so helpful to me."

Lizzie boxed up the suit and hat and handed the garment box to Mrs. Donaldson. "I'll see you when it's time for Edward's initial fitting. We'll be in touch."

Mrs. Donaldson winked. "And maybe I'll be back for another of your wonderful creations for me as well."

Surely, Mr. Calloway was standing on the other side of the curtains listening. Probably rubbing his hands in anticipation.

Lizzie stayed bent over the Singer the rest of the day, skipping her lunch, trying to keep up with all the alterations tasked to her. What had he done prior to her coming? Doubtful the man could wind a bobbin himself. Yet his business seemed to be thriving, so was it her own ineptness that was causing the backload?

At this rate, she'd never be able to find information to help Mama and Papa save the Double E. And if she couldn't keep up, Mr. Calloway might order her to stay late again—and then she'd miss serving supper and Mrs. McPhearson might fire her —or charge her for Josiah's room. And Josiah. If he came by to escort her after work today as he said he would, what if she couldn't leave on time?

So she threaded the machine faster, cut ribbons and trims faster, talked to the customers faster. Recorded measurements faster.

As soon as Mr. Calloway left with nary a good evening, Lizzie straightened her sewing area. Did she dare lock the door and dart behind the curtains? No, not in the daylight. What if he returned unexpectedly? He had another key, that she knew.

She exited, locked the door, tested the knob. When she turned and looked up—there was Josiah, lounging against the candy store window, arms and ankles crossed.

He grinned, and there went that flutter again. His eyes lit, as if he'd been waiting for the moment she spotted him.

"Lizzie." Within moments, he was at her side.

"Hello, Josiah." She couldn't help her own smile. The hope of this moment was what had kept her going through the day.

He took her elbow in gentlemanly fashion, and with just the slightest tug, she was pulled closer to his side. Mercy. He was strong, confident, sure. And tender. Lizzie snuck a peek up at him. He looked down into her eyes, and as she sank into the warmth of his, she missed a step. In almost the same movement, he righted her and tucked her arm through his. Oh, she was very secure now.

"I'm not sure I should even ask how your day went. You look exhausted." He gazed so deep into her eyes, it was like truly being seen. Cared for.

Somehow, at his side the weariness vanished. "It was a long day, but the lady I was making a new hat and suit for loved both of them." In spite of what his father thought.

"That's a nice affirmation of your work to receive."

"It was."

But there had been an underlying tone in his voice, an ache? For something he didn't often—or perhaps ever—receive himself?

No, surely, he heard praise. He was a good man. A kind man. Going out of his way to help others. To try to live in a godly manner.

But she could imagine the one person in his life who probably never said a kind word to him. His own father. Was that why Josiah never poked his head in the door or came in while the shop was open to greet his father? She'd never seen them together. Not once.

"Josiah?" She pulled him to the edge of the sidewalk, out of the way of other pedestrians, then to a halt.

"Yes, what is it?"

"Thank you for all you've done for me. Everything. You're one of the kindest, most generous, godliest men I've ever met."

He gazed at her wide-eyed. Pulled her a little closer. And if she didn't know any better, from the longing in his eyes, he was going to kiss her. Right here on the sidewalk.

"Um, thank you." He shook his head. "I guess we'd better get on to the boardinghouse."

"Yes."

He started walking again, keeping her tucked securely against his side. And she was content with that, for this was where she belonged. Oh, the initial spark was still there—right where her arm looped through his—but it had grown into a companionship that cocooned itself around her in his presence.

Neither spoke until they reached the back porch of Mrs. McPhearson's house. "Here you go, Lizzie."

"Thank you."

He hesitated a moment before releasing her arm from his. "I'll see you inside."

She watched him disappear around the corner of the house before she opened the back door and stepped in.

Mrs. McPhearson took a roasting pan out of the oven and set it on top of the stove. "You look tired, girl. That calls for tea and a moment of rest before I put you to work."

Tea. Maybe Mrs. McPhearson's philosophy that tea was the start of a solution to most everything was right. Plus prayer, of course, she liked to add. Much like Mama, who'd probably be serving up supper to Papa and the youngsters about now also.

"No, I'm here to work. I hope I'm not late." Lizzie glanced around to determine how much preparation had already been done.

"There's nothing here that can't wait a few minutes. And even the men can wait a few extra minutes for their supper. Now sit."

Lizzie obeyed while Mrs. McPhearson puttered around preparing tea. When she placed two steaming cups on the table, she joined Lizzie as well. "So...tell me about your day, what has you so tuckered out."

She wouldn't tell Mrs. McPhearson her suspicions about Mr. Calloway, but perhaps she could clear up any lingering questions about Josiah. "I had a lot of projects to work on today, so I'm just feeling overwhelmed. But I'll wade through everything in time."

"Of course, you will." Mrs. McPhearson took a sip of her tea. "I didn't see Josiah. Did he walk you home today?"

"He did. And actually, I wanted to speak to you about him, something he left in his room."

"Oh, of course. Anything he left just box up and we'll get it back to him."

"Well, there's something about what I found, a ledger that was hidden. It's an accounting of debts owed. Your name is in it, and—"

"That dear boy." Mrs. McPhearson shook her head.

"I don't understand." Lizzie drank from her own cup to keep from fidgeting. To let Mrs. McPhearson talk.

"He doesn't owe me anything, Lizzie. I've tried to tell him that. But his— Someone cheated my husband years ago, God rest his soul, and others with various ruses. Josiah is paying back all the debts."

Not all of them, according to the ledger. But Lizzie didn't mention that. Nor her suspicions of Benton Calloway stealing more than money—how he was undermining the Double E's reputation and thus chipping away at its sales. Oh, wouldn't he love to run the ranch into the ground?

"Why would Josiah be paying the money back if he wasn't the one who stole it?"

Mrs. McPhearson looked her straight in the eyes. "Because that's the kind of man he is, Lizzie. God-fearing, upright, honest. A man who cares more for righteousness than his own reputation or personal gain."

"But the ledger has others, including—"

"Lizzie. He's trying to make something of himself, of his name, and paying people back is his way of doing it. I believe what you found is proof of someone else's wrongdoing and proof of Josiah's godliness."

Shame blanketed her for any of the doubts she'd had about Josiah. But, yes, that was exactly the kind of man he'd already shown her he was. When he didn't even know her, he'd given her a safe place to stay at his own inconvenience. And the way he'd cared for Mrs. Farber... He'd not only paid her in full but took money for her train ticket out of his savings. Yes, Josiah was exactly all those things Mrs. McPhearson saw in him. Even if it didn't explain the zero repayment in the Morgan column while there was money sitting in the envelope.

Lizzie took another sip of tea. "If I give you his belongings, could you return them to him?"

"Of course. I'd be glad to." Mrs. McPhearson stood and walked over to the roast and picked up a carving knife. "But perhaps you could."

Lizzie gulped. What would she say when she handed the ledger and his poetry book over? Admit she'd looked in them? Not say anything unless he asked? And, of course, the money. But she'd have to look into his brown eyes—eyes full of mystery, compassion, kindness—and see his disappointment when he realized she had questioned his character. And read the words of his heart.

Lizzie drank the last of her tea and stood also. "I'm ready to help serve the boarders. Shall I take the rolls out now?"

"Yes, start with those and fill the water pitcher, please."

Lizzie did so and grabbed the basket of rolls and headed into the dining room as the men took their seats. Everyone but Josiah.

"Hey, doll, I'll take one of those." Hugh reached into the basket and grabbed a roll before she even set it down.

"Me, too, honey." Markos also tried to grab one.

All jesting broke off as Mrs. McPhearson entered behind Lizzie.

"There will be no talk like that around my table—and hopefully, nowhere else as well."

"Yes, ma'am," most of them chorused.

"Yeah, Hugh, cut it out." Peter sent him a glare.

Mrs. McPhearson set the platter of roast beef on the table and walked out. Lizzie made her way around the table, pouring water into the glasses. But still no Josiah. Where had he gone?

When she got to his empty seat, he walked in.

"Hey, Holier than Thou. You're late." Hugh, of course.

Josiah ignored him—though his jaw tightened—and took his seat as Mrs. McPhearson returned with a dish of potatoes and a bowl of gravy.

"Did anyone say grace?" she asked.

All the men turned to Josiah.

"I will." He waited until each man closed his eyes. "Dear Lord, thank You for our food and for Mrs. McPhearson, who prepared it, and Miss Morgan, who is serving us. May You use it to strengthen our bodies, and may we serve You daily. In Jesus's name, amen."

A couple mumbled amens mingled with the scraping of food onto plates and the clatter of passing bowls and resumed conversation.

Lizzie poured water into Josiah's glass. He turned his head, and there she was, looking into his kind brown eyes.

"Thank you." He smiled, and her heart went and did that

little dance again. So maybe, yes, she'd gladly be the one to return his items to him.

Right as she looked away, she caught the eyes of Hugh on her. And a slow smile that reminded her of a fox. How would she be able to ask Josiah to wait after he ate so she could give him his books without the others overhearing?

On a trip back to the kitchen, she checked on the coffee percolating and pulled a golden pie out of the oven. Apple and cinnamon mingled with the scent of rich coffee, just like back home with Mama's pies and her evening coffee with Papa on the back porch. That's the kind of a man she wanted—like Papa.

Not that anyone like him would ever look at her twice. Though being around Josiah gave her a taste of what that might be like.

She wasn't a beautiful, successful businesswoman like Mama. She was just plain.

Like the sentiment in Josiah's poem.

> Just a bitterbrush bloom left behind,
> Crushed underfoot.

Even though Mama claimed she had been plain when Papa courted her, she was beautiful. Maybe it was more her smile and her joy, rather than her actual features, that gave her that glow.

When the men finished eating, Lizzie cleared plates, refilled water glasses, and served the pie and coffee. Still with no idea how to get Josiah alone to return his books and envelope.

"Hey, Busy Lizzie." Hugh snagged her wrist as she set a dessert plate in front of him. She jerked free. "Want to go for a walk with me after supper?" He winked.

"No. Thank you."

"I'll meet you on the front steps as soon as the last dish is cleared."

Lizzie shook her head.

"You know you want to. I'll even clear it with—"

"She said no." Josiah's words were calm yet spoken like steel.

"Stay out of it, Straight and Narrow. I'm asking her, real nice and polite like." Hugh turned to Lizzie. "What do you say, sweets? You wanna—"

Mrs. McPhearson stood in the doorway, arms crossed. "Supper is over."

The men with bites of pie still on their plates groaned and glared at Hugh. They wolfed down what they could before Mrs. McPhearson snatched their silverware. "Josiah, will you please bring the plates into the kitchen?"

"Yes, ma'am." He scooted his chair back, stood, and set to work.

Lizzie scurried to the kitchen clutching the coffeepot. "Mrs. McPhearson, I'm so sorry." She swiped an arm across her eyes.

"Nonsense. It's not your fault Hugh is ill-mannered. Josiah—pour yourself and Lizzie a cup of coffee and sit on the back porch here while I prepare a plate for her."

Lizzie shook her head. "I couldn't eat—"

"Of course, you can. After a hard day's work, you need to sit and eat. So go on out. I'll bring pie—and another slice for you, Josiah—in a bit."

"Thank you, ma'am."

He poured coffee and carried the cups behind Lizzie out onto the porch, then sat on the top step next to her. "Listen... The frogs are starting to come out. Hear them?"

The frogs. She did hear them, along with Papa's words. *"And when you hear the birds singing in the sun and the frogs croaking on a moonlit night, think of us here. And know you're loved."* Was this what Mama and Papa did out on the porch with their coffee and pie and the nighttime noises singing to them? Just rested in being together, another day done? Praising God?

"An evening like this makes me want to praise the Lord." Josiah spoke reverently, turning his eyes heavenward. "'For thy mercy is great above the heavens: and thy truth reacheth unto the clouds.' His mercy and truth. That's something to think about, isn't it?" He turned his eyes from the sky to look at her. "How about you, Lizzie? What do you think of when sitting in the still of the evening?"

"My family. My home in Caldwell." *Their love. My failures.* "Josiah, wait here."

She jumped up and hurried through the kitchen. "I'll be right back," she whispered to Mrs. McPhearson, who was humming as she washed dishes—just as Mama often did.

"That's my girl." Her landlady smiled and continued with her tune. A hymn.

Lizzie ran to get the two books and money to return to Josiah before she lost her courage. For what would he do once he surely guessed she'd read some of them, pieces of his heart?

~

Where had Lizzie fled to? Josiah would have left and headed back to the accounting office, now his home and his workplace, had it not been for Lizzie's "*wait here.*"

And wait he would. Her sweetness, her simple beauty, her forthrightness, her courage spoke to his heart. So, yes, he'd wait for her. And not just for her to return to the step.

He again looked heavenward. *The heavens declare the glory of God; and the firmament sheweth his handywork.* "Lord," he whispered into the night, "I know You're there. Please show me Your way. How to protect Lizzie from my father." Should he urge her to find another job? Move to another boardinghouse or back to

117

Caldwell? But knowing his father, there was nowhere she'd be able to hide from him. "Please show me Your way."

The creak of the kitchen door behind him alerted him to Lizzie's return before her breathlessness did. But she didn't sit back beside him on the step. She stopped at the door, holding her hands behind her back.

"Lizzie." He spoke in the gentle tone his mother had taught him to use to not spook their horses. No longer was she relaxed, but she shifted from one foot to the other. And still held her arms behind her back. Hiding something.

He patted the spot beside him that she had vacated. "Please sit back down."

"Here." She thrust her arms out and—

His ledger and envelope—and his poems!

Shock at having them in his hands overrode his initial question. Had she—

"I read them." She covered her mouth and ran back into the house, the door firmly voicing her departure.

Josiah scrambled to his feet. But he'd stayed on the hard step too long, and now his leg was cramped. He stumbled before he reached the door.

"What's wrong, Straight and Narrow?" The voice sounded from the bushes beside the house. "Can't walk? No wonder your girl ran off." Hugh's laughter was echoed by Markos's cackle.

Josiah hobbled through the door and would have slammed it behind him if Mrs. McPhearson hadn't been standing but feet away.

"I'll be heading home now, ma'am. Thank you for supper." He stuffed the envelope into his pocket, tightened his grasp on the ledger and poetry book, and turned to head back outside. By now, Hugh and Markos had had their fun, so they'd probably gone around to the front. He'd just slink back to the office. His home.

Like the worthless man he was.

Only when he could repay his father's debts in full could he prove himself otherwise. Before it'd been perhaps only himself he needed to prove it to. But now that Lizzie Morgan had found —and, of course, read—his ledger, he needed to prove it to her too.

"Josiah, sit a moment with me, won't you?" Mrs. McPhearson wiped her soapy hands on her apron and took a seat herself.

He remained standing. "You've been most generous, but I don't think I should continue eating meals here. I'm no longer a boarder."

"Josiah. This is my house, and I make the rules. You will continue eating here. The truth is, you're family. Now, will you please sit with me for a few minutes?"

He took a seat across from her, set the two books on the table, and folded his hands on top of them.

"This"—she tapped the ledger—"is not who you are, Josiah. And yet it is."

His heart had quickened when she said he was family. He'd taken it to mean he was loved. But, of course, she'd meant he was cut from the same cloth as his father. He hung his head.

"Josiah." Mrs. McPhearson put a hand on his arm, waited until he looked at her. "By that, I mean your entries of money stolen represent the wrongs your *father* has done. But each time you pay someone, sacrificing your own needs, and record the deductions, that, my dear Josiah, is who *you* are. Selfless. Giving. Caring. Loving. Always remember who *you* are. Those debts are not yours, nor are they yours to repay."

"My father is not going to repay a single penny. So who is?"

"That's where the two of you are so different. I didn't say you can't repay them. I said they're not your debts. You are a godly man for taking on the debts of someone else, to pay who you do not owe. Does that remind you of anyone? Someone who paid your own debt?" She smiled at him.

And finally, he returned her smile. "Yes. Jesus."

"Ah, yes. Jesus, who owed no debt of sin but who took on our heavy load of debt Himself to pay." She patted his hand. "So when you record each deduction as you repay your father's debts, do it in love for the recipient, even if not for your father. Not as an obligation but a gift. That's all I ask you to think about. I do love you like a son, Josiah Calloway."

"Thank you...well, for everything." The words so reminiscent of Lizzie's words to him this evening on the edge of the sidewalk. *"Thank you for all you've done for me. Everything."* He stood, gave Mrs. McPhearson a hug, then stepped onto the back porch before heading to the accounting office for the night. The first shades of a brilliant sunset had begun to fill the sky.

No matter what Lizzie thought of his poems or seeing her parents' names in the ledger with nothing repaid as of yet, he was thankful for so much. Mrs. McPhearson's mothering ways, meeting Lizzie, and for Jesus being the ultimate debt payer.

He left the boardinghouse with his head held high, looking forward to escorting Lizzie home again tomorrow after work.

And hoping she'd never find out about his father's threat.

CHAPTER 11

Josiah Calloway would never speak to her again.

Lizzie blinked fast before tears fell onto the red brocade she was sewing. A ball gown for some society lady. She didn't care about balls or high fashion or any of those things—but she did care that she'd wronged a man of right and courage. Certainly, she owed him an apology—but she couldn't utter it at Mrs. McPhearson's table in front of Hugh and his cronies. And Josiah was sure to avoid any possibility of time alone with her. Reading his ledger, his poems—it was like reading someone's private journal.

The clock crept toward five, but the stack of garments awaiting her attention had not diminished. Surely, Mr. Calloway was going to require her to stay late again. Or her other fear was in his displeasure he'd fire her. That would end any chance she had of sneaking into the back room of the tailor shop. Without that or even being able to talk with Josiah to find out what he knew about his father's plans, she might as well leave Boise and return to the farm. At least she was good at slopping the old pigs. And wouldn't her brothers be glad for her return if it meant taking that unsavory chore back?

As if on cue, Mr. Calloway swooshed through the curtains. "Miss Morgan, you've been hard at work today." She blinked at him, and he looked at her ever-growing stack of projects. "I see you're making progress. It's almost closing time, so you should prepare to go home."

What? But she brushed loose threads into her hand, eager to get out of here as quickly as possible. "Why—yes, Mr. Calloway."

The door opened, and under the jangling bell walked in Josiah, of all people. "Father. Lizzie." He nodded at them in turn.

As glad as she was to see him, what was he doing here? In the time she'd worked here, he'd never once entered the premises while his father was here, always waiting rather furtively across the street.

"Good evening, Josiah," his father said and smiled. Not quite the welcoming smile of a father seeing his son, but at least what appeared an actual attempt. "What brings you this way?"

"I've come to..." He cleared his throat. "I've come to escort Miss Morgan to the boardinghouse."

Mr. Calloway grinned. "Ah, yes, of course. She was just getting ready to leave, in fact."

Josiah turned to her. "If I may?"

Lizzie opened her mouth, but nothing came out. This was what she wanted, wasn't it? What she'd hoped for all day while sitting at the sewing machine. A chance to speak in private with Josiah. But now her mouth was so dry—how could she form the words? She hadn't yet even composed them in her head.

She picked up her pocketbook and edged toward the door. "Good night, Mr. Calloway."

"Yes. Enjoy your walk home."

On anyone else, the smile accompanying his words would

have been a benediction of sorts—but on him it was a smirk, as though enjoying some private joke.

"Thank you." She didn't speak again until Josiah had ushered her out the door and well into the next block.

"Josiah, I'm sorry. For reading your ledger and your private journal...for my curiosity, for my rudeness—"

"Ah, Lizzie. That's enough to be sorry about already, don't you think?"

In the depths of his chocolatey brown eyes, a glimmer of a twinkle appeared. "Well, I'm sure there are a lot more things I could name."

He pulled her out of the main stream of pedestrians, over to the side of a brick storefront. "As could all of us. Thank you for returning them to me. Now you know my big secret. I'm not an accountant at heart but a poet."

...But sobs of sorrow pierce my heart. Oh, she wished she could ask him about those words. What sorrow was he carrying? Was that what made him a compassionate man?

He reached for her hand as naturally as if he'd done it a hundred times before. And this time, there were no flutters or tingles. Not one. But in their place was something so much better.

Belonging.

He tightened his grip, as though he'd never let her go. Which was fine with her. With a grin, he led her back into the parade of people heading home for the night.

"My father thinks poetry is useless. And that writing it, no less, is a waste of time."

"He's wrong, Josiah. I said I read them, but you should know, not all of them. The ones I did, though, were moving. Deep and with passion." Lizzie's heart ached for him. But the words she wanted to say—*They show your kindness and compassion*—didn't come out.

"Thank you, but I know in his eyes, they're worthless. He

values physical strength, especially ranching. With my bum leg, I'm prevented from doing that." He shrugged. "But he doesn't even know the extent of it."

"What do you mean?"

Even above the cacophony of the crowded sidewalk, she heard his intake of a deep breath and felt his heavy silence. Perhaps it hurt too much to say the words aloud. Yet when he did, his trust of her settled into her heart.

"I wanted to be a rancher. I loved riding and roping growing up."

He fell into silence again, as if thinking, remembering.

Lizzie shuddered. "I grew up on a horse ranch. The Double E. My mother is a trainer—the Angel from the East, she's known as. And Papa is a saddlemaker." Though he must know this since their names were in his ledger. And probably also knew the rumors that were spreading about their reputation. "Except"—with her free hand, she fingered the scar over her right eye, pulled her hair back over it—"I hate horses."

He took a few strides, seeming to let the words settle in. "Horses are like people, Lizzie. Some are kind and gentle, others are mean. Test each one on its own merits."

Did he mean horses—or people?

"Did you learn riding and roping from your father?" Benton Calloway fit more the image of a man riding tall and statuesque on a stallion than he did cooped up inside a tailor shop.

Again, a deep breath and a moment of silence before answering. "No. I worked on a neighbor's ranch, and the ranch hands taught me. For a while, I did have a horse, though. Brownie. I even dreamed of buying my own place one day. Until..." He cleared his throat. "Lizzie, I don't want to speak ill of my father, but he'd been in and out of jail. This particular time for starting a barn fire." He looked at her, and she nodded, hoping he'd continue. "When he got out and decided to come back to my mother, I was twelve. He moved us to Boise, then disappeared for months at a time. My mother was so strong. And godly. And kind and hard working. By then, I was able to get a job to help her and was trying to save money for a small ranch. Then I fought in the Great War and..."

> Firing and explosions echo as villagers hide
> and dart
> but sobs of sorrow pierce my heart.

He shook his head. "I was blessed to make it out with only a leg wound. Shrapnel. But that was enough that I wouldn't be able to run a ranch. And in the time I was gone, my father had cheated yet more people and ended up in jail again. I put my ranch money toward his debts. He's out now and I hope is running his tailor shop honestly. But how long before he fulfils the biblical proverb? 'The dog is turned to his own vomit again; and the sow that was washed to her wallowing in the mire.'"

He stopped in the middle of the sidewalk and pulled Lizzie to a halt. People from behind bumped them and walked around, muttering.

"Lizzie." He led her over to a store window. "For all I know, he's following us. You have to leave Boise. It's not safe for you. Your family is who he's targeting. You must leave."

Leave? She couldn't. "No, Josiah. I came to help my family. And that's what I must do."

"But surely, they wouldn't want you in danger."

Definitely not—if they knew. "I'll be fine."

"At least get a different job. You can't be around him day after day—especially alone in the shop. I know he's my father, but he's vengeful—he's not safe for you to be around."

That was probably true. Yet as she looked into Josiah's eyes, another truth buried itself even deeper into her soul. That awful man had a son who was a man of honor, one she could trust wholly.

    Even with her heart.

CHAPTER 12

That Lizzie Morgan was a stubborn one. It'd been three days since he'd begged her to leave his father's employ, yet she was still there.

Josiah bent over the desk in the second-floor office, writing numbers into the ledger and double-checking them. In a way, he did like numbers. They were predictable. Entered correctly, they always came out perfectly. And his boss had been in today to bring more ledgers to balance—thanks to the excellent work Josiah was doing, he said.

The clock on the wall indicated it was 4:45. In fifteen minutes, he'd see her. Josiah closed the ledger, put his pencil in the drawer, and cleared the desk. Since he hadn't been able to persuade Lizzie to find another job, he made certain he was standing outside the Boise Tailor Shop each workday at five o'clock sharp to escort her to the boardinghouse. Not to satisfy his father's demand, but to protect her.

Though his father waited at the accounting office door now each evening when Josiah returned after supper and badgered him to tell what he'd learned from Lizzie, Josiah shared only a few tidbits. Nothing that would further his father's interests.

Lizzie hated horses. Lizzie didn't like ranching. She was learning to make delicious cherry pies.

And her eyes lit up when she saw him. He would never tell his father that. Lizzie treated him as if he were special to her. Someone to listen to her. To share their hearts with each other. To laugh with.

Last night, they'd sat on the porch until the stars came out. Then he'd walked home in the dark, feeling accepted, only to find his father waiting, livid that it was late.

> Under the stars in the soft hush of moonlight glow
> Amid a chorus of frogs and trumpeting crickets

He'd have to write it down later—adding the words he longed to say to Lizzie. If he could feel them, write them first, maybe then he'd have the courage to say them out loud one day.

Now that he'd gotten sidetracked, he'd have to hurry. He descended the stairs at a faster pace, ignoring the throb that jabbed through his leg on each step. Just as he arrived at his spot in front of Mrs. Brighton's window, Lizzie walked to the door of the tailor shop.

Since that one occasion three days ago now, he never stepped inside, just stood at the candy store window until she exited. Then he'd cross the street. Twice his father had parted the black curtains just enough for Josiah to catch a glimpse of him, no doubt making sure Josiah showed up each evening.

"Josiah!" Lizzie smiled up at him as she stepped outside, and in a flash, he was there to greet her.

He grinned and took her hand. Somehow after that evening of baring his soul to her, this had become their habit. "At last, this long workday is over. I hope you didn't think I wasn't coming. I got to thinking of a poem after I put the ledgers away, and..." He shrugged.

Lizzie's tinkling laugh seemed for his ears only. "I hope someday you'll share it with me."

"That I plan to do. Once I finish it." Hopefully, that'd be soon. They swung their hands in silence for a few steps. "Have you heard anything from your parents?"

"Yes. Mama is putting testimonials of satisfied customers on her sales leaflets, and Papa is too. They said little things like that seem to be helping sales for both saddles and horses to be picking back up some."

"That's great."

"And at the auctions, Mama is also setting up appointments with possible buyers to sit down and discuss questions they have. She said if she and potential buyers can get to know each other, they can start to build trust."

"Your mother is a good businesswoman."

"She is. I hope..." She looked at him shyly.

"What?"

"Well, maybe that you could meet Mama and Papa someday."

That would be a big step to meet her parents. But it would also spell the end of his dreams with Lizzie, as they'd never allow her to be courted by a Calloway. Did they not know about him yet, then? With her hand securely in his, now wasn't the time to voice those worries. "And your brothers too?"

She laughed. "Well, yes, them too—if you insist. Though they'll be underfoot whether you do want to meet them or not." But the twinkle in her eyes said she loved them all.

"I do. I want to know everything about you, Lizzie Morgan."

She smiled up at him ever so sweetly.

"Even how you got that scar over your eye you keep trying to cover up with your hair."

She brushed her hand over it. Though faded and barely noticeable, it held a story.

But she said nothing.

"I'm sorry, Lizzie. I got ahead of myself. It's none of my business, and I—"

"No, that's all right, Josiah. It's the reason I hate horses."

"I thought as much, that it had to do with that."

"I used to love seeing the ones Mama and Papa brought home. Scared, untamed ones that Mama taught to trust." She lapsed into silence, and Josiah squeezed her hand as different emotions flitted over her face, some seeming to bring happy memories. Then as the saddest one landed, she spoke again.

"Mama had two rules around the barn. Never startle a horse. And never enter a stall with these new ones. When I was ten, they brought home a beautiful white horse. Mama was so thrilled with her purchase. He had the potential of being their best horse yet and was going to help make a name for the ranch into other states as a possible stud horse, if they ever ventured into breeding.

"He hadn't yet been gentled nor was used to having people around, much less a ten-year-old. Mama hadn't even had a chance to win his trust. But he was so majestic and magnificent, I envisioned myself on him like a princess riding her royal stallion before her subjects. So I ducked into his stall while he was lying down. I thought I could climb on his back..."

"Lizzie—"

"He jumped up, and I scrambled into the corner, trapped. When he reared, his hoof caught me here." She again touched her forehead. "Then he came at me with bared teeth—"

"Oh, Lizzie." Josiah pulled her into an alcove of a store entrance and into his arms. Her body shook, and she buried her head against his shirt. This was where she belonged, in his arms, where he could keep her safe. Right next to his heart.

Finally, she looked up at him, tears on her cheeks. "Mama

and Papa heard the ruckus. She got the horse out of the stall, and Papa ran in and carried me out. The next day, she took that horse into Boise and sold him to the first person who'd take him."

Josiah pushed her hair back and laid a finger on her scar. Proof that Lizzie's parents loved her at any cost. "You're so blessed."

She swiped the tears away, then gave a weak smile. "I thought so, too—until I got the job of feeding the pigs instead of having to help with the horses."

She'd grown up around pigs? His heart double-timed. Was this confirmation that he should pursue his new dream? And wonder of wonders, that Lizzie would be part of it?

For it sure seemed an answer to his unformed prayer, that God had led him to a girl who loved pigs as much as he did.

~

Lizzie could have stayed in Josiah's arms there in the shoe store alcove, cocooned in his embrace, all because of that frantic white horse.

With the telling of the story, her blame of the horse lessened. She'd been disobedient, yet Mama and Papa had never said a word about that. Never was a mention made of the income lost from that beautiful horse Mama had pinned her hopes on. And that made it all the more imperative that she now help with sustaining the Double E.

She'd stopped crying but didn't move out of Josiah's arms. Nor did he move away, either, just letting her lean her head against his heart. She could feel each thud beating against her cheek.

But thankfully, he was the practical one. "I guess Mrs. McPhearson will be wondering where you are."

Lizzie looked up at him and smiled. "Yes, we should go."

He grabbed her hand and held on all the way to the back porch of the boardinghouse. "I'll be waiting right here after supper, whenever you finish up in the kitchen...if you'd like to sit again under the stars."

"I would." She turned the doorknob before she ended up taking his face in her hands and kissing him. As it wasn't just his cheek she wanted to kiss. With one last glance back and before her cheeks got any hotter, she dashed inside.

But the promise that he'd be right here waiting for her after work hurried her steps in every task Mrs. McPhearson gave her to do.

At the end of the meal, Lizzie poured coffee around the table while the men waited for dessert. When she reached Hugh, he put his hand on her arm as she poured his cup.

"So, Busy Lizzie, has Straight and Narrow kissed you yet?"

Her cheeks burned, and she jerked her hand, sloshing coffee into Hugh's saucer.

He laughed. "I'll take that as a yes."

Josiah scraped back his chair. "Apologize to Miss Morgan."

A sneer crossed Hugh's face. "I don't think so. If you're not man enough to kiss her, I will."

Josiah stood and started around the table.

"Oh, dear me." Hugh ducked behind Markos's shoulder in a fake cower. "Straight and Narrow is going to get me." He quaked, and Markos howled in laughter.

Josiah had reached him now. "I believe you owe Miss Morgan an apology."

"And how are you going to make me? Remember, you're supposed to turn the other cheek."

Lizzie stepped back. "Josiah—please—"

Mrs. McPhearson came through the doorway holding a pie, and Hugh turned to Lizzie.

"Miss Morgan, I'm sorry I spoke out of turn. Please forgive me."

Lizzie nodded, even though she doubted his sincerity.

But Mrs. McPhearson stood stock still, taking in the exchange and staring at Josiah.

She finally set the pie on the table and started passing out the dessert plates. And no one at the table said another word.

Lizzie slipped into the kitchen and started the dishes.

"Lizzie, dear." Mrs. McPhearson came up behind her and turned her around into a hug. "There are days I so miss Mr. McPhearson. He'd set those boys straight in a man-to-man way. And not to make excuses, but perhaps that's why some of them behave as they do—they didn't have a father teaching them. But I'm proud of our Josiah. He'll defend you. Now, while I don't condone fighting—and it is not allowed in my house—if Hugh insists on besmirching your honor, I just might happen to not notice if Josiah teaches him a lesson. However he best sees fit." She winked, and Lizzie managed a smile.

"Now, get on out there on the back porch. I'll fetch Josiah and let him know he's always welcome there."

"Thank you, Mrs. McPhearson."

"You're welcome. But first, I'm going to put on the teakettle."

Lizzie stepped outside into the crisp night air, a welcome relief from the heat of the oven inside. Evening sounds sang around her—a hoot owl, the frogs, a neighborhood dog. Pleasant sounds reminding her of Caldwell nights. She could hear Mrs. McPhearson puttering around inside, then a voice. Josiah's. Had he walked through the dining room door right into the kitchen?

"I'm sorry, Mrs. McPhearson. I let my temper get the best of me—but no one is going to talk to Lizzie like that."

"Of course not. She's worth standing up for."

"She is."

More puttering and clanging as Mrs. McPhearson must have been pulling teacups down, and then the kettle whistled.

"Thank you for letting me spend time with her on your porch."

"Indeed. Mr. McPhearson and I spent many a night out there ourselves. We had countless conversations and milestones under the starry sky. And numerous talks with our Lord as well."

"He sounds like a fine man."

"He was. You remind me much of him, Josiah. Now"—she must have taken the kettle off the stove, as the whistling stopped—"go get on out there with your girl. And stay again until the stars come out."

"Yes, ma'am." Lizzie could hear the grin in his voice.

The back door opened and closed, and then Josiah was standing beside her, pulling her into his arms once again.

"Lizzie, I'd do anything to protect you. I hope you know that."

She nodded against him. And wished he would take a hint from that horrible Hugh—and kiss her.

CHAPTER 13

This should be payday again.

Though as Lizzie sat at the sewing machine Saturday morning, she didn't have high hopes. Here she'd been in Boise almost two whole weeks and had nothing to show for it. No money sent home. No proof of what Benton Calloway was up to. And, of course, no job in the roadhouse. She was barely keeping up with helping Mrs. McPhearson as she was supposed to do.

But, oh, the memory with Josiah last night on the back porch. No, he didn't kiss her under the stars. But he held her hand from the time he sat beside her to the time he stood to leave. Every little squeeze, each time he ran his thumb across the top of her hand—that made the days in this shop bearable.

A clatter, then a shout sounded outside. Lizzie jumped up and ran to the window. Lying on the sidewalk across the street was a boy.

She dashed out the door and darted across the street. "Gideon!" Lizzie looked up and down the street to see if anyone was around to help, but the usually busy sidewalk was empty.

The boy looked up, tears in his eyes but blinking fast as though he was trying not to let them out. "Miss Lizzie."

She knelt beside him. "What happened? Are you all right?"

He didn't say anything, just stared at the concrete under him.

"Do you think you can sit?" At his nod, she helped him up enough so he could lean against the front of the store.

"Gideon, were you working in the candy shop?"

He nodded.

"Were you supposed to be outside?"

He shook his head.

Ah. "All right, then"—she pointed to his scraped leg—"it looks like you fell. Are you hurt other than this?"

"I don't think I can stand up."

Oh dear. "Is your grandmother here?"

"No. She left me in charge and said she'd be right back."

"How did you end up out here?" Lizzie used a tone she would with her brothers—firm enough to say she expected the truth but gentle enough that they knew she was for them.

"I had an idea for the display window. But I needed to see it from outside to know if it'd work."

"I'm sure your grandmother appreciates you taking an interest in the shop."

"Well, I am going to own it one day." He started to smile, then winced.

"Yes, I believe you will. Now, tell me what happened."

"No customers were here, so I got thinking. How could I get them to come inside and to buy something? I'd talked to Grandma about adding ice cream and a soda fountain, but she said no, we're a candy store, and it'd cost too much, anyways. I thought maybe they needed to notice the display better. So I came outside. Shelves."

"Shelves?"

"Yeah. If I built shelves in the window, we could put more stuff out and up higher for people to see it."

"What does this have to do with hurting your leg?"

"Because I needed to see what was the tallest you had to be on the sidewalk to still see over the shelves into the store. The customer needs to see the inside to want to come in, you know."

"Of course. But...?"

"I'm not tall enough. And there wasn't anything to stand on." His gaze darted to the window.

Lizzie spotted the narrow ledge under the window. "No..."

Gideon grimaced. "I thought standing on it and jumping up a little would work."

"It didn't, though, right?"

He rubbed his leg. "No, ma'am."

She checked the sidewalk again, but still no one was around to offer assistance. "All right. If I help you up, do you think you can stand now? And then maybe get you inside?"

"Yeah. Grandma will be hoppin' if I'm not inside when she gets back."

"I'm sure she'll be more concerned about you. I'll put my arm around you and—"

"Miss Morgan." Mr. Calloway stood in his doorway across the street, hands on his hips, wrath coloring his words. "Why are you not at the sewing machine?"

"I'm helping this young boy who's injured." Under her arm, Gideon stiffened, and Lizzie squeezed his shoulder to reassure him.

"He's of no concern to you. You have a job to do. Inside *my* shop."

Gideon's eyes went wide, and he tried to rise on his own.

"It's okay, Gideon." Lizzie held him still.

"Then get him inside or wherever he belongs and get back to work. Know I'll be deducting a day's wage for this incident."

"What?" That man was beyond awful.

"Now get back in here." Mr. Calloway whirled around and slammed his door.

Gideon again struggled to stand, and Lizzie helped heave him up. "Little by little, Gideon."

"Gideon Brighton!" Mrs. Brighton came from around the corner. Looked between Lizzie and Gideon. "What happened?"

"I'm all right, Grandma."

Lizzie stayed quiet, letting Gideon tell the story.

"I fell, but Miss Lizzie was helping me, and that mean man at the tailor shop came outside and yelled at her for helping me. Said he's not going to pay her 'cuz she helped me."

Mrs. Brighton looked over Gideon's head, a question in her eyes, and Lizzie nodded. "Let's get you inside, mister. And then you can tell me what brought you out here, when you were supposed to be inside taking care of the store."

"Yes, Grandma."

Together Lizzie and Mrs. Brighton got Gideon inside and seated on a chair.

"Thank you, Lizzie, for taking care of my grandson, but now you'd better be getting back to work before you get fired. That man—" With a look at Gideon, she didn't finish. "You'd better go."

"But..." At the fear in Mrs. Brighton's eyes, Lizzie nodded. "I guess so." She'd quit the moment she stepped inside the tailor shop if she could. But until she got her hands on proof of what Mr. Calloway was up to, she had no other option than to stick it out. If she left before that, then her whole time working for him was for nothing—and he would still ruin her parents and the Double E.

"Lizzie?"

"Yes?"

"Don't forget—ring my bell if you ever need me."

"I'll remember. Thank you." She turned to leave.

"Wait." Gideon tried to stand until his grandmother held him still. "Grandma, can Miss Lizzie have my wages today?" He looked at Lizzie, sadness in his eyes even as he gave her a brave smile. "It's chocolate fudge day."

Oh, she couldn't take that from him. Except...she understood what he was offering her. "Thank you, Gideon. That's most kind of you."

After Mrs. Brighton wrapped and handed her his daily wage, Gideon studied Lizzie a moment. "Just be careful not to get any of it on your sewing."

Oh, that would further infuriate Mr. Calloway. "Yes, I'll be very careful. Good day, Mrs. Brighton, Gideon."

Lizzie crossed the street, and the bell jingled as she opened the door to the tailor shop. Though she'd expected Mr. Calloway to emerge from his secret lair the moment she entered, he did not. Not a sound came from behind the curtains.

In the silence, she pulled out Edward Donaldson's measurements and the black fabric his mother had chosen. Working on the sweet little boy's suit kept her fingers busy and even brought a smile as she pictured the bag of candies he'd presented to her.

Had Josiah been as precious as Edward as a child?

At lunchtime, she ate her fudge from Gideon, careful to heed his admonition to not get any chocolate on the garments.

When five o'clock arrived, there was still no sign or sound from Mr. Calloway. Stuffing down the growing anger in her heart, Lizzie packed away her work and headed to the door.

Not only had Mr. Calloway kept his word about deducting her pay for the day—he'd managed to avoid paying her at all.

Well, come Monday, he was in for a surprise himself.

*J*osiah was only a minute late arriving at his father's shop, and yet Lizzie was already striding down the sidewalk. Had she thought he wasn't coming?

"Lizzie—wait up." Not that she heard him over the growing crowd that seemed to appear out of nowhere to join her. He walked faster, slipping in and out between people, until he was even with her. "Lizzie."

She turned her head, and her eyes—red-rimmed eyes—widened at the sight of him. He gently tugged her out of the sidewalk traffic and stopped under a lamppost. "What's wrong? Did something happen at work?" Of course, it did. His father could not be trusted.

Lizzie drew in a deep breath. Weighing what was safe to tell him, seeing her boss was his father? Or lumping him in together with the misdeeds of Benton Calloway—like father, like son?

"I hope you didn't think I wasn't coming, Lizzie."

"I don't know what to think anymore. About anything." She moved back into the flow of pedestrians, and he followed. "Except that I need to hurry to help Mrs. McPhearson."

"Of course." They walked in silence, his leg starting to ache at the pace she set. Even though Lizzie was hurrying to presumably get to the boardinghouse on time, her steps pounded out an underlying something. Maybe not quite anger. Determination, perhaps? Whatever it was, he was exhausted by the time he walked her around to Mrs. McPhearson's back steps. And how they called to him. But if he sat, he'd probably not move until Mrs. McPhearson herself kicked him out.

"I'll see you in the dining room," he murmured as she clomped up the few stairs. With no reply before she closed the back door, he walked around to the front and climbed those steps. He hadn't once regretted giving up his room, his bed, for Lizzie, but right about now, it sure would have been welcome.

Maybe supper would fortify him enough for the walk and climb back to the accounting office for the night.

Josiah headed straight to his seat in the dining room, where Peter and Melvin were already in conversation.

"Hello." They greeted Josiah almost in unison.

"We were just discussing how Mrs. McPhearson keeps us all fed so well." Peter stretched an arm in the direction of the kitchen.

Tonight's dinner smelled like roasted chicken. Probably with carrots baking in the juices and fluffy potatoes with gravy to accompany it all. And if the warm smell of chocolate drifting through the closed door was any indication, a layer cake would be coming out at dessert time.

Melvin took a big whiff of the air and sighed in contentment. "You can't go away hungry here."

"I can't argue with that." Josiah grinned, momentarily at ease. Maybe Hugh and his crony wouldn't show up. As if.

And right on cue, here came Hugh and Markos, followed by Walter and Frederick. They each took their seat, and mercy be, Hugh didn't even look at him. Which would have been fine, but knowing Hugh, he had something planned.

Mrs. McPhearson entered the dining room with a platter of carved chicken encircled by carrots. "Peter, would you ask the blessing this evening?"

"I'd be glad to." He waited as each man bowed his head. "Dear Lord, thank You for this bounty that You've provided through the hands of Mrs. McPhearson. Please bless it and her and each of us. Amen."

"Amen. Thank you, Peter." Mrs. McPhearson set the platter on the table just as Lizzie appeared behind her with a bowl of the fluffy potatoes in one hand and a silver gravy boat in the other. Mrs. McPhearson took the bowls one at a time from Lizzie and set them on the table, and they both returned to the kitchen.

141

Something definitely was wrong as Lizzie had not smiled. Had not spoken or even nodded to a single man. And most definitely had not looked at Josiah once.

The men passed the food around and chatted among themselves. When the platter of chicken and carrots came around a second time, Josiah speared a thigh and a carrot. Then the bowl of potatoes followed, along with the gravy boat. Men helped themselves and passed the food on to the next person. By the time dishes were collected and Mrs. McPhearson and Lizzie served slices of the still-warm chocolate cake, Lizzie still had not made eye contact with him nor smiled.

While delicious, the dessert would have been more enjoyable served on the back steps with a cup of coffee and Lizzie at his side as they watched the stars together. But with each trip Lizzie made into the dining room, that scenario was becoming less likely to happen.

Once the meal was finished, Josiah placed his napkin on the table and stood. After giving a cordial nod, he walked out the front door as fast as he deemed decorum dictated. Then he hurried away from the boardinghouse, each step taking him farther away from the one person he wanted to be with. But who definitely had signaled she didn't want to be with him.

Maybe tomorrow at church, he'd see Lizzie and all would be back to normal. But a gnawing in his chest jabbed him with little whispers that something wasn't right.

And if he didn't know what it was, how could he fix it?

CHAPTER 14

Monday morning, Lizzie trudged through the door of the Boise Tailor Shop. Instead of walking confidently in to implement the plan she'd come up with for Mr. Calloway, all she managed was a dejected plod. All due to Reverend Matthews's sermon yesterday on forgiveness, of all topics.

And he had to pick Papa's favorite verse to start with. *As far as the east is from the west, so far hath He removed our transgressions from us.*

And of course, he'd made it a point to add in words from Jesus Himself. *"For if ye forgive men their trespasses, your heavenly Father will also forgive you: but if ye forgive not men their trespasses, neither will your Father forgive your trespasses."*

Nor was she as generous as Peter had been in asking if forgiving someone seven times was adequate. She'd been ready to crawl under the pew when Reverend Matthews read the answer to that. *Jesus said to him, "I do not say to you, up to seven times, but up to seventy times seven."* That was four hundred ninety. And she was struggling with forgiving Benton Calloway once.

And yet God had forgiven her multitude of sins totally. Completely.

So she had tried forgiving once.

And the anger came right back at Mr. Calloway for docking her a day's wage for helping Gideon.

Father, forgive me. Two times.

Mr. Calloway was so mean. Not even paying her for her work the other days.

Dear Lord, please forgive me again. Three.

Each thought of him on the way into work this morning was one of grumbling, then one of forgiving. And she was still a long way from four hundred ninety.

The shop door jingled, announcing her presence instead of allowing her to sneak in and get to work silently.

"Well, well. You came back." Mr. Calloway looked up from the counter, surprise quickly replaced by that smirk he often sported.

Lord, please help me to forgive another time. Four.

"Good morning, Mr. Calloway." Lizzie took off her coat and walked to the sewing machine. Pulled out her chair and laid her coat over the back. Then walked to the counter. *Lord, give me boldness.* She drew a deep breath. *And kindness.* "You left on Saturday before you had a chance to pay me."

He narrowed his eyes. "As you should remember, I said your wages would be deducted as you weren't at your station the entire workday."

"Yes. I stepped out for a matter of minutes to help a boy who was injured. But did you have any problem with my work the rest of the week?"

His head jerked back. "It was adequate, I suppose."

"Then I should be paid fairly for that work."

He speared her with his pale blue-eyed glare but reached into his cash drawer and withdrew some bills. Of course, not a fair amount, but she took the proffered bills and put them in her pocket.

"What are you standing there for? If you don't get sewing and put in a full day's work today, you shall again be docked accordingly."

Of course. *"Forgive, and ye shall be forgiven." Lord, I forgive another time.* Could that count as five? Or should she start all over?

Lizzie retreated to the sewing machine and set to work. She would put in a full day's work, whether or not he ever paid her for a full day.

Finally, Mr. Calloway stomped back into his secret area, and Lizzie didn't see or hear from him all morning. Well into the afternoon, he parted the curtains and stepped into the front room, dressed in his suit coat and top hat.

"I'm going out for a while to attend to some business. Take care of things. And keep working."

"Yes, sir." Good thing she hadn't stood at that moment to stretch, as he'd accuse her of being idle. "Will you be back for closing?"

He scowled. "I don't report to you. I'll get back when I get back. Lock up at five if I'm not here." He strode to the door and exited.

What a mean-hearted man. If it wasn't for needing to find physical proof he was cheating Papa, she would be gone from here.

The bell stopped jingling after his departure. She was all alone in the shop now, and the curtains would hide her if—

No. She squashed the tantalizing thought of darting back there. He could return at any moment.

Or was this an opportunity?

Definitely no. She had work to do, or he'd dock her pay yet more. And it wasn't likely he'd ever give her a full week's wages, anyway, let alone any compensation for the extra hours she labored.

Lizzie scooted her chair off-center so the temptation of the back room was not in her view at all.

Stick to your work. Stick to your work.

Since she'd again skipped her lunch break, her stomach was now registering a complaint. She couldn't stay a minute past five tonight. Of course, she had to help serve supper—but after that...

Ever since Saturday when she'd been so angry with Mr. Calloway, she regretted her treatment of Josiah. Josiah was nothing like his father, and she'd been wrong to treat him otherwise. And how she'd missed sitting with Josiah on the back porch that night after supper. But he'd disappeared as soon as he'd taken his last bite of cake. And she hadn't seen him at church yesterday. Perhaps he'd come in late and sat in the rear pew and left at the final amen. But a whole day without even seeing him, especially as she'd wrestled with forgiving his father, left her so empty.

But if he came to escort her home this evening, words of apology would be the first she uttered to him. And if she could have another evening on the back porch with Josiah in the moonlight...

The humming whirl of the Singer machine became the background music for the song in her heart. Josiah's soft laughter and quiet manner of loving her were the trills and crescendos.

Lizzie's feet stopped on the treadle. *Loving?* Yes, in his unhurried, gentle way, that was what he'd been telling her by every one of his actions.

Before she could get back to her thoughts and the song in her heart, a lady came in.

"Good afternoon, Mrs. Crenshaw."

"Hello, dear. I'm just stopping in since I was nearby to see if my mending was completed yet."

"It is." Lizzie stood and found the woman's skirts on the jobs-completed shelf. "I have your skirts all ready for you. On the ripped pockets you said you were having trouble with, let me show you what I did." Another trick she'd learned from her mother in repairing four boys' ripped pants. "I fixed the tear and then double-stitched the seams to give them more durability. Now, if you still have any problem with them, just bring them back in."

"Thank you, dear. I appreciate your skill, as I'm not handy with thread and needle, much less sewing machine repairs. I'm sure Mr. Calloway knows how valuable you are to his shop and treats you well."

Lizzie almost laughed at the absurdity of Mrs. Crenshaw's mistaken assumption. "I'm still learning, so I'm probably not up to his standards yet. But he is giving me more and more responsibility." That was true, as he dumped project after project on her.

Forgive.

That would tick off one more toward the four hundred ninety times—though Reverend Matthews said even that was not the stopping point. But each instance of forgiveness put her a step closer—and humbled her more. Especially when she considered how she needed to ask Josiah to forgive her. Would he issue forgiveness freely, not bothering to count how many times she needed it?

After showing Mrs. Crenshaw each mend, Lizzie took the garments to the counter. "Let me wrap these for you. And while I do that, is there anything else I can help you with? Or maybe you'd enjoy browsing the shelves of fabrics?"

"That I would. I have an upcoming dinner event and would love a new dress."

"Then by all means. Feel the fabrics. Unfold them a bit and

let them drape over you. Take your time to first simply dream about the color and style that would make you feel most elegant. And whenever you're ready, or if you'd like some help deciding, just let me—us, I mean—know." Mr. Calloway would want his clients to think he was involved in guiding them.

Mrs. Crenshaw smiled and walked over to the bolts of fabric as Lizzie finished up.

"There." Lizzie patted the wrapped package. "You keep looking, but you're all set with your skirts. I'll leave your package here. If you have any questions, I'll just be over at the sewing machine." Trying to finish the piles of work she'd been left with.

And keeping an eye on the candy store window across the street, watching to see if Josiah would be standing there at five o'clock. Or had she chased him away a final time with her anger on Saturday?

~

*J*osiah took his place in front of Mrs. Brighton's shop at five o'clock. Whether Lizzie ignored him or not, he was here, showing his commitment to her. And if she allowed him to escort her this evening, that'd be the perfect ending to the wearying day.

Lizzie was putting garments on shelves and tidying up around the Singer. The glare on the front window made it difficult to see more than Lizzie, but Josiah could tell someone else was inside. A woman. Within minutes, Lizzie and presumably a customer, as she was carrying a wrapped package, walked out together. Lizzie stopped and locked the door behind her.

But the woman said something, and Lizzie focused on her, spoke a few words, and laughed. Then waved goodbye to her.

Immediately, he pushed off from the candy shop window and headed straight across the street to Lizzie.

She looked his way, right into his eyes. A welcoming grin lit up her face a fraction of a second before it disappeared. But now he was next to her.

"Lizzie, I wondered if I may—"

"Josiah." She held up a hand. "I am so sorry for the way I treated you on Saturday. Will you please forgive me? I—"

He captured her hand with his. "Of course, I do."

She crinkled her nose. "Don't you want to hear why I was so rude?" But she didn't extract her hand from his clasp.

"Not unless you really want to tell me. I forgive you, and as far as I'm concerned, that's all there is to it."

"I— You—"

He grinned at her, her stumbling for words so adorable. "Just say 'thank you' and allow me to escort you home, if you will."

She returned his smile. "Thank you. And I would be honored for you to escort me to the boardinghouse."

He tucked Lizzie's hand through his arm, as though they were a twosome heading off somewhere together after a day's work. With her at his side, close to him like this, his day was complete.

They blended in with the crowd of pedestrians bustling along the sidewalk, not speaking until the foot traffic had cleared some.

"Were you at church yesterday? I didn't see you." Lizzie's tone hinted at an underlying reason for asking.

He'd been there, in the back. But so convicted with the topic of forgiveness, he'd rushed out immediately afterward, needing time to think. As he had plenty of forgiving to do. Toward his father. Hugh. "I was. But I left right away."

"Oh. But you heard the sermon?"

"On forgiving. Yes." If Lizzie knew what an unforgiving man he was, she'd want nothing to do with him. As well she should. Another reason he was unworthy of her.

"It made me realize many things. That I have forgiving I need to do."

"You, too, Lizzie?"

She tipped her head up, meeting his eyes. Searching deep, as if seeking something. "Yes. My mother grew up out East, in New York City. Often, in her stories, she'd tell me she had to come as far as the West to learn God's truths of loving and forgiving. And she learned them right on our family's ranch in Caldwell, where her grandmother had left a legacy of the bitterbrush bloom."

"The bitterbrush flower—is that why you had one on your hat the day you arrived in Boise?"

"Yes. My great-grandmother had also come from the East, far out to the West. Her first winter here was filled with hardships and bitterness. Until she learned God's ways. On the edge of the yard behind the house is a lone bitterbrush bush she said must remain there—her legacy to the generations who live there of God's faithfulness. Of His promise of hope and provision."

"Your family sounds so godly. So loving." And kind. How was it both he and Lizzie had been born to parents of Caldwell, but she was born into a God-fearing family, while his was... At least his mother had had a change of heart through the years and reared him in a godly manner.

"Oh, they're wonderful. And my brothers, too, even though mostly they're nuisances." She laughed and her eyes twinkled.

Before he got drawn too deep into her sweetness, he needed to know something else. "Lizzie, can I ask you something?"

"Of course. What?"

"Aren't you embarrassed to be seen walking in public with me?"

She stopped so abruptly, he was thankful the people walking this direction had thinned out so they didn't get rammed into.

AS FAR AS THE WEST

"Why would you ask such a thing? Of course not."

"Because of my limp."

"What are you talking about? It's barely noticeable, but why would that even matter?"

"It matters to my father. He sees me as weak."

"Well, I don't. Anyway, my father has a bit of a limp, too, and that's just part of who he is. He's just Papa to me. Not a man with a limp."

"Really?"

"Yes, really."

"Aren't you curious as to how I got it?"

"Only if you want me to know."

Strangely, he did. "Let's sit a minute." He stopped beside the steps of a closed business, shrugged out of his coat, and laid it on the top step for her. They sat side by side in silence until he could get the images under control. "Shrapnel. I served in the Great War in France. There was this little town where the villagers welcomed us. Even with our limited French, we enjoyed being with them when off duty. One of the guys would play his harmonica in the town square at night, and some of the children would edge around. There was one little girl—Victoria—who had especially won our hearts with her smile and big brown eyes. Anyway, that night, we were ambushed." He gulped back a sob, and Lizzie took his hand. "I tried to get to Victoria and her mother sitting not far away, but I didn't make it. I was shot, and when I went down, I landed on top of someone. I don't even know who."

"Oh, Josiah." Lizzie scooted closer to his side. "You started a poem about that night. About her…"

He nodded. "I tried but ended up not saving anyone."

"But you did. That one person you fell on was protected under you."

"That was an accident."

"But if they were alive, it was because of you. You're a man

151

of honor, Josiah Calloway. And that limp you're worried about? It's a symbol that you cared, that you were trying to save lives. That you did everything you could. And to that one person, you are a hero, Josiah."

A hero. With Lizzie at his side clinging to him, tears in her eyes, encouragement in words he'd never heard before, he believed her. At least for a moment. But it was enough to lift the weight of guilt, to see a ray of hope beyond the hopelessness he'd felt for so long.

He didn't even try to speak past the lump in his throat, but she seemed to understand.

"Thank you for telling me, Josiah. Should we continue on?" At his nod, they stood, her hand still in his.

They walked in silence the rest of the way to the boardinghouse. And, as was his custom, he accompanied her around to the back.

Lizzie slowly withdrew her hand from his when they reached the porch, as though she also hated to break their connection. "I'll see you in the dining room in a few minutes. And maybe on the porch later?" Her cheeks turned red, and she quickly climbed the steps.

"For sure." He hoped she heard his words before she slipped inside. *Thank You, Lord.* Things were back to normal with Lizzie, all the awkwardness of Saturday night gone. Forgiven. And something new and wonderful was growing in its place. Perhaps similar to that bitterbrush blossom she'd spoken of. From bitterness to living in God's faithfulness.

Josiah walked to the front of the building and entered properly through the front door. He had plenty to ponder this evening.

At the table, the men—minus Hugh—spoke congenially among themselves. No one asked about Hugh or seemed concerned about his absence. And without him there, even Markos joined in the conversation. But this was unlike Hugh to miss supper. Josiah couldn't recall a single time he'd been absent. Maybe instead of speculating on his absence, Josiah should enjoy the peace around the table.

And enjoy it he did, especially when Lizzie sent demure smiles his way. And she grazed his hand when he lifted his glass for her to refill with water.

After dishes were cleared, Mrs. McPhearson stepped into the dining room with a tray of dessert. "Gentlemen, tonight we have a special dessert. Victoria cake."

Murmurs of delight filled the room, as Mrs. McPhearson's sponge cake with red jam—hopefully, strawberry—and icing sugar on top was the best. Lizzie appeared at her side and passed out the plates of dessert as she followed Mrs. McPhearson around the table.

Mrs. McPhearson bent close to him as Lizzie lifted his plate off the tray. "Meet Lizzie on the back porch where I'll have another piece waiting for you." She winked and he wanted to shout. Just as he hoped—another evening under the stars with his Lizzie.

After supper, Josiah walked out the front door, as usual, and made his way around to the back. He rapped lightly on the door, and Mrs. McPhearson opened it, grabbed his arm, and pulled him inside. "Come in, come in. I want to talk with you about something privately."

"Is something wrong?"

She bustled about and cut a generous piece of cake and placed it on a dessert plate. "You take this out, and I'll have Lizzie join you when she gets down."

"Mrs. McPhearson, you wanted to talk about something?"

She looked over her shoulder at the back stairs. "Yes." She sat—or with the weight of sadness that seemed to shroud her, it was more like plopped—on a kitchen chair. "This may be the last Victoria cake I make for you boys."

"Ma'am?"

Josiah sat across from her and placed a hand over hers. Underneath his, hers was trembling.

"Someone reported my boardinghouse to the city for some infraction."

"What?"

She shook her head. "I don't know why or for what. Just that an inspector is set to come out for a look around. If I have repairs to make, I don't know how I'll continue to make ends meet. After the loss of my husband a few years back, I opened my home to boarders as a way to keep the house and pay my bills. You came after the worst of the great influenza last year, but God protected this place, and I lost not one boarder. But this?" Her shoulders shook. "I don't know if someone in the neighborhood brought the attention of the city to my home or who. Have I offended one of them somehow? The nearby boardinghouse owners all said they're not being inspected, so it seems I'm being singled out."

"I'm so sorry, Mrs. McPhearson." And if Mrs. McPhearson closed down, where would Lizzie go?

"Please don't say anything about this to anyone yet, as my plans are uncertain." She pushed the plated cake across the table to him. "I made this as I know it's a favorite of yours. Tonight, it's meant to be a celebration cake for you and Lizzie."

"I'm so sorry," he repeated, as no other words came to mind.

"Thank you. Now you take this and go on out. I'll get Lizzie. I sent her upstairs to change into a pretty dress. And I'll bring out coffee."

Josiah picked up the dessert that now would be tasteless to him. Or maybe he should concentrate on it being extra sweet, considering Mrs. McPhearson had made it with love and had happiness in mind for it. He took it outside and sat on the porch floor, resting his feet on the steps below.

With minutes, Lizzie appeared, carrying her own plate of cake. Indeed, she had changed into a pretty dress—light pink and pale gold fabrics intertwined in some surely fashionable pattern that swished as she walked. He didn't know fabrics or styles, but even he recognized shining eyes and a becoming smile.

"You look lovely." He helped seat her beside him.

"Thank you." She looked up into the sky, now filled with sunset colors which easily matched her dress. "It's such a beautiful evening."

He couldn't take his eyes off her, though. "Yes, lovely." He was still processing how she'd been raised in such a loving home. And, yes, how he still owed her parents money to pay off his father's debt to them. How were they managing without that income? "Tell me more about your family. What are your parents like? In their day-to-day running of a ranch."

"Even though Mama's busy with buying and training the horses and Papa with building his saddles, they always find time for each other and for each of their children. This is something they do almost every night after supper—sit out on the front porch together in my great-grandparents' rocking chairs and talk about their day, watch the stars come out."

Maybe share a kiss or two in the moonlight? What if that scenario could one day be him and Lizzie? He took her hand, and she wound her fingers with his. He could so easily turn his head and kiss her. But now wasn't the time. He cleared his throat to chase away the urge. "So you said business is picking up some for them now?"

She looked sideways at him. "It's getting back up there. As I said, they're trying some new things. Someone had been spreading rumors around horse people, just enough to shed doubt on their reputation for fine training and saddle making. So they're making every effort to counteract that and let people know the truth."

Given that slightest shift in her tone, did she suspect it was his father? He couldn't look her in the eye. "But they'll be fine?"

"Of course. Especially once I'm able to send money back home, that will help." She picked up her dessert plate. "We'd better eat our cake. Mrs. McPhearson was perking coffee when I walked through the kitchen."

Josiah reached for his plate and took a bite of the Victoria cake, any thought of romance gone. The cake that had been moist and delicious at supper now went down like dry crumbs. Would he never be able to get ahead? To live his life free from his father's transgressions?

He'd keeping whittling down the amount due to Mrs. McPhearson regardless of what she said each time he gave her a pittance. She might not want it, but it appeared she'd be needing it now.

That would put him even further away from repaying Caleb and Eliza Morgan. And until they were repaid, no thanks to his father, he could make no claim on their daughter.

CHAPTER 15

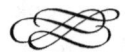

Mr. Calloway greeted Lizzie with a deeper scowl than usual the moment she walked into the shop in the morning. What was wrong now? She was early even by his standards.

He held up the receipt book. "I see Mrs. Crenshaw picked up her garments yesterday."

"Yes. She happened to stop by, and they were ready for her ahead of schedule—"

"As they should have been."

"Is there a problem, then?"

"A problem!" He shook the record book at her. "I don't see a new order in here for her."

"I don't understand. She was looking at the fabrics, but that was all. Were you expecting her to place an order yesterday?"

"'Were you expecting her to place an order yesterday?'" He mimicked her question. "That's your job—to see to it that customers always place a new order or bring in new mending or alterations. Always."

"Even if they don't want one or don't yet know exactly what they do want?" The words rushed out before Lizzie censored them. Oh she was going to have to start counting all the way over again for times she forgave him.

"Such insolence." His face turned red with his words. "I should have expected nothing but impudence from a Morgan."

Yes, there was no doubt now that he knew exactly who she was.

He slammed the receipt book down and strode to the curtains. "Now get to work." He ducked into his private quarters, and she didn't see him the rest of the morning.

Lizzie had no idea what he was doing back there, but out here at the sewing machine, she was fuming.

She couldn't take any more of him. This week, she would get some proof and be done here. After she walked out of the Boise Tailor Shop for good, she'd be free to look for another job. A decent one. Surely, someone in Boise was looking for a hard worker. Someone who would be kind and fair. Now that she had a place to live and knew a little of the city, she could take more time looking and hopefully fare better in her search. Maybe with the experience she'd gained here, she could apply for another seamstress position—if Mr. Calloway didn't spread rumors about her around town too.

The shop door jingled, and Lizzie looked up. "Mrs. Donaldson, Edward, how nice to see you this morning."

"Good morning, dear. I ran into Mr. Calloway last evening, and he suggested I stop by for Edward's fitting at our convenience. Is this a good time for you?"

How dare he imply she had the boy's suit ready for a fitting without checking with her? Or was it another ploy to dock her wages? Well, the surprise was on him, because it was ready for Edward to try on. Or had he known that from snooping around on the shelves when she wasn't here?

"Now is a perfectly good time. Are you ready to try your new suit on, Edward?" She waited for his nod, then selected his coat and pants from the shelf of items ready for fittings. "I want to thank you again for your lovely gift of candy the last time you visited." She lowered her voice and winked. "I ate all the Mary Janes before I left work that day." Which was true, as they had been her lunch. She handed the garments to Edward. "You can go right behind the screen and try these on."

When he returned dressed in the suit, Mrs. Donaldson put her hands on her cheeks. "Oh, Edward. You look so handsome, just like your father. And Lizzie, you are such a talented seamstress."

No doubt, Mr. Calloway was standing at the curtains listening. If only they weren't so long, but if he was there, even his shoes were hidden from sight. Now would be when he'd say she should push Mrs. Donaldson into a commitment for another garment for herself. But if the Donaldsons had the money to spend and wished to use it on clothing, that was their decision alone. Let him dock her, as if not for this, he'd find some other excuse to do so.

Mrs. Donaldson stepped up close to Lizzie. "I wanted to let you know how much I love the skirt you made." She looked around the room, then lowered her voice. "I'm just about ready to take my first pleat out." She placed a hand on her middle and smiled at Lizzie with that motherly glow Lizzie had seen on her mother and some of their neighbors.

"If you need any help with them, just bring the skirt in one day, and I'll show you how to release them."

"Thank you. And when you're finished with Edward, I would like to discuss a dress for me. I would again value your expert advice."

"Certainly." Lizzie could hug Mrs. Donaldson for bringing up the topic herself—and Mr. Calloway was probably in the back wringing his hands in glee. "Edward, let me pin the sleeves and pant legs for you, and you'll be all done." He stood still like a gentleman while she measured and pinned.

"You didn't stick me once," Edward said.

Lizzie grinned at him. "I try not to, but you helped because you were so still. I'm all done, so you can change into your own clothes now. Let me help you with the jacket sleeves so you don't stick yourself on the pins. Then just be careful with the pant legs." She inched the jacket off him. "And now it's your mother's turn."

"Yes, I would like one nice dress while I'm with child. Can you make a dress similar in style to the skirt? With pleats?"

"Indeed. I have an idea for a style that would be practical yet stunning. Let me sketch it for you, and then I'll show you which fabrics I think it would look pretty in."

Mrs. Donaldson sighed. "Thank you. You don't know how grateful I am that you're still here. I hope you stay throughout my entire time."

"Ma'am?"

Mrs. Donaldson glanced toward the curtains and dropped her voice to a whisper. "I probably shouldn't be saying this, but I know it's been very difficult for Mr. Calloway to find women of excellent skill. He's had to let the last couple of girls go after only a few days. So each time I find you still here, I'm so relieved. He surely recognizes the talent he has in you."

"It is a demanding job, but I love helping each customer." She glanced toward the curtains herself, then picked up a pencil and drew a quick outline of what she envisioned for Mrs. Donaldson's dress. "What do you think?"

"I love it."

"Wonderful." Lizzie led Mrs. Donaldson over to the wall with fabrics and pulled out the teal-blue bolt. "This is the one I think would drape well, and the color is beautiful with your skin and hair. If not this particular color, any of these jewel tones in this section would be very becoming."

Mrs. Donaldson ran the fabric between her fingers. "This is it. Definitely."

"You think it over, and you can let me know your thoughts. I

AS FAR AS THE WEST

already have your measurements since we'll do the pleats again, so if you do decide to proceed, it's just a matter of letting Mr. Calloway know." She purposely raised her voice just a bit to make sure the words carried clearly through the curtains. So Mr. Calloway would have no doubt she was not pressuring Mrs. Donaldson into anything.

"I've made up my mind, and I'm sure Mr. Donaldson would agree. Please write the order up, Lizzie. The only stipulation is that you must be the one to both start and complete it."

Lizzie could barely restrain a smile of victory. Either God was blessing her with this, or Mrs. Donaldson had some inkling of the true workings of the Boise Tailor Shop. With satisfaction, she walked to the counter and noted Mrs. Donaldson's request on the order form.

"Mr. Calloway sets the prices and requests payment be made at the time of the order, so I'm not sure what to charge you." How Lizzie hated even asking for money before Mrs. Donaldson saw the finished product.

"Oh, don't worry. I'll leave a generous down payment, and Mr. Donaldson will settle up with Mr. Calloway as to the exact amount." She pulled out several bills from her pocketbook.

"Thank you." What should Lizzie do with the money? Mr. Calloway wouldn't trust her with it. She set it down.

"Edward, are you ready to go?" Mrs. Donaldson took his hand.

"Yes, Mama. Are we going to the candy shop next?"

She ruffled his hair. "I believe we can do that."

"Well, well." The curtains parted, and Mr. Calloway strode out. "How good to see you, Mrs. Donaldson." His eyes skimmed over the money still lying on the counter and then to Edward. "I see you came in for your son's fitting. Was everything to your satisfaction?"

"Yes, as always. You have an excellent seamstress in Lizzie. I'm sure you're as blessed with her as I am." She pointed to the order and her payment. "I placed an order for a new dress, which Lizzie agreed to make for me. Let me or Mr. Donaldson know if we owe more."

"Excellent. Excellent. I look forward to seeing you soon, then, for your own fitting and to pick up the final suit for Master Edward."

"Yes, thank you. Good day to you both." With that, she and Edward left with the jingle of the door.

Mr. Calloway crossed to the counter and grabbed the money and order slip. With a glare at Lizzie, he slid back between the curtains and disappeared for the rest of the day.

Lizzie retrieved the teal fabric and cut off a length that would be plenty for the new dress. Because she wouldn't put it past Benton Calloway to tell some other lady how lovely she'd look in it and leave Lizzie with insufficient material for Mrs. Donaldson.

Speed was of the essence now. She'd promised to sew this dress for Mrs. Donaldson, but once that was completed and she found the proof she needed in that back room, she was done here.

Unless Mr. Calloway found yet some devious way to stop her.

~

Josiah needed help. Someone who had connections with people who bought horses and saddles. Whose only world wasn't accounting and numbers. Someone like Conor O'Shannon.

Josiah didn't really know the man, but he'd helped Lizzie. From what he'd heard in the neighborhood when people gathered at Mrs. Farber's, he helped whoever he could. So Conor O'Shannon it was.

If Josiah started work early and took no break, he could leave early, talk to Conor, and still get to the shop to walk Lizzie to the boardinghouse. And if all went well with Conor, that was one step closer to the day he could pursue Lizzie Morgan.

Finally, the long day passed to where Josiah could leave the office. He followed the route where he'd seen Lizzie on the evening of her first day in Boise over to Conor O'Shannon's livery.

Josiah walked into the barn, quiet for a stable. "Hello? Conor O'Shannon?"

"In here." The voice came from within a stall at the end of the aisle. Then a head appeared, and the man walked through the door. "What can I do for you?"

"I'm Josiah Calloway—"

"Calloway." Conor rubbed his chin.

Josiah kept his sigh to himself. Conor would find out, anyway, so he might as well jump right in. "Do you know Benton Calloway?"

"Yes, that's the name." His eyes narrowed.

"He's my father."

"Your father." Conor crossed his arms. "Why are you here?"

"I'm here to ask for your help. I know you've helped Miss Lizzie Morgan, and I want to help her too. I think my father is behind rumors that might be keeping people from buying horses and saddles from her parents' ranch in Caldwell, the Double E. I don't know horse people in Boise, but I'm sure you do."

Conor nodded. "What can I do to help?"

"Can you find out what the rumors are? And talk to people to combat them? And most importantly, find out, if you can, who bought either a horse or saddle elsewhere based entirely on these rumors."

"What are you going to do with this information, assuming I'm able to find it?"

"Make sure the Morgans receive their lost monies." By the time he was finished paying off this increased debt, he'd be old and gray, sitting alone on a boardinghouse rocker the rest of his life. Without Lizzie. "So do you know horsemen you can contact?"

"I do." Conor clapped Josiah on the shoulder. "Leave it to me."

"Thank you, thank you." Now he could hurry back to meet Lizzie on time with a lighter heart, now that he was doing something to help. But helping widened the distance separating them yet more in his ledger until he could declare his feelings for her.

He arrived in front of the candy shop a few minutes early and waved to Mrs. Brighton's grandson inside at the counter. With a quick glance at the tailor shop window, he assured himself that Lizzie was deep in work and wouldn't be closing up for yet a few minutes at the least.

He stepped into the candy shop, and the boy straightened.

"Welcome, sir, to Brighton's Candy Shop, Boise's finest in chocolates, candy, and handmade fudge."

"Why, thank you." Josiah had rarely been inside for candy, only coming to repay Mrs. Brighton a bit here and there when he could. She always took the money with a nod but said nothing about his father to him. "What would you recommend for a pretty lady?"

The boy eyed him. "Someone you're sweet on or just a grandma or someone like that?"

Josiah pointed across the street. "For the seamstress."

"Oh, Miss Lizzie? She likes everything. But her favorite is Mary Janes. And the chocolate fudge."

"You're sure about that?"

The boy puffed out his chest. "Of course, I am. I know my customers."

"All right, then. I'll take a piece of fudge and a handful of

Mary Janes." Today the extravagance would show Lizzie she was worth it to him, even if it set him back a bit. He'd scrimp on his own needs, as not a penny would come from his savings toward ledger payments.

"Whose hand—yours or mine?"

Ah, the lad was clever. Josiah's own hand would be a bigger deduction in the ledger, but the boy looked so hopeful. "Mine, if the jar is self-service."

"It is." The boy handed Josiah a small paper sack. "Go ahead, mister. Miss Lizzie really likes those Mary Janes."

With the boy watching, Josiah couldn't skimp. He took a normal-sized handful, which filled the little candy bag.

"You still want the fudge, mister?"

"I do. Are you sure Miss Lizzie likes that too?"

"I know she does. But she can't eat it while sewing, as those fancy people who go into her shop don't want chocolate on their clothes." He stepped out from the counter and went to the fudge-making table. "Fudge isn't self-service. I'll get that 'cuz I have to use special paper to pick it up. Grandma showed me how to do it."

"Of course. Thank you—what's your name?"

"Gideon Brighton."

"Thank you, Gideon." Josiah held out his hand, and the boy shook it with a good, strong shake.

"And who are you?"

Josiah darted a glance at the tailor shop. Who knew what Gideon had heard about Benton Calloway from his grandmother, so no use opening the door for questions. "Josiah."

Gideon cut and wrapped the fudge and laid the package alongside the candy bag on the counter. "That'll be twenty cents."

Josiah fished out the coins and placed them on the counter, then picked up his purchases. "Thank you for your assistance, Gideon."

"That's my job. I'm in training, as one day, I'll be taking over for my grandma."

"Good for you. Keep up the good work."

"Th— Mr. Josiah!" Gideon pointed out the window. "You'd better hurry. Miss Lizzie is locking up."

Josiah nodded and quickly stepped outside and waved. "Lizzie!" What was he doing, yelling across the street? But it didn't matter whether his father saw him or not, as he was doubtless expecting him to show up, if not watching in secret.

Lizzie turned after locking the door and smiled, her eyes lighting up as he made it to her side.

"I, uh, got you something."

"From the candy shop?"

"Yes. I was thinking you'd like something sweet to eat on the way home. To brighten your day." How corny was that? But maybe Lizzie didn't think so, as she grinned at him as she reached for the bag. Her eyes grew wide when she peeked in. "Mary Janes—my favorite. And what else—fudge? Oh, Josiah, you're so sweet. Thank you."

"I had a little help."

"From Gideon?"

"Yes. Fine boy, but quite the salesman."

"He is. He has hopes of taking over the store one day."

"So he told me. But I just wanted you to know…"

Lizzie looked at him expectantly.

How awkward was he? But he'd never spoken words of endearment to a young lady before. He cleared his throat. "How much you mean to me."

"Thank you, Josiah. That's as sweet as the candy." She dug into the bag and unwrapped a Mary Jane. She stuck it in her mouth so fast that maybe she didn't know quite what to say either.

With Lizzie's mouth full of chewy candy, he reached for her free hand, and they walked in silence for a few blocks. But what was he doing? He shouldn't pursue her until he'd paid the debt to her parents. And he couldn't let Lizzie go. With just the thought of Lizzie not in his life, he tightened his fingers around hers.

Finally, they arrived at the back door of the boardinghouse. They bid their goodbyes amid promises of seeing each other in the dining room and later out on the back porch. After supper, that's exactly where Josiah went, not even waiting for an invitation from Mrs. McPhearson. As if even she knew that was where Josiah belonged.

He intentionally set the plate of pie Mrs. McPhearson handed him right between him and Lizzie, far enough away from her so he didn't automatically reach across for her hand. Or turn to kiss her. Just until he figured out how to keep her in his life and still be honorable to her parents.

But when her head rested against his shoulder as the sun sank, he didn't move a muscle. For this was where someday he hoped she would fully belong.

With an evening chorus of birds surrounding them, he reached over and enveloped her hand in his.

Lord, help me to find a way.

CHAPTER 16

The next two days, Lizzie worked steadily on Mrs. Donaldson's new dress. It must get done before she could implement her plan. And if she didn't finish it today, she only had two more days left of this week, or she'd be stuck here even longer. Obviously, Mr. Calloway was trying to goad her into walking out, as he made the days more and more unbearable. But she would not quit until her mission was completed.

When he wasn't staring at her with arms crossed or finding some new infraction to dock her for, she dreamed of seeing Josiah again. Reliving their walks and talks and back porch evenings. How she longed to talk with Mama. Was this how she'd felt with Papa when she'd moved to Caldwell? When he'd courted her? And even now?

Not that Josiah had ever said anything about courting, but would he treat her as such a treasure, tucking her hand into his, holding her close, if that wasn't on his mind?

Silently, Mr. Calloway appeared from behind the curtains late that morning.

"I'm going out." Without another word he left, and true peace reigned in the shop.

But Lizzie didn't have time to once even consider sneaking into the back, as customers flowed in one after another to pick up items, expressing their thanks and chatting. While she was glad for the break from sewing and a chance to talk with someone, it put her further behind in constructing the teal dress. And then another two customers brought in tailoring to add to her pile of work.

At four-thirty, Mr. Martin stopped in to pick up a dress his wife had ordered even before Lizzie's first week here.

Lizzie held up for his approval the lovely red silk dress with the daring calf-length hem she'd sewn along with a matching hat. "What do you think?"

He grinned. "I'll be proud to have her on my arm in this, indeed."

"I'm sure your wife will be very beautiful in this dress." Someday maybe Lizzie could purchase fabric and sew something so elegant in contrast to her own sturdy black-and-white-checked serge skirt. She consulted the slip of paper Mr. Calloway had stuck in with the dress. "That'll be twelve dollars."

Mr. Martin cocked his head. "There must be some mistake, Miss Morgan. I paid Benton for this when I placed the order."

And that was Mr. Calloway's normal practice. So the unpaid ticket didn't make sense. Benton Calloway was a precise businessman when it came to finances. And the attached slip said Mr. Martin owed money. "Are you sure, sir?"

"Quite. Could you please check with Benton?"

"He's not here right now. Would you be able to return tomorrow when he's back?" Her heart was pounding so hard. What if he said no? And he was bound to let Mr. Calloway know about this.

"No, that won't work. Mrs. Martin needs the dress for dinner at the mayor's house tonight. I'm already on a very tight schedule."

"I don't know what to tell you. The slip here says it hasn't been paid for yet…"

His hands clenched as though he was trying to hold in his frustration with her. "Could you go in the back and check the records?"

"I'm not allow—" Wait. Hadn't he just given her the perfect —and legitimate—opportunity to look in the books? "Yes, let me do that. That's a good idea. I'll be right back." She slipped between the black curtains and stepped into the private office of Mr. Calloway.

For all his pomp and secrecy, the space was spartan. A wooden filing cabinet stood on one wall and a large mahogany desk and a chair on the opposite side. And that was it, besides the back door that led to the alley. Perhaps that was why she never heard sounds from behind the curtains—he wasn't even in the shop most of the time.

But she couldn't stand here gawking or speculating, as he could return any moment. She stepped to the desk, and right on top of the ink blotter was a ledger. She opened it and matched the date of the order to the entry—and sure enough— Mr. Martin was right. Twelve dollars had been paid in cash on the day of the order. So Mr. Calloway did make a mistake occasionally.

She flipped through the previous pages and skimmed the entries. But they all seemed correct, simply the careful entries of sales and payments from customers she'd seen come in.

She closed the book. Was Mr. Calloway really a legitimate businessman? He couldn't be. Maybe he had a secret ledger, but did she dare look?

She darted a glance at the curtained entrance. Mr. Calloway couldn't sneak up on her, as the bell would ring, and he'd stop and talk to Mr. Martin first even if he did return. And she had a valid reason to be here at Mr. Martin's insistence.

Lizzie opened the narrow middle drawer. Inside was

another ledger, but no entries were recorded in it. She pulled open a side drawer. Nothing there except some pencils and pens. The next drawer held a half-empty bottle of some liquor. The bottom drawer held a couple of used ledgers—but a thin black leather journal was wedged between them.

Lizzie looked up again to check if anyone was coming, then opened the journal. Just random jottings were in the front part. She flipped through a few pages, then stopped as she stared at the heading and entries recorded toward the end of the book.

Sales Redirected:
  December 6, 1919—Turner Horse Market, Caldwell
  -$45 – C. Morgan Saddlery – stock saddle

  January 10, 1920—Auction, Boise
  -$75 – Double E – palomino

  February 21, 1920—Auction, Boise
  -$125 – Double E – bay

A few more entries were on the back, all with dates up until recently.

Lizzie looked at the rear door, expecting Mr. Calloway to fling it open. And if her heart wasn't pounding so hard, she'd do a jig right here. Should she tear the page out? No—that would raise suspicion. But this was the proof she needed.

At the jingle of the front door, Lizzie ripped the page loose and shoved it into her dress pocket. Hurriedly, she smoothed down the remaining ragged edges.

Please be another customer.

"Mr. Martin—good to see you, as always." Mr. Calloway used his charming, cultured voice.

No. Lizzie stuffed the leather journal back between the ledgers and softly clicked the drawer closed.

"Good evening, Mr. Calloway." Mr. Martin's voice carried clearly. "I was just picking up my wife's dress for the mayor's dinner tonight." Then he lowered his voice, and Lizzie couldn't hear the rest of his reply.

With a deep breath, she exited through the curtained doorway.

"What were you doing back there?" Mr. Calloway's tone was calm—no doubt for the benefit of Mr. Martin—but his pale-blue eyes, now steely, said he wouldn't believe a word of her explanation.

"I..." She looked at Mr. Martin. "He asked me to check on his payment, so—"

"He said you told him he owed twelve dollars. Of course, he paid me when he ordered the dress. Again, I'm sorry for my employee's mistake, Mr. Martin. Please accept my sincere apologies."

Mr. Martin looked from Lizzie to Mr. Calloway. "Uh, of course. No harm done." He gave Lizzie a smile. "Fine work, Miss Morgan. Thank you."

"You're welcome." She'd best not say she had found the paid entry herself, too, as that would confirm that she'd been looking in the ledger.

"I'm glad that's settled, Mr. Martin." Mr. Calloway turned to Lizzie. "Alas, it's closing time, Miss Morgan. You may leave, and I'll wrap the dress and close up."

Leave? It wasn't even five o'clock. She glanced out the front window. Josiah wasn't waiting in front of Mrs. Brighton's yet.

With Mr. Calloway surely watching her as he spoke pleasantries to Mr. Martin and packaged the dress and hat, she moved to the sewing machine. Quickly, she cleaned up the area, then donned her coat. And still it was too early for Josiah to be waiting for her. Should she just go on to the boardinghouse? But he wouldn't know why she had left unless he came inside and spoke with his father.

"Miss Morgan?" Mr. Calloway lifted one brow and tapped his foot.

"Yes, sir. Thank you for allowing me to leave early." With her coat on, at least she wasn't holding her hand over the pocket containing the journal page. Now that she had proof that Benton Calloway was involved somehow in both Mama's and Papa's businesses losing sales, did she dare tell Josiah? Or keep him from knowing what his father was capable of? Though she had no idea why Mr. Calloway would care about the profitability of the ranch, other than trying to ruin her parents out of spite.

Mr. Martin took his package and shook hands with Mr. Calloway. "I need to be on my way, too, and get this dress home to my wife. Miss Morgan, I'll walk out with you."

"Thank you." She was in trouble for sure with Mr. Calloway, embarrassing him in front of a customer.

Lizzie hurried out the door with Mr. Martin right behind her. Papa needed this journal page, but the interurban would take too long. If she could hire a carriage—

Yes, from Conor O'Shannon. He'd help her.

But she had to move away from the front of the tailor shop. She'd wait in the candy shop and would easily spot Josiah when he arrived, as he always stood in front of their window.

Mr. Martin turned to the left after bidding Lizzie good day. She crossed the street and pulled Mrs. Brighton's door handle. It didn't budge.

Locked? How could that be? It wasn't even closing time for her.

Lizzie had to get off the street, though. The bell—

She reached to ring it but stopped with her hand in midair. If Mr. Calloway even suspected what she'd done, he'd come after her. And she'd be drawing Mrs. Brighton right into his path.

Going to Conor O'Shannon's stable was her best option. If she could find it from here.

She turned in the direction she and Josiah usually walked, daring every few steps to turn and search every face behind her on the crowded sidewalk for him. No Josiah. She was on her own, then. She took off running until the buildings thinned out. The O'Shannons' home must be near here somewhere, but she didn't recognize anything now.

"If you lose your way back here, just ask for Conor O'Shannon. Everyone knows where my stable is."

Lizzie stopped a couple strolling along.

"Excuse me, do you know where Conor O'Shannon's stable is?"

They looked at each other and shook their heads. "No," the man said, "never heard of him."

An elderly lady stood at the edge of her yard leaning on her fence. "Ma'am," Lizzie called, "am I in the neighborhood of the O'Shannons' house?"

"Mercy, girl. You're going the wrong way—two blocks that way." She pointed down a side street. "You'll smell the horses way before you get there."

"Thank you, ma'am!" And Lizzie took off again.

Once she located the residence and business—both by sight and smell—she knocked on their house door and waited. No answer. She knocked again, then peered through the kitchen window, but the inside was dark. Where were they?

Against all hope, she headed to the stable. Maybe Molly had gone shopping, but perhaps Conor was back here feeding his horses.

The heavy door scraped across the brick floor as she opened it.

"Conor?" Lizzie took a step inside. "It's me, Lizzie."

The horses stirred and whinnied, shuffling in their stalls.

Rebel stuck his head out to greet her.

"Hi, fella." She took a step closer to him and cautiously patted him on the forehead. "Mr. O'Shannon—Conor—are you here?"

"No, but I am."

She whirled around and was face-to-face with Benton Calloway.

"I knew you were trouble the moment I met you." His voice was hard, his usually perfectly brilliantined hair flopping above his steely eyes. He stepped up to Lizzie. Too close.

"Mr. Calloway. I—"

"Hand it over."

"What?"

"Don't play dumb with me. You know what you took. You Morgans are all alike, every last one of you. You think you're better than everyone. That you can take what belongs to me. You're a thief just like your pa. Well, you can have my worthless son if you want him. Can't ranch. He's of no use to me. He has more in common with my enemy. Your father."

"Mr. Calloway." Lizzie was backed up against Rebel's stall with no place to run. "I don't understand. What do you want?" The journal page in her pocket, or was he bluffing? She refrained from moving her hand over the pocket under her coat where it was hidden.

"Payment for what he stole from me."

"Papa didn't steal anything."

"Oh, yes, he did. The Double E was to be mine. As was Eliza."

Lizzie gasped. "Mama?"

"Yes, your mother. Your pa stole her just as surely as he stole the ranch from me."

That was twenty-some years ago. And Mama never would have married this man.

"I made them a promise years ago that one day I'd own the

ranch and even the score. Now I'm making good on my word to pay them back."

"P-pay them back? How?"

"How? A little trade." His cackle lifted to the rafters of the barn. "You for her. Or her for you. We'll see who he loves the most. Doesn't matter much to me anymore."

"Papa will never do that!"

"Oh, but he will. First, hand over the page you stole." He thrust out his hand and took a step closer. "Now."

Lizzie unbuttoned her coat and pulled the journal sheet from her pocket. With a shaking hand, she held it out. He snatched it away, and now she had no proof at all.

"Get into that stall."

Lizzie's legs were about to buckle. She couldn't. Rebel was a nice enough horse from the other side of his gate. But get in the stall with him? With any horse? Where was Conor?

"I...can't."

Mr. Calloway pulled a gun from his pocket. "I think you can. Move!"

Rebel pinned his ears back and tossed his head. In a half rear, his front leg banged against the stall door.

"I ca—"

"Now!"

He slid the stall latch back and swung the gate open mere inches. Just wide enough to shove her inside and slam the door as Rebel reared again. She stumbled in the hay, ducking under the hooves flailing above her head. Half crawling, she scrambled to the back of the stall and huddled in a corner, hands over her head.

Lord!

"Father!"

Josiah? How had he found her? Lizzie wanted to weep, but she couldn't move. Couldn't speak. And Rebel continued to rear and kick. She was going to die in this stall with Josiah standing in the aisle.

She closed her eyes as Rebel's hooves crashed against the stall just overhead.

~

*J*osiah had to get that horse calmed down before he harmed Lizzie. He had no idea what his father was doing here, but he shoved past him to the stall.

"Lizzie—"

"Shut up." His father swung Josiah off the door and around in one motion.

Now facing his father, Josiah actually looked at him. Or rather the gun aimed at him. "What are you doing?"

"Step away and maybe no one will get hurt."

Maybe? The seal-brown horse continued to thrash, and if Josiah didn't do something fast, it'd be Lizzie who was hurt. That stall wasn't big enough for both a frantic horse and her.

"Lizzie!" Why didn't she answer? Had she already been kicked in the head? Lying there bleeding? Or worse?

"Shut up and get me a saddle for him."

"No, Father."

His father's eyes seemed to glow with fire. "No?" He leveled the gun at Josiah's chest. "Do it or you'll go in there too."

Yes—then he could calm the horse.

"Choose who you're going to stand with—your own flesh and blood—or the daughter of my enemy."

"I choose her. I'll always choose Lizzie. So go ahead and put me in—"

A shot rang out, and the hay at Josiah's feet puffed from the force of the bullet. The dark horse reared yet higher, and now all the horses up and down the aisle were kicking their stalls and neighing.

"You'd like that, wouldn't you? To be the hero? Well, that's never going to happen. You're no hero. You're as worthless as you've always been. Now"—he waved the gun—"get in there and calm that stupid horse. Then saddle him."

Josiah caught the nameplate before his father pushed him in and slammed the gate closed behind him. *Rebel*. "It's okay, Rebel." He used the soft tone he'd heard so often from his mother around frightened animals. "Easy, boy." He reached up and grasped Rebel's halter, pulling his head down. "I'm not going to hurt you. Easy, there."

Rebel still shook his head and pawed but was starting to quiet down.

Josiah risked a glance at Lizzie balled up in the corner, hands over her head, shoulders shaking. Hopefully, unharmed, but he couldn't tell. He just knew he had to get Rebel away from her. Either get Lizzie out of the stall or Rebel. If he could get Rebel out, Lizzie would certainly be safer there than facing his father.

With the gun aimed at the stall, his father one-handedly lugged a saddle over.

"Now nice and slow, bring him out and saddle him up. No funny business, or I'll shoot the Morgan girl. Or you."

Josiah believed him.

He'd just as likely shoot Rebel too.

"Psst. Josiah."

He turned his head toward the corner as much as he dared and raised his eyebrows, barely catching Lizzie's whispered words.

"Don't saddle him—he hates the saddle."

Josiah nodded with the slightest gesture he could in return.

With a deep swallow, he reached over the gate and released the latch as a plan developed.

Lord, please save us.

Holding onto Rebel's halter, Josiah led the horse from the

stall and stopped him in front of his father. Throughout the barn, neighs still sounded here and there, but hooves striking wood had mostly stopped.

"Saddle him."

"Yes, Father."

Rebel pranced around skittishly, and Josiah eased him forward a few discreet inches with each step, closer and closer to his father.

"Hold that beast still and get to it." His father waved the gun as if backing up his words.

Josiah stopped Rebel next to the saddle. He picked up a Navaho horse blanket lying on a trunk and slid it onto Rebel's back. The horse swung his hind quarters around, and Josiah positioned him again in front of his father.

"Father, this horse is going to take more control than I can manage. Could you hold his head while I put the saddle on?" Josiah bent and picked up the fine leather western saddle his father had deposited on the brick floor.

"Can't you do anything?" His father grabbed the halter with one hand, and Rebel tossed his head, jerking loose from the grip. "You stupid horse." He reached for the halter again and yanked Rebel's head down, holding the gun on Josiah with his other hand.

Josiah swung the saddle onto Rebel in one motion and jumped back. Rebel jerked his head free again and reared, the saddle sliding off. On his way down, his hoof clipped his father's gun-hand shoulder, and his father went down, face first. The gun skidded across the floor.

Josiah grabbed Rebel's halter and spoke gently, but his father was now scrambling, looking for the gun. Out of the corner of his eye, Josiah saw Lizzie dart from the stall and beat his father to the pistol. She picked it up and aimed it at his father. And Josiah was sure she knew how to shoot it.

"Hey!" Steps ran across the floor, and Conor O'Shannon

appeared. He grabbed a pitchfork leaning against the wall and held it aloft. "What's going on here?"

Josiah's father grasped Rebel's stall door and pulled himself up. "The fool girl and this wild beast tried to kill me!" He nodded to Lizzie still holding the gun trained on him.

Lizzie's mouth dropped open.

"She opened the door and let him loose to attack me." He grabbed his shoulder where Rebel had clipped him.

A woman with bouncing red curls entered the stable just steps behind a policeman.

"Molly!" Conor waved her back. "What are you doing here?"

"I heard a shot come from the stable, and I called the police station, fearing you might be the one being shot at."

Josiah could hug this woman.

But apparently, his father didn't feel the same, as he glowered at her and the policeman. "Arrest this girl! She and this crazed horse both tried to kill me."

The officer looked at Lizzie. "Put the gun down, miss."

She laid it on the floor, and he edged toward her and picked it up. "I'll have to take both of you down to the station to straighten this out."

Josiah rushed to Lizzie's side. "Are you all right?" Barely waiting for her nod, he turned to the policeman. "She didn't do anything—"

"Shut up," his father hissed. "You're more than worthless." He turned to Lizzie. "Are you sure you want me arrested? If so, your dear Josiah will be implicated too."

"He has nothing to do with this."

"Ah, but he does."

"I know he doesn't. He's honorable. Unlike you."

"Oh, really?" His father turned to Josiah, his thin smile failing to cover the evil of his heart. "Tell her, Josiah. Tell her how you agreed to meet her each evening at my shop to escort her to the boardinghouse—at my request."

"I did that to keep her safe. From you."

"Oh? And you never once asked about her life on the ranch? About her parents? What steps they were taking to hold onto the Double E?"

Lizzie looked at him. Her face was white, as if—

Surely, she didn't believe him. But he could see his father's words sifting through her. Josiah had rarely missed meeting her a single day. And he had asked just the other evening about how her parents were doing with the ranch.

"Lizzie, you know that's not true!"

"What I know is that maybe your father *is* telling the truth for once." She turned her back to him.

The policeman grabbed Josiah's father's elbow and pushed him toward the door. "Get moving. Miss, you too." He gestured to Lizzie to move along.

Conor O'Shannon took Lizzie's arm as she turned back to glare at Josiah. "I'm coming with you. You're not alone, Miz Lizzie."

But Josiah was. So alone.

CHAPTER 17

Each evening for the past week, Lizzie had been afraid of finding Josiah sitting at the supper table. But each day, he'd been missing. So where was he taking his meals? Not that she cared. She was just thankful to have been released down at the police station and given a chance to finish the orders at the Boise Tailor Shop, even with Mr. Calloway sitting in jail. At five each evening, she left to return to the boardinghouse to help. Unescorted.

"Hey, Busy Lizzie." Hugh eyed her from his rocker on the front porch of the boardinghouse as she marched up the steps. He winked at Markos rocking beside him.

"Leave me alone." She kept walking, sorry she'd come up the front steps.

"Leave you alone?" He grabbed his chest. "Oh, my heart!"

Markos grinned, then jabbed Hugh in the ribs. "All right, knock it off. Just do what you were paid to do."

"Ah, yes. Straight and Narrow showed up and—"

"I don't care." Lizzie glared at him. Not running into Josiah was one thing, but she didn't need any reminders of him.

She'd spent hours finishing up the alterations and new

garments clients had paid for. Clients who fully expected their work to be done before the Boise Tailor Shop closed for good. And the police promised she'd be paid for her hours out of Mr. Calloway's profits.

"Hey. He paid me to give you this"—Hugh waved an envelope at her—"so you'd better take it. Or else I just made some easy money."

"Josiah wouldn't give you anything to deliver to anybody."

Hugh burst out laughing. "You don't believe me?"

"No."

Markos stopped rocking. "Cut it out, Hugh." He turned to Lizzie. "He really did, Miss Lizzie. That envelope is from Josiah for you. What Hugh's not telling you is that he was the only person here when Josiah came by—Mrs. McPhearson wasn't even here at the time—so he had no choice but to leave it with Hugh if he was leaving it at all."

She stretched out her hand. "Then give it to me."

Hugh winked. "Here." He handed her the sealed envelope.

Why should she even read it? It'd be some flowery apology from Josiah embedded in a poem and how she should believe him.

She headed into the kitchen, where Mrs. McPhearson, now back from wherever she'd been when Josiah had stopped by, was bustling about. Lizzie tossed her envelope on the table, put on an apron, and set to work pulling down serving dishes.

"Dear, you look exhausted."

"I'm fine."

Still, Mrs. McPhearson filled the teakettle with water and set it on the stove. She nodded at the envelope. "Did you receive bad news?"

Lizzie shrugged. "I haven't read it."

"Then by all means, take a moment to do so."

"It's from Josiah."

Mrs. McPhearson's eyes lit up, and she looked toward the dining room. "He's here?"

"No. Hugh and Markos said he dropped it off when you were gone."

"Then all I can say is, I'm glad it reached your hands. Now, sit."

"I'm fine," Lizzie insisted, though since she could barely stand, she did sit.

Mrs. McPhearson shook her head. "I'll fix you a plate of supper and a cup of tea, and you'll take them up to your room. I'll serve supper by myself tonight."

"No, it's my job. I just need a moment, then I'll do it."

"Child." Mrs. McPhearson placed an arm on Lizzie's. "You more than do your job. Here and at the tailor shop. Now it's time for you to rest." She scurried about and prepared a plate of chicken, carrots, and biscuits while she steeped the tea. Then she handed the cup and plate to Lizzie along with the envelope. "Off with you now, dear. If you want to talk this evening over another cup of tea, I'll be here. Or in my sitting room."

"Thank you." Lizzie climbed the stairs to her room. Josiah's room, which he'd given up for her. She could at least read whatever he'd sent. After placing the food and tea on the small desk by the window, she sat and opened the envelope. Two pages. One a poem, of course. One a letter. She read the poem first.

On the Back Porch

> Under the stars in the soft hush of moonlight
>   glow,
> Amid a chorus of frogs and trumpeting crickets
> I discovered true love, so beautiful, so full,
> Unexpected, nourishing, drawing me with its
>   pull.

Deserving of her precious love I'll never
achieve.
But oh the delight of knowing the beautiful
heart
of my Lizzie. Always, only, the one for me.
She my true love will always, only be.

Lizzie stared at the words. Reread them. Refused to let her heart dwell on what he'd written. She picked up the second sheet of paper instead.

Lizzie,

This is the poem I was writing, searching for the words to declare my love to you. I guess I'll never get the chance now to say these words to you, but I mean them with all my heart. I never expected to find love, let alone encapsulated in such a spunky, adventurous, courageous, beautiful woman as you. You have opened my eyes to what love means, to what love is. My heart truly will only ever be yours.

I will always be a Calloway, though, and bear my father's legacy. But knowing you has been such a gift in this dark world.

Thank you for the light and joy you have brought to me.

You may consider the room at Mrs. McPhearson's boardinghouse yours permanently, for I will have no need to ever return to it. And you need not fear running into me at suppertime, as I have made other arrangements.

Yours, with a grateful heart always,

Josiah

Lizzie read the poem and Josiah's letter again. Josiah loved her. How could he still? After she'd made it clear who she believed. Even though he'd tried to warn her about his father, tried to get her to go home or at least find a different job.

"I choose her. I'll always choose Lizzie." In the confrontation in the barn with his father, he had shown his true heart. Chosen her.

Was he leaving the city? Was that why he wouldn't need his room?

She really shouldn't care what he did—because he'd decieved her, working for his father, the enemy. He had done exactly all the things his father had gloated over. Walking her home each night, all the while asking about her life, her parents. The Double E.

But—

"I'll always choose Lizzie."

One tear, then another slipped down her cheeks.

Could she have seen things wrong somehow? She'd been cornered again, nearly crushed in that stall. But worse than being trapped by a horse, was she not trapped in her unforgiveness? Even if Josiah *had* done his father's bidding, was she any better for not forgiving him? Benton Calloway was a crafty man. But was it not God's place to execute justice, not hers?

She'd had the love of a wonderful man and had thrown it away. Why? Because of her pride and unforgiveness. She certainly wasn't worthy of Josiah's love.

Oh, Lord, please forgive me. And here I am asking You to forgive me while I need to forgive Mr. Calloway. Please help me to forgive him—but most of all, Josiah.

Lizzie tucked the poem and letter into her pocket, and when she was sure the boarders had finished supper, she headed to the kitchen. Mrs. McPhearson was humming while washing the dishes.

As soon as Lizzie entered the room, the humming stopped, and the whistle of the teakettle filled the room. "Hello, dear. I put the kettle on, hoping you'd be down."

"Thank you." Lizzie sat at the table.

Mrs. McPhearson prepared the tea, the peppermint already starting to soothe Lizzie just from its fragrance. She set two cups on the table, then sat and patted Lizzie's hand. "Now, tell me what's wrong."

"I finished all of the alterations today for Mr. Calloway's customers. With him in jail, the tailor shop will now close down. So since I don't have a job anymore, I've decided to go back home to Caldwell."

"Hmm. I'm sure you'll be welcomed. But what about Josiah?"

"He can have his room back, if you can get word to him." Unless even that was too late. What had he meant by *I will have no need to ever return to it*?

"No, dear. I mean what about you and him?"

Lizzie took a sip of tea and fingered the envelope in her pocket. *"I'll always choose Lizzie."*

If only the peppermint could warm her heart as well as her insides. "There's nothing between us." Thanks to her.

"I beg to differ."

"Perhaps there might have been, but I didn't trust him. And he needs someone to believe in him."

"I think you do."

Lizzie gave a sad smile. "It's too late."

"Have you spoken with him since everything happened?"

"No...he...he..." Wouldn't want to talk to her. She finished her tea and pushed the cup away. "I'll help with breakfast in the morning, but then I need to catch the train. Josiah said he won't be taking meals here, but once I'm gone, he can return to his room and the meals. Could you please let him know?"

Mrs. McPhearson clasped Lizzie's hand in hers. "I'll be telling the boarders soon, but I want you to know. Since someone complained about this house and a city inspector visited, I've been debating whether to keep running a boardinghouse. And if not that, what to do with this big house. I'm getting too old for running it by myself, and the repairs the inspector cited are just overwhelming. But if you truly are leaving...?"

Lizzie nodded.

"Well, I'm hoping my son and his wife will move out this way from New York City one day so they'll be close by when they have children. I was thinking of dividing this big house into two homes instead of a boardinghouse, so if they ever do come, I can have them right next door. And until that day, I'll rent out the other half. But if you'll stay, you'll keep your room next to mine, on my side of the house."

Lizzie stood and hugged her. "Thank you, but no. I need to return home." There was nothing left for her in Boise now that all her plans had fallen through. Mrs. Farber's roadhouse. The tailor shop. Any possible future with Josiah.

"Please, Lizzie, before you leave, won't you talk with Josiah?"

Lizzie's mouth dropped open. "I—can't." She couldn't bear to look at him now, always seeing him as another scheming Calloway. Not after her heart had seen him as so much more.

"Lizzie." Mrs. McPhearson took Lizzie's hands. "Perhaps it's not my place to say this. But I think it needs to be said. It's fine for you to return home to your family. But if you return without speaking to Josiah, without hearing him out, then you will be running away. Return home honorably, having faced your problems."

"Mrs. McPhearson—"

"Please, Lizzie. Just think about it."

And while Lizzie could ignore the plea, she could not dismiss the love in Mrs. McPhearson's eyes. Love like Mama's eyes always held when she looked at her children. At Lizzie. But there was also an underlying sadness, as though Mrs. McPhearson knew exactly what she was asking. As if she also meant the words for herself. Could she have run from forgiving someone once upon a time and regretted it herself?

And it was that possibility that struck Lizzie. Perhaps Mrs. McPhearson was right. Even if the only thing Lizzie accomplished with listening to Josiah—being able to say she'd faced his duplicity head-on—she supposed she could hear him out. "All right. I'll try."

"Good. That's all I ask." With a squeeze, Mrs. McPhearson released Lizzie's hands.

"I'll stop by his workplace before I leave. If you could tell me how to get there."

Mrs. McPhearson smiled and drew a map. "There you go. I don't believe you'll be sorry."

At least one person was hopeful.

After breakfast the next morning, Lizzie packed her carpetbag and hugged Mrs. McPhearson goodbye. Three-and-a-half weeks ago when she'd placed her cloche hat on her head, it had been with a twig of bitterbrush blooms. God's promise of hope and provision, a reminder of His goodness and faithfulness. That she'd lost the flowers upon arriving in Boise should have told her something.

She set the drab brown hat on her head and set off to fulfill her promise of talking with Josiah. Before going to the train depot and purchasing her ticket to Caldwell, she'd find him and give him a chance to explain.

"I'll always choose Lizzie."

Would he truly choose her over his own father?

But wasn't that exactly what he'd done? What if even in the facts his father had ticked off one by one, Josiah had only been trying to help her? He had been there helping even before he knew who she was. At the train depot the day of her arrival. The first night out on the streets of Boise when she was all alone. Giving up his room and comforts for her. Warning her about his own father. Yes, he had chosen her all along.

And she'd turned her back on him.

Following Mrs. McPhearson's directions, Lizzie walked past

the burned-out roadhouse of Mrs. Farber. Soot-covered boards and a blackened oven were all that she could distinguish amongst the rubble. That and the lingering smell of smoke were all that was left of Mrs. Farber's building. Mrs. Farber had left this behind to move on to a new and different life. So maybe Lizzie's return to Caldwell, her own moving on, wasn't exactly a setback either.

With Mr. Calloway in jail, Mama could resume building her horse-training business unhindered by him trying to sabotage her reputation and Papa's saddles. Maybe Lizzie could find a way to help the Double E while living on the ranch.

Though she still didn't want to be near the horses, she could make flyers to distribute to townspeople. Or perhaps travel with Mama and speak to customers when she went to buy new horses. Or stay home and watch her brothers so Papa could travel with her. She would find a way to be useful. Somehow.

Whatever the outcome, she'd always be welcomed home. And very eagerly, from Mama and Papa's response to her telegraph that she would arrive today.

She reached the address Mrs. McPhearson had given her.

But this couldn't be right. She checked the paper again—then the hand-scrawled sign on the door at street level. *This office is closed.*

No, it couldn't be. How would she find Josiah if he wasn't here? No contact information was given on the notice. What even was the name of the company he worked for? No name was on the door, and she'd never asked.

Her chance at reconciling with Josiah was gone, as she had a train to catch and no way to find out where he was. Maybe that was what he'd meant in his letter—*You may consider the room at Mrs. McPhearson's boardinghouse yours permanently, for I will have no need to ever return to it.*

But where had he gone?

She made her way to the depot and had the entire trip to ponder that, but no answer came by the time the train pulled into Caldwell. Lined up against the depot and waving were the boys. Isaac. Winston. Zephaniah and little Sammy. And Papa, with his arm around Mama.

Lizzie stepped off the train straight into Mama's arms. Then Papa's. Sammy crowded in to be part of the hugging. Even the older boys circled around with pats on her back.

"I'm glad you're home, Lizzie." Winston thumped her harder. "Now you get your job of feeding the pigs back."

Papa placed an arm around Winston's shoulders. "Maybe, maybe not. You keep feeding them until it's decided what Lizzie's jobs will be."

"Aw, Papa—"

A look from Papa silenced him, likely before he could be assigned more chores or even feeding the pigs forever.

"Let's just enjoy having Lizzie back home with us." Mama pulled her into another hug.

Then Papa held her tight again. "Yes, indeed. Welcome home, Lizzie girl."

Maybe the boys had been warned not to ask the reason she was back, but at least here Lizzie was wanted. All she needed to do was find a new purpose on the ranch.

And a way to forget that Josiah Calloway loved her.

CHAPTER 18

Josiah walked the familiar blocks to the boardinghouse. He'd promised Lizzie in his letter yesterday that he would not make suppertime awkward for her by being at the table. But as he turned the corner onto Mrs. McPhearson's street and the aroma of pot roast wafted from an open window into the air along with cinnamon—maybe from an apple pie Lizzie had baked?—he almost wished he hadn't made that promise.

A dreadful thought stopped him. Hugh had given her the envelope, hadn't he? He really wouldn't put it past that troublemaker not to, but he hadn't had much choice when he'd stopped by. Mrs. McPhearson had been out, and Josiah certainly wasn't allowed upstairs, especially as he no longer lived there. So he couldn't slip the letter under Lizzie's door.

Hugh had been the only boarder home from work already, and Josiah had been at his mercy. But—and even worse—what if Hugh had not only not delivered it but had read the contents? Josiah's love letter and poem were meant for Lizzie's eyes alone. Yes, he probably was a fool for trusting Hugh with anything—and to have paid him for it as well. He should have waited—

what would one more day have mattered? But yesterday he couldn't bear for Lizzie to go one more hour without knowing his heart, that she was loved.

And today, he needed to say one more thing to Lizzie. If she'd let him.

Mrs. McPhearson's words spurred him on. *"...that, my dear Josiah, is who you are. Selfless. Giving. Caring. Loving. Always remember who you are."* He wanted to be all those things to Lizzie, for her to see that even though he was a Calloway, he was not following after his father.

If he hung around on the back porch until Lizzie finished in the kitchen, maybe she'd join him so he could explain. Even though she'd thrust a dagger into his heart when she believed his father over him, he had forgiven her for that. His father was practiced at twisting words to use against people. If only he could convince her that he had been watching out for her, loving her.

The birds chirped their songs in the ever-lengthening daylight, and he quickened his pace, eager to make sure Lizzie had recovered after her scare from his father and being trapped with a frenzied horse. And even if he couldn't win back her trust, he would not leave until he'd looked her right in her eyes and told her clearly, boldly, that he loved her.

Another whiff of pot roast reminded him that he sure would have appreciated a hot dinner tonight, but that wasn't an option.

He hiked his duffel bag higher on his shoulder. He still had to find a place to sleep tonight, as his boss had closed the upstairs office where Josiah had worked alone—and lived for these past weeks—to save on rent by consolidating his two offices. He'd talk to Lizzie and be on his way. To somewhere. Maybe Conor O'Shannon would allow him to spend the night in the hayloft for a night or two.

Josiah reached the boardinghouse, ready to go around to

the back when he spotted Hugh sitting in the shadows on the front porch in a rocker.

"Well, Straight and Narrow, what brings you this way again? You checking up on me to see if I delivered your letter to Busy Lizzie?"

Josiah scowled at him. "Did you?"

Hugh smirked. "What, don't you trust me?"

Hardly. But Josiah held his tongue.

"Of course, I delivered it. I'm your faithful servant, am I not? Paid and everything." Hugh laughed and slapped his knee.

"Thank you." Josiah started to head around the house.

"But she ain't here."

He stopped. Not here? She should have been here almost an hour ago after work. Where was she then?

"I'll wait." Or should he go looking for Lizzie? Mrs. McPhearson would know what to do.

"It'll be a long wait, then. She left."

"Left?" To buy food supplies, or, surely not— "What do you mean?"

"She left today with her belongings. You can get your room back, I suppose. Until the old lady closes the boardinghouse down. She announced it this morning. She's tired of us all and cooking and cleaning for us. She's getting old, you know."

"Hardly. Mrs. McPhearson isn't anywhere near old."

"Well, then, maybe it's because of your old man."

"What's that supposed to mean?" Josiah balled his hands to keep from swinging out.

"In the interest of establishing safe residences for boarders, he let the city know of some irregularities here, and now she says running this place is too much for her."

"And how would you know that?"

Hugh's face turned red. Beet red. And it dawned on Josiah. "You. You let my father use you."

"I didn't mean no harm. It was just an anonymous phone

call for easy money. You Calloways pay good." He shrugged. "But now I'm gonna be out of a room. All of us men will."

Oh, Josiah really needed to sit. The damage his father caused just kept growing and growing. He'd never be able to repay it all. But if Lizzie didn't forgive him, it didn't really matter, as he'd have the rest of his life working to pay it off.

Hugh scowled. "But you don't have anything to worry about."

"And why is that?" How Josiah wanted to grab Hugh and shake him. Did he not even grasp the consequences of what he'd done for some quick money? Had putting each of the men, including Hugh himself, out of a home been worth it?

"Because all you need to do is go tell Mrs. McPhearson what I did—just like before—and she'll believe you and reward you."

"Hugh, it's not—"

Hugh jumped from the rocker and swung. Josiah ducked, but Hugh came at him again and shoved him to the porch floor. Crouching over Josiah, Hugh pulled his fist back, fury in his eyes.

"Hugh—stop!" Markos ran up the steps. "What are you doing?"

His fist still poised in midair, Hugh turned his head. "Finally paying the snitch back, that's what."

Markos jerked Hugh away from Josiah. "He didn't do it."

Josiah got to his feet and stepped back from them both.

"So now you're taking his side?" Hugh sneered at Markos. "You're a goody two-shoes now too?"

"No, but the truth is the truth. And Josiah was not the one who told Mrs. McPhearson what you were doing in the kitchen that day."

"And how do you know? He was the only one who came in after I took a few measly dollars from her hiding place. And by raising my rent, she got way more back."

"It wasn't him," Markos insisted.

Even Josiah wondered how he was so sure, as Markos hadn't been there.

Hugh narrowed his eyes at Markos. "I'm beginning to think it was you, then, since you know so much."

"Mrs. McPhearson knew all along."

Hugh scoffed. "She'd left to do her grocery shopping."

"She did, but I was on the porch and saw her come back. Maybe she forgot something. Anyway, she went around to the back of the house. Did she come into the kitchen while you were busy helping yourself to her money?"

"No."

"Then she saw you from the window and decided not to say anything."

Hugh stared at Markos. "Well, it doesn't matter now, does it? As we're all getting kicked out." Then he seemed to realize Josiah was still there. "You knew all along, didn't you?"

Josiah nodded. If Mrs. McPhearson hadn't confronted Hugh directly, it hadn't been his place to. Perhaps she'd been waiting for him to pay her back or to confess. Or to give him a second chance? The only thing she'd done was to make the kitchen off limits to the men after that. And, according to Hugh, to raise his rent.

Hugh scowled at Markos. "Well, you can hang around with your new friend"—he jerked his head toward Josiah—"from now on. I'm done with this place." He stomped off down the steps.

Markos watched him leave, then walked over to Josiah. "I'm sorry. I should have said something sooner. I shouldn't even have been hanging around with him. But"—he looked Josiah in the eye—"all those names he called you? If they mean you're a godly man and trying to live by the Good Book, then they're good names. I think everyone here except Hugh knows what you stand for."

Josiah held out a hand, and Markos shook it. "Thank you.

And I pray you and the others all find another home as good as this one has been."

"Yeah," Markos said. "Hey, we'd better get in for supper."

Josiah couldn't go in for supper, but he had to find out about Lizzie. *"She left."*

Josiah jerked the door open and strode through the dining room to the kitchen. Surely, Mrs. McPhearson would forgive him for entering this way, as this was an emergency. If she suspected a problem with Lizzie, she'd send him out looking for her.

"Mrs. McPhearson—"

"Josiah!" She held a roasting pan. Her hair was straggling out of its bun, and perspiration beaded on her forehead. "I can't talk now, but after I serve everyone, I'll put on tea."

"What can I do to help?"

"Oh, you're a sweet one, you are. Bring in the bowl of potatoes and the gravy bowl, if you would."

"But where's—"

"After supper, Josiah. After supper."

Maybe he'd get a plate of this hot meal, after all. But he had a feeling that by the time he talked with Mrs. McPhearson, he wouldn't be hungry.

And he was right. When he sat at the kitchen table with a plate of pot roast, carrots, and potatoes, he could barely swallow the food as Mrs. McPhearson confirmed that Hugh had been telling the truth about Lizzie. She was gone for good, back to Caldwell.

Finally, Mrs. McPhearson set a slice of apple pie in front of him—not the one he'd imagined Lizzie baking when the cinnamon aroma had wafted out the window earlier.

"Here we go." Mrs. McPhearson brought over two cups of tea and seated herself across from Josiah. "A cup of tea does wonders for muddled thoughts."

While the scalding brew did nothing for his dilemma, it at

least gave him something to do with his hands as he gripped the cup. One he'd seen Lizzie drinking from.

"I don't understand." Mrs. McPhearson studied him over the rim of her cup. "You didn't see Lizzie before she left? She promised she would stop by your work before she caught the train."

And that right there was the problem. "Whether she did or not, I don't know. As I wasn't there. As of this morning, the office is closed."

"Closed?"

"My boss notified me last night that he had to make a quick decision on the property. He's consolidating it with his main office. And unless I wanted to pay rent on the room and continue living there, I needed to be out by this morning."

Mrs. McPhearson's face turned red. "You have no place to sleep?"

"No, not yet, ma'am."

"Well now you do. You shall have your old room back. But back to Lizzie…"

"Even if she had come by, she would've had no idea of where I was, what with the sign he left on the door stating it was closed."

"But you know where she is."

"Mrs. McPhearson—"

"No buts. You go up now to your room and get settled in."

And just like that, he was dismissed. He climbed the stairs, thankful for a room—his room. And once he'd unpacked his few possessions from his duffel bag, he had nothing to do but pour out his heart. In prayer. And in poem.

> The birds sing their evening chorus from the
>   branches
> The sun sets bold and strong
> But I sit in this room with no song

Because I am alone
Alone
Alone
Always alone.

~

*L*izzie had been back home just over a week, and June had crept in along the way.

If she'd hoped cooking and ranch work and the saddlery and horse training business now booming again would keep Mama and Papa so busy they wouldn't have time to ask details about Boise, she was only partly right. They might not ask out loud in words, but their eyes asked plenty of questions.

She'd told them about Mrs. Farber and the fire, of course. And that she'd had a room at a boardinghouse with dear Mrs. McPhearson. And that she'd found a job as a seamstress at a tailor shop. And that the shop had closed so she no longer had a job. And that she'd wanted to return home.

All true.

Except she hadn't dared to mention the who, where, and whys of the tailor shop and its closure. And most of all, she hadn't mentioned Josiah. Even if she was stuck here and had to feed the pigs the rest of her life, she couldn't bear to mention Josiah to her parents. Mama and Papa had found true love, while Lizzie had been naïve and a fool.

"Lizzie." Mama called from the kitchen doorway where she stood with Papa. "While the boys are doing their outside chores, we'd like to talk with you. To finally get a chance to sit and really learn what you've been up to in Boise."

Of course, she wouldn't be able to evade questions forever. But did today have to be the day?

Slowly, she moved to the kitchen table and sat. Her parents

seated themselves also, and Papa took Mama's hand and smiled at her. Still so much in love. And now that Lizzie had had a taste of someone looking at her like that, she would rather remain a spinster than settle for less. Knowing what she'd thrown away.

The aroma of a bountiful supply of coffee percolating on the stove drew her attention. In minutes, it would be ready. And Mama's coffee, just like Mrs. McPhearson's tea, was the thing in the Morgan house to hold while discussing matters.

"We're so glad to have you home again." Mama started the conversation. "You're such an adventurer, Lizzie."

"Just like you were at her age, Eliza," Papa said.

Was that a look of pride in his eyes? Lizzie blinked. It wasn't aimed just at Mama but at her too.

"Well, yes." Mama rolled her eyes at him but blushed under his gaze just the same.

Papa grinned. "The fire may have destroyed your dream, but you certainly bounced back and found a new job. A place to stay."

Lizzie squirmed in her chair. She was hardly someone to be proud of—but with both Mama and Papa beaming at her like that...

"Poor Mrs. Farber." Mama's blue eyes clouded with concern. "We have to find out where she is and see what we can do for her."

"I heard from— Someone in Boise said she went to be with her sister in California. Maybe I can get the address." From Josiah, somehow.

"I'll always choose Lizzie."

Where was he? What if she never saw him again? It'd serve her right for how she'd treated him. But if she never found him, she'd never be able to ask his forgiveness either.

"Yes," Mama said. "Please do find out her address if you can. Now tell us about Mrs. McPhearson and your job. A seamstress

—that must have been lovely. You've always been very handy with sewing."

"Oh, Mama, the fabrics were so beautiful. And the threads—they were lined up like a rainbow of colors under the large front window. I also got to learn what fashions are popular in Boise. Some of the ladies asked me for advice in choosing fabrics and styles for them, so I suggested tips I learned from you. They turned out so beautiful, and the ladies loved them." Not Mr. Calloway, but that was not something she'd add.

"Speaking of being stylish, I got a letter from Aunt Belinda in New York. My cousin, Olivia, is engaged to be married."

"Do you think we might be invited to the wedding?" She'd never met any of the New York City family, as they always refused to come to Idaho and rarely corresponded. Maybe Mama's cousin, who was closer in age to Lizzie since Aunt Belinda married later in life, would be more adventurous.

"I would hope so, even if we can't attend. It would mean so much to draw the whole family together one day."

"If we do get to go, I'll help design our dresses."

"I know they'll be beautiful." Mama covered Lizzie's hand and winked. "And we'll fit right in with their society lives."

Papa laughed. "Enough about fabrics and threads and styles. Tell us about the tailor you worked for. What was he—"

"Papa!" Sammy burst through the door. "When is Lizzie coming out to help me with the pigs? Winston made me feed them, and they don't like me."

Lizzie could have hugged Sammy. She jumped up and grabbed his hand. "I'll come right now. I know what you mean—the pigs don't like you, and the horses don't like me." She ruffled his hair.

"Sammy." Papa put on his stern look. "Tell Winston to come see me."

"Yes, Papa." He turned to Lizzie in a stage-whisper. "He's gonna be in trouble."

He probably was, but Lizzie could hug Winston too. For being such nuisances sometimes, her brothers had just rescued her.

"It's so good to have you home, Lizzie girl," Papa called as Sammy tugged her out the door.

"A blessing, indeed," Mama added.

If Lizzie turned around to look back, Papa would be smiling into Mama's eyes as they held hands across the kitchen table. She'd seen it so many times, it was just part of daily life at the Double E. The ache in her heart pressed harder, as there was only one man she wanted to hold hands with.

But even if she could find Josiah, would he ever want her back in his life again?

CHAPTER 19

Josiah stood at Mrs. McPhearson's sink with his hands in dish suds. After a week of working two jobs, morning to night, he was worn out. But it was worth it.

A raise with working at the main accounting office and pleasing two new clients added a hefty chunk toward paying down the amounts owed in the ledger. Plus, Mrs. McPhearson had offered him an unexpected exchange. In payment for doing repairs around the house and washing and drying dishes after supper and cleaning the kitchen, he now received free room and board, giving him more money to apply to the accounts.

That gave him enough money now to repay everyone in the ledger in full with only twenty more dollars needed to reach the three hundred owed the Morgans. Finally, even that was now within sight. And when he took the entire amount to the Double E, he'd be able to face Lizzie with his head high.

As he put away the last of the supper dishes, Mrs. McPhearson came through the door from the dining room.

"Josiah, you have a visitor."

He inhaled, his heart soaring. Could it be? He whirled

around, but no one was with Mrs. McPhearson. "Who? And where?"

"It's Conor O'Shannon. He's coming around to the back door, as I thought you might want some privacy. He's welcome to come inside if you'd like, and I'll fix you both a cup of tea."

Did he have news of Lizzie? He wiped his hands on a towel and stepped onto the back porch. It'd been almost three weeks since he and Lizzie had sat on these steps. When he'd almost taken her in his arms and kissed her. Now with her gone from his life, he wished he had kissed her even against his better judgment. For then he'd have that memory to carry him through the days. Through his life.

Conor O'Shannon was rounding the corner of the boardinghouse. "Mr. O'Shannon—Conor. What can I do for you?"

"You're a hard one to track down, boy." Conor climbed the steps and clapped Josiah on the back.

"Mrs. McPhearson is fixing us some tea, if you'd like to come inside and talk."

"Fine by me. It'll give me a rest before I head back. I should have rode one of my horses, but I do like an evening walk."

Together they went inside and sat at the table while Mrs. McPhearson bustled about. "Thank you for making the trip over." If Conor had news about Lizzie, Josiah wanted to hear that first.

"Ah, yes. I did what you asked. You know, inquiring about rumors on why people were buying saddles and horses elsewhere than from your Miz Lizzie's parents."

Josiah leaned forward with his arms on the table. "What did you find?"

Conor pulled a paper from his jacket pocket. "I wrote down the names of a couple people who told me they'd heard talk that the Double E was skimping on saddle materials and bought elsewhere. Not that they were happy with their other purchases, anyways. And one person—Hank—who had liked a particular horse Miz Lizzie's mama, the Angel from the East, had showed him. But he said a man told him he'd be swindled if he bought from her, as she didn't spend enough time training her horses and this one wouldn't be safe for his boys to ride."

"Any idea how much those losses amounted to?"

"No. Oscar was just grumbling and didn't want to admit how bad a decision he'd made. Morgan custom saddles are the best there are, but they sell for a pretty penny, though, I'll tell you that. The other fella walked away before I could ask him. And Hank, with the horse, said he wished he'd gotten the Angel of the East's one, as his turned out to be as mean as all get out. There's no telling at an auction how much he could've gotten the Double E's for. But the one he did get was pretty high by the time someone was bidding against him."

Josiah ran a hand down his face. Now instead of only twenty dollars to go for the Morgans, he'd have to figure out how much more these losses had cost them. And even with that, would Conor discover yet another horseman who had bought elsewhere based solely on rumors manufactured by his father?

"Here you go, gentlemen." Mrs. McPhearson set steaming cups of tea in front of them. "I'm slicing up some cobbler right now. Peach. If you'll stay for that, Conor?"

"None for me," Josiah said.

But Conor patted his belly. "Gladly. Thank ye much. So, Josiah, is there anything more I can do for you?"

"Thank you for what you've done already. And I just want to say again I'm sorry for the ruckus of my father in your stable. I hope it didn't tarnish your reputation at all, what with a gunshot and arrest on your premises."

"I'm sorry about your father, too, that he's landed himself in jail again. But I'm mighty glad you and Miz Lizzie are safe. Where is she, by the way? My missus and I miss her."

Josiah looked at Mrs. McPhearson to answer.

"She's gone on back home to her family's ranch in Caldwell." She gave Josiah a pointed look as she set cobbler in front of Conor.

Yes, he knew very well her stance on what he should do. But until he could repay her parents for his father's debts, he could not ask Lizzie's father for anything. Most of all his only daughter.

"Caldwell." Conor seemed to chew on that along with a bite of dessert. "Not so far from here. When you see her, give her my and Molly's regards. Tell her Rebel is expecting her to visit him."

Josiah held back a grunt. She probably wanted to see Rebel about as much as she wanted to see him. He gave Conor a noncommittal smile. "Thanks for coming over to inform me of what you found out. I'll see that it's taken care of."

"Mighty glad to be of assistance." Conor finished off the cobbler in two more bites and gulped the last of his tea. "Thank you, Bea, for the hospitality." He stood and headed to the door, then turned back. "Josiah, if you do think of anything else, let me know." With that, he let himself out.

Josiah gathered the plates and cups and took them to the sink and ran water again.

"And what do you think you're doing?" Mrs. McPhearson crossed her arms.

"Dishes."

"No. You're finished for the night. You go on up and get yourself some rest. You're working too hard. Both here and at your accounting job."

She was the one working too hard, but he'd never convince her of that. But there was one thing he could do to relieve some of her burden. "If you insist."

"I do."

He hurried up to his room and pulled out the ledger and his money envelope he'd re-hidden under the floorboard. Marked an entry *paid*, fortified himself against an argument, and slipped back into the kitchen.

Mrs. McPhearson turned from the sink at his footsteps. "And what are you doing back after I relieved you for the night?"

"Please sit."

Alarm flashed across her eyes. "What's wrong, dear boy?"

He took her elbow and guided her to a chair, then sat across from her. "Nothing is wrong. I'm making something right." He placed bills in the remaining amount of debt to her on the table. "You are now paid in full."

"Josiah, I told you long ago that—"

"I know what you told me. That the debt is not mine to repay. But for the Calloway name to have any honor, I have willingly sought to right the wrongs. I'm sure this isn't even the whole amount that my father cheated your husband out of, but I ask that you please take it. Perhaps it will help toward keeping your boardinghouse open or at least in making repairs or changes to the house."

Mrs. McPhearson wiped her eyes with a corner of her apron. "I don't know how such a callous man as Benton Calloway has such an honorable son." She patted Josiah's hand and reached for the money he pushed her way. "Thank you. I'll accept it as an answer to prayer, then."

"Thank *you*. Now how about let me finish up here and you be the one to go upstairs and rest?"

She dabbed her eyes again and nodded. "You're a dear man, Josiah Calloway. I'm sure Lizzie would agree."

Lizzie. If only.

She headed upstairs, and Josiah finished the last of the cleanup in the kitchen. Back in his room later, he studied the ledger again and made his new entries.

Mrs. Farber had been paid when she departed for California. Mrs. McPhearson now had a zero balance. And Mrs. Brighton had only five dollars left, which he'd pay tomorrow.

He pulled out his money envelope again and recounted the bills, though he knew exactly the total. After paying Mrs. Brighton her remaining five dollars tomorrow, there would be the two hundred eighty dollars left for the Morgans. Twenty dollars short. And once he took action on Conor's report, the amount due would grow yet again. He'd been so close.

Fury at his father roared up again. The only consolation was that he was back in jail.

Lord, please help. Help him to forgive. Help him to somehow earn this extra money. Help him to be worthy of Lizzie. He fell asleep with one word on his lips. *Help.*

In the morning, he pulled five dollars from the envelope. Maybe he'd gone about his repayment method wrong. Maybe he should have been repaying the Morgans bit by bit all along like the others.

Was it pride that had slithered into his heart as a seed and grown into the resolve that they must receive their total at once? Or shame? Facing Caleb and Eliza Morgan as the son of their adversary from years ago was a mighty humbling prospect. One he only wanted to encounter once.

He accepted a steamy cup of morning coffee from Mrs. McPhearson and a cinnamon roll just out of the oven but didn't stay to enjoy the scrambled eggs.

When he reached the candy store, the *Open* sign wasn't yet out, but Mrs. Brighton stood filling the jars of candy in the front window. She walked to the door and let him in.

"Good morning. What brings you by so early?" She glanced at the vacant tailor shop across the street, clearly puzzled as to his presence, since neither his father nor Lizzie brought him to this street any longer.

"I came to bring you the last payment of my father's debt."

"Josiah." She shook her head. "You're a faithful son to do this. But it's not necessary."

"To me it is." Didn't anyone understand? He could never be free of his father's legacy until those debts were paid. And even then, he'd still be a Calloway, with the stains of Benton Calloway's wrongdoings clinging to him like a stench.

She accepted the proffered bill and nodded at his father's former store. "I don't even know what to say. I do miss seeing your Lizzie there, though. What a joy she was." She dumped another bag of candy into a glass jar. "Have you seen her since she closed down the shop?"

"I haven't." And there was no use explaining that she wasn't "his" Lizzie.

"When you do, greet her for me and Gideon, will you?"

"Sure." He could do that someday. Once the amount owed the Morgans was ever marked *paid*. "I'd better get to work as it's on the other side of town now."

"Of course." Mrs. Brighton fluttered the five-dollar note in her hand. "Thank you for this. Now I can pay Gideon a little bit of real earnings on top of his candy allowance."

Josiah smiled and waved. He knew nothing about Gideon's life other than that he had a grandmother who loved him. And that might just be enough to keep him on the right path.

~

Lizzie had soap suds up to her arms as she did the morning dishes, alone in the kitchen except for Sammy at the table.

With sales for Mama's trained horses and Papa's custom saddles picking back up, the family was already outside tending to their jobs.

"Hey, Lizzie. Do you like the chickens?"

"I suppose so. Aren't you supposed to be out collecting their eggs?"

"I don't like them too good. They peck at me. But they're better than those old pigs."

"I agree with you there. Why don't you start with gathering the vegetables first today, then?"

"I don't like doing that either."

Lizzie rinsed the suds off and faced Sammy, trying hard not to show her exasperation. "As a family, we all pitch in to help on the Double E."

"I know." He swung his feet back and forth, kicking his chair, but made no move to get to work.

"Of course, you do. So what's the problem this morning?"

He looked up at her. "I want to be a trav'ler like you. And tell stories."

There was such longing in his eyes that she wanted to scoop him into a hug like Papa would have. Though Mama probably would have told him to go out and tell the chickens his stories. Or perhaps he just wanted someone to listen to his dreams.

Lizzie sat in the chair across from him. "Made-up stories or real ones?"

"Ones like in the newspaper Papa reads."

"Ah, I see. And that's a very important job. But travelers and storytellers have to do chores first, too, you know. Look at me"—she pointed to her apron—"cooking and doing dishes and mending. It's all part of helping each other. I'll tell you what. You do your chores without complaining—and do them well—and I'll help you write a story."

"Really, Lizzie?" He hopped up and hugged her.

"Yes. Now, who do you think has the most interesting job on the ranch? Isaac learning to train the horses?"

"No." He sat again and wrinkled his forehead in thought.

"Hmm. Winston, feeding and watering the horses and chickens?"

"Nope."

"Zephaniah?"

"No." Sammy shook his head vehemently. "Poor Zephaniah. He has to do the pigs now. And pull weeds."

"I think he's the only one who likes those pigs, so don't feel bad for him. So, who, then?"

"Papa."

Such a good answer for a little boy. "Then we'll start with him and make a list of questions you can ask to interview him."

Sammy again ran over and threw his arms around her. "Thank you, Lizzie." He grabbed the egg basket by the door and was gone in a flash.

Now all she had to do was take her own advice. Do her never-ending chores before she could do what she really wanted to do, which was—

Find Josiah.

A rap at the door and Kep's happy bark sounded about the same time. And standing on the porch was the white-haired man who was like a grandfather to her and the boys. Gus, Mama's original mentor in horse training, must be in his eighties, but he still showed up to watch Mama work or give Isaac tips.

"Lizzie, other than your hair and eye color, you're a-looking more and more like your ma each time I see you."

She searched his eyes to see if he was joking, but he seemed quite serious. "Thank you. Are you looking for her? She and Isaac are out in the training corral." He should have spotted them on his way in. "Or did you come to see if there are any biscuits left?"

Now his eyes lit up.

"Do you want butter or honey on them?" Lizzie snatched both jars, anticipating his answer.

"A bit of both. So...how were things during your stay in Boise?"

The change in his tone told her exactly why he'd come to the house first. Fishing, what Gus did best. Just what did he know about her time in the city? She hadn't told Mama and Papa about meeting Benton Calloway, much less working for him. Or being threatened by him.

But had Gus heard something? He and his sidekick Mr. Jacobs, who owned the mercantile, always seemed to know what was going on from Caldwell to Boise.

She split two biscuits and spread both butter and honey on them. "It was fine. But I'm glad to be back home now." She plated the biscuits and handed them to Gus.

"Thank you. Any, um, adventures?"

"Of course." She wasn't about to take his bait. "You know Mama says I can find adventure in everything." She motioned to the plate of biscuits. "Take these, for instance. When I was making them, I forgot to add in the salt and then burned them until they were so hard and awful that Winston said even the pigs wouldn't eat them."

Gus turned the biscuit in his hand around and examined it. "Looks okay to me."

"I had to make another batch—and it put everyone behind this morning. But we all had a good laugh to start the day. But here I am rambling, and I imagine you came to instruct Isaac. I'd better get back to finishing up here so I can start the mending. It was nice seeing you, Gus."

He held his biscuit up in a salute. Maybe he realized he'd been outwitted. But she wasn't about to tell him anything about Boise, especially not until she told Mama and Papa. Which would be never.

But what if Gus or Mr. Jacobs did know something and they told her parents first?

CHAPTER 20

*A*t last, the end of the week had come, and Josiah didn't have to rise extra early to get across town to the office. But even at night, he didn't find real rest in his longing for Lizzie.

"But you know where she is." Even in his dreams, Josiah couldn't erase Mrs. McPhearson's admonition that he should seek Lizzie.

But he hadn't been dreaming. He'd been wide awake, watching the early light of Saturday creep into his room. And the voice wasn't exactly Mrs. McPhearson's this time. It wasn't even a voice. More like a resonance in his heart.

A nudge from God?

He reached over to the desk for his paper where he'd finished his poem last night. After crying out to God, the words had finally come.

> The birds sing their evening chorus from the
>   branches
> The sun sets bold and strong
> But I sit in this room with no song

> Because I am alone
> Alone
> Alone
> Always alone.
>
> But I am not alone, never forsaken
> For God always sustains.
> He walks with me even through the valleys of
>   the shadows
> I am not alone for I am loved by God above.
> Loved
> Loved
> Always loved.

And with those words, Josiah knew finally what he needed to do. He had to see Lizzie. Even without the total payment to her parents. He would work something out with them for the remainder or do whatever he had to pay it off. But he had to see Lizzie.

He jumped out of bed and packed his duffel with the money envelope layered between two shirts, keeping the new poem in his pants pocket. If he hurried, he could catch the first interurban of the day to Caldwell.

He bounded down the stairs, following the aroma of coffee and cinnamon into the kitchen.

"Good morning." Mrs. McPhearson took a tray of rolls from the oven and set it atop the stove. "You're up early. I barely have the coffee made. Would you like some—and a cinnamon roll?"

"Yes, ma'am. Thank you."

"You look like you're going someplace." She eyed the duffel slung over his shoulder. "It wouldn't be to see Lizzie, would it?"

Mrs. McPhearson was indeed direct. Though she hadn't spoken outright to him again of going to see Lizzie since the night he first came back, she apparently thought it was time to do so now.

Josiah nodded. Then grinned.

"Good. Go after your girl."

His smile dimmed. If only she were his girl. "I just...just want to make sure she's safe. I can at least do that much."

"And so much more. You're a good man, Josiah Calloway. Don't let anyone persuade you otherwise." She handed him a cup of black coffee and a hot cinnamon roll. "Don't go after her, though, with unforgiveness in your heart."

Josiah choked on the mouthful of coffee he'd just taken. "What?"

"Unforgiveness eats away at a person is all I'm saying."

"If you're talking about my father, he doesn't deserve it."

"You're right. He doesn't." She wrapped another roll in a cloth and handed it to him. "But neither do we." She reached up and kissed him on the cheek. "Now go and, Lord willing, bring our Lizzie back."

"Thank you, Mrs. McPhearson, for—well, everything."

"You're welcome. Godspeed."

Josiah left and hurried toward the depot. The Caldwell car was just pulling in. If he could catch this train out—

"Tell her, Josiah." His father's words burst into his head, and he stumbled mid-step. *"Tell her how you agreed to meet her each evening at my shop to escort her to the boardinghouse—at my request."*

He'd never forget Lizzie's horrified look as the indictment had filled the barn, settled in her heart.

"What I know is that maybe your father is telling the truth for once."

Her words of condemnation left him gasping for air.

He spun around on the sidewalk, almost colliding with the gentleman behind him. "Excuse me, sir. I'm sorry."

He was going to the jail to confront his father. Now. And

then he'd board a train and go find Lizzie, to talk with her. He had to see her.

Even if she sent him away.

When Josiah reached the jail, he approached the man at the front desk.

"My name is Josiah Calloway. My father is here—Benton Calloway. I'd like to talk with him before I go out of town."

"Sit there." He pointed to the bench against a wall. "I'll check."

The man left and was gone several minutes. When he returned, he shook his head at Josiah. "I don't know who you are or what you want, but Calloway said he has no son. So beat it. And don't come back."

No son? Josiah couldn't stand if he'd wanted to.

"But—"

"I said beat it."

Josiah forced himself up. "Could I just—"

"No. Now get out of here before I throw you in your own cell."

Josiah staggered out the door.

No son.

He slowly worked his way back to the train depot. If he could just pour out his heart to Lizzie, wrap her in his arms, and let her comfort him. But what if she disclaimed him too?

"What I know is that maybe your father is telling the truth for once."

He bought a ticket for the next train to Caldwell and went outside to wait. He sat on the bench under the wide eaves of the depot, his back against the sandstone wall. The exact spot Lizzie had sat when she'd arrived in Boise with that yellow bitterbrush bloom stuck in her hat.

"Unforgiveness eats away at a person is all I'm saying."

Oh he had plenty of time to sit here and think about unforgiveness until the train arrived. How could he ever forgive his father? For what he did to the Morgan family, his own family, Mama. For intentionally turning Lizzie from him? And the deepest wound of all—*"Calloway said he has no son."*

Unforgiveness was becoming like a posting in his accounting ledgers. The heavy debt was like an anvil, crushing his heart. His entries of Benton Calloway's wrongs were rising higher and higher, with nothing to cancel them, no way to pay them. Except for forgiveness.

But how could Josiah forgive all that?

He'd been working and sacrificing to pay his father's debts against others, to reclaim decency for the Calloway name. And yet—*"Calloway said he has no son."*

Josiah looked up at the clear sky, the sun warming his face. *Oh, Lord, please hear me. You're my true Father. Please help me.*

Finally, the train arrived and Josiah climbed aboard, staring out the window the entire trip. When he debarked in Caldwell, he surveyed the town where his father and mother had met years ago. Where they'd married during a short time his father was out of jail. He shuddered with the thoughts of what his father had done then. And now.

Oh, that he'd never follow in his earthly father's footsteps.

Help me to cling to You, Lord. Always to Your goodness.

With his duffel bag over his shoulder, Josiah searched for the local mercantile. Most likely, someone there could point him to the Double E.

When he found it, he entered, and two older men playing checkers looked up.

"Howdy." The one with a shopkeeper's apron smiled.

The grizzled-looking white-haired man just nodded.

"Hello." Josiah walked up to them. "I'm looking for the Morgan ranch, the Double E."

The two men exchanged a glance. "Is that right?" The shopkeeper spoke, but the other man's eyes bored into Josiah. "And who might you be?"

Josiah swallowed. "Josiah Calloway."

Scowls appeared on both men's faces. Of course. Anyone with the name Calloway would likely still be persona non grata in Caldwell.

"Calloway, you say," the shopkeeper finally said. "Any relation to Benton Calloway?"

"Yes, sir. He's my father."

"What business do you have with the Morgans?" The question may not have had a snarl to it, but the crossing of the man's arms silently voiced the equivalent.

Probably no business being here at all. Lizzie had made it plain she didn't want to see him. And yet, according to Mrs. McPhearson, maybe she did.

"It's of a personal nature. I come on my own, not on my father's behalf, I can assure you."

The man looked him up and down. "They live outside of town a few miles that way." He moved his head in the direction.

A few miles. It'd take him a while, so he'd better get started.

The grizzled man stood. "It's okay, Daniel. I'll take him."

Another look passed between the two men, and the storekeeper nodded. "Very well, Gus."

"Let's go. I have my wagon out front." Gus hobbled to the door.

Josiah climbed onto the rickety one-horse wagon and clung to the seat on the ride out of town. The trip wasn't unpleasant —as long as he could skirt Gus's grilling. But he wasn't confident the man wouldn't give up trying to be polite and ask pointblank what he wanted to know before they reached the gate of the Double E.

The mountains in the distance, the sprawling land, the sagebrush like a silver carpet climbing up the hillsides—this was the embodiment of the ranch he'd envisioned owning one day. The days before his wound in the war. Before he'd learned of his father's debts.

"Here we are." Gus pulled the horse to a stop in front of a gate. The overhead sign boldly proclaiming the *Double E Ranch* was like a welcome banner. But would he be welcomed by Lizzie? Or her father?

"I'll get the gate." Josiah climbed down from the wagon.

Gus urged the horse forward onto Morgan property, and Josiah closed the gate behind them, then pulled himself back up onto the seat. Gus opened his mouth but closed it, apparently thinking better of whatever he'd wanted to say.

They'd no sooner started down the lane than a collie bounded out to meet them, barking and running alongside them.

"Howdy, Kep," Gus called out to the dog.

As the wagon approached the homestead, horses with their heads hanging over the paddock adjoining the red barn nickered. Outside a lower building, pigs grunted and rolled around in the dirt. The pigs Lizzie had had to feed because she was scared of the horses. Was she here? Still feeding them?

Gus stopped the wagon near the house. "End of the line."

Perhaps his words were prophetic. Lizzie's—or her father's—reaction could seal his fate, stomping any remaining hope he had.

"Thanks for the ride." Josiah grabbed his bag and climbed down again from the wagon.

"Let me know if you need a ride back to the train. Or"—his eyes lit up—"should I wait?"

Should he? "I don't know how long I'll be, so that won't be necessary." The route back to town was straightforward, so if Lizzie rejected him, the walk would do him good.

Josiah reached into his pocket. "What do I owe you?"

"Nothing. Much obliged to help out. That's what we do round here."

"Well, thanks again, then."

As Gus left, Josiah took a few steps toward the front porch

of the well-maintained white farmhouse. Two rocking chairs all but beckoned a husband and wife—or a courting couple—to come sit as the sun set and to share their hearts into the evening hours.

The collie circled him, sniffing, ears alert.

Josiah set his bag down, crouched, and held out his hand. "Here, fella. Kep. Hello there. I'm here to see your Lizzie." The dog came closer, and Josiah tentatively patted the dog on the head. The collie licked his hand, so Josiah gave him a rub on the back.

"Who're you looking for?" A man's voice came from the barn doorway. Definitely not as welcoming as the dog.

Josiah stood, and the man walked toward him with a bit of a limp. A ranch hand? Or could this be Lizzie's father?

"Kep. Down."

The collie immediately sat, and the man came abreast of Josiah.

"I'm Josiah Calloway."

The man frowned but said nothing. Just gave a nod.

"Are you Mr. Morgan?"

"I am." His eyes narrowed, and he looked Josiah over, searching deep.

Caleb Morgan, Lizzie's father. The man his own father had tried to discredit and even worse years ago. But Josiah stood still, not daring to look away. "I'm glad to meet you."

Mr. Morgan studied him in silence. "How may I help you?"

"I met your daughter in Boise. She was working for my father, Benton Calloway."

His lips tightened into a line. "And where was this?"

"My father ran a tailor shop—Boise Tailor Shop."

Mr. Morgan folded his arms and looked hard into Josiah's eyes, his stare intimidating.

Josiah swallowed. "But I was trying to watch out for her,

keep her safe. I wanted to get her away from him, but she wouldn't leave her job."

Mr. Morgan shook his head as if Lizzie's stubbornness wasn't news to him. "Go on."

Before he could, a woman stepped onto the porch with three boys behind her vying to see out the door. "Caleb?"

"It's okay, Eliza. I'll be up in a bit. Boys, stay inside and help your mother." He turned back to Josiah. "Continue."

"Yes, sir. My father followed Lizzie after work three weeks ago and tried to attack—"

"Attack!" His head jerked back, and his fists clenched.

Josiah had no idea of the man's temperament, but he held his ground. "She's fine, sir. But my point is, he's in jail now, and she's safe from him. And I...just wanted to make sure, since she left Mrs. McPhearson's boardinghouse, that she's somewhere safe now."

Mr. Morgan nodded. Lizzie had returned to the Double E as Mrs. McPhearson thought, hadn't she? Was she inside even now? Peeking out a window after her brothers surely reported on the presence of a strange man? Being questioned by her mother?

But her father offered neither any information nor indication. Not even a furtive glance that might give away her whereabouts, if she indeed were here at the ranch this moment.

Josiah scuffed his shoe in the driveway. "She...left before I could say a proper goodbye. And I wondered if—if she's here, if I might...see her."

Lizzie's father didn't say anything for a few moments. Josiah concentrated on keeping his feet still, not shifting from foot to foot. Not to do anything to make him look weak. Or suspicious.

"She is here."

A puff of breath escaped. "Then may I see—"

"But she hasn't mentioned your name. Not once."

Oh. "I see." He could barely speak around the knife in his

heart. "Thank you for your time, sir. I won't bother you—or her—anymore."

Josiah shouldered his duffel bag and turned to leave. He should have asked Gus to wait a few minutes until he'd been sure, but oh, he'd really thought—

It didn't matter what he'd thought...that Lizzie would be here. That she'd run out to see him. That she'd include him in her family. That she would have at least mentioned his name, whether good or bad.

The walk back to Caldwell—a few miles—would do him good. Let him wallow in his pitiful life of copying numbers on his way back to the main accounting office.

"Josiah. Wait." Mr. Morgan clapped his shoulder, and Josiah turned. "If you are leaving, we'll take you to the depot. After supper. Come up to the porch and sit."

"Yes, sir. Thank you." Together they walked to the porch.

"You can sit in a rocker here." Mr. Morgan pointed to the slightly larger one. "I'll be right back. Just need to let Eliza know to set another plate."

Voices filtered through the screen door and feet scurried about. He set the rocking chair in motion, letting the rhythm and the view of the mountains in the distance lull him into what-could-have-beens.

If only he could have bought a ranch like this one. Growing up, he'd never expected he'd set foot on the Double E, home of his father's enemy. If he didn't have a bum leg, he'd be able to ranch, even be able to buy one if he didn't have to repay his father's debts.

But setting the accounts right, balancing the debts, was the only way he could make the Calloway name stand for something good. Or at least erase some of its tarnish. And in his earlier dejection that Lizzie had not mentioned him at all, he'd forgotten the other reason he was here. To pay Mr. Morgan the money he did have and to arrange the remaining payments.

If only—

"Josiah." The sweet voice filled the summer air like a gentle wisp of breeze.

Lizzie came out the screen door and closed it quietly behind her. He stood.

"No, sit." She sat in the other rocking chair, giving the aura of a couple sitting side by side in the evening. Just as he'd pictured minutes earlier.

"Lizzie, I—"

Snickers at the door caused them both to look that way. The three boys were back, whispering and pointing.

Lizzie jerked up. "Isaac, Winston, Zephaniah! Get away from the door."

"And Sammy, too," one of the older boys sang out as a grinning boy of about five pushed past them and onto the porch.

"Boys." Mr. Morgan's stern voice got the boys' attention. "Into the kitchen to help your mother."

"But that's Lizzie's job," one of them complained.

"It's your job today. Now get to work with no grumbling, or it'll be your job tomorrow also."

They all scrambled away, and Mr. Morgan stood in the doorway a moment, winked—whether at him or Lizzie, Josiah wasn't sure—and closed the outer door.

Josiah could breathe easier now, knowing Lizzie was here, safe. But his breath caught.

Was she glad to see him—or sorry he came?

CHAPTER 21

Why had Josiah come? Oh how her heart wanted to hope for...foolish dreams. Because the reality was, Lizzie had pushed him away and believed the worst about him.

"What I know is that maybe your father is telling the truth for once."

If only she could take back those horrid words.

"Why are you here, Josiah?" Dare she hope that he could forgive her?

"I wanted to make sure you're safe."

Safe. Oh.

"I am." Physically safe, but still trapped in her own cowardliness, her unbelief in him, her running away without doing more financially to save the ranch.

"Good. I was worried." He scraped his feet across the porch planks in front of his rocker. "I'm here for another reason also. I came to speak with your father about a matter and to say I'm sorry."

About his part in aiding his father? She might be able to

forgive Josiah. But she was still struggling with forgiving Benton Calloway.

Except...Papa's words the day she had left for Boise pricked her heart.

"Bitterness does no one any good. I had to learn to forgive as God has forgiven me. 'As far as the east is from the west, so far hath He removed our transgressions from us.'"

And that was Benton Calloway he'd forgiven. Yet...it was God's place to execute justice. His alone. Was that what Papa had meant?

Josiah sat quietly, looking at her. Waiting for her to say something.

"I—"

Sammy burst onto the porch. "Food's ready!"

Josiah stood. "Perhaps I should head on into Caldwell to catch the train back to Boise."

"Hurry up." Sammy tugged Lizzie's hand. "Mama said to come. You, too, mister."

Lizzie turned to Josiah. "Please stay. For supper."

With no more words between them, they followed Sammy inside and took seats around the table overflowing with food. Judging by Mama's glances at Josiah, Papa had told her whatever Josiah had shared with him. Who he was. At least who his father was and enough of what had happened for Mama to send concerned looks her way as well.

During the meal, her brothers peppered Josiah with questions about Boise, but Lizzie didn't join in the conversation. Mama and Papa listened intently, studying him, giving a nod to each other occasionally. And the way her mother's eyes lit up when Josiah spoke to her and Papa—well, Lizzie knew she'd be sought out later for questioning.

Finally, the meal was over and dessert served and cleared away.

"Mrs. Morgan, may I wash the dishes? I'm pretty good at it."

Josiah grinned. "That's one of my jobs at the boardinghouse where I live."

Had he returned to his old room and taken over Lizzie's job there?

Again, Mama's eyes twinkled. "Thank you, but no. You go on out to the porch and enjoy the evening."

Josiah turned to Papa. "Mr. Morgan, may I have a word with you, please?"

"Of course. The porch is always the best place to sit and talk. Especially at sunset." He winked at Mama and followed Josiah outside.

"We'll bring coffee out," Mama called after them and set Lizzie to work preparing it.

"Mama..." Lizzie turned to face her mother once the coffee was set up to percolate. "I know I should have told you everything. But I was...ashamed."

"Oh, Lizzie..."

"And I know you're bursting to know more about him—and at one point, yes, I did have dreams of Josiah. But he is like his father—Benton Calloway—after all."

"Oh? Do you really think so? In what way?" Her mother sat at the table and motioned for Lizzie to join her.

"Years ago, when you told the story of how you and Papa met and about Mr. Calloway, you said he was charming."

"Yes, he certainly could be. But it was a ruse to gain people's trust."

"Exactly. And that's what Josiah did. He gained my trust, only to turn on me, to give what I told him to his father to use against the Double E."

Mama frowned. "What makes you think that?"

"His father said so."

"Benton Calloway said so." Her mother reached across the table for Lizzie's hand. "And you trust his word more than Josiah's?"

"He— Well, I also found Josiah's ledgers where he was trying to pay back the people his father had cheated."

"That sounds honorable to me."

"It had your and Papa's names in it for three hundred dollars. But not one cent was repaid on it."

"Did you ask him about it?"

"No…"

"Lizzie, I'm going to tell you this woman-to-woman." She squeezed Lizzie's hand. "You know the main parts of my and your father's story."

Lizzie nodded. "Of course. How Benton Calloway stole from the ranch and attacked you—"

"Yes." She waved her hand as if that part of the story didn't matter anymore. "But now I want you to hear the rest of it." She folded her hands on the table. "The worst of it isn't what Benton did to us. The worst is that I didn't trust your father. I let distrust and unforgiveness and bitterness come between us."

Lizzie's eyes opened wide. "Mama?"

"Yes. It's nothing I'm proud of—and that was my problem—pride. Then God showed me how He feels about bitterness. 'Let all bitterness, and wrath, and anger, and clamor, and evil speaking, be put away from you, with all malice. And be ye kind one to another, tenderhearted, forgiving one another, even as God for Christ's sake hath forgiven you.'"

"I know those verses."

"Of course, you do. I made sure each of you children learned them early on. What a difference it would have made in my life had I applied them earlier. I needed to learn about true forgiveness. And as I asked the Lord's forgiveness and then asked Caleb to forgive me, that's when our firm foundation was laid to build our marriage on."

She sat in silence a moment, perhaps weighing how much to tell Lizzie. "Unforgiveness breeds bitterness. We did forgive Benton, but he apparently didn't learn anything from his prior imprisonments. However"—she rubbed Lizzie's cheek—"we will forgive again. Though this time it may be harder. Not for trying to ruin the Double E but because he attacked one of our children. But, yes. We will forgive again."

"I don't understand. How can you?"

"That, my sweet girl, is not something we can do on our own. It is only possible if we let the Lord do it in us. Because God for Christ's sake has forgiven us."

"The Bible verse?"

Mama chuckled. "Yes, the Bible verse."

Lizzie leaned over and hugged her mother. "I love you, Mama."

"And we love you so much too." Mama wiped her eyes. "And you know, from what I've observed and you've told me, Benton's son doesn't sound anything like him."

"No, he's not." And the truth of those words sank into her soul. He had been watching out for her, helping her. He had chosen her.

Mama looked over at the coffeepot bubbling away, the aroma filling the kitchen. "I think once the coffee is perked and after your papa and Josiah are finished talking, perhaps you should go out and have a talk with Josiah."

"You approve of him?"

Mama smiled. "Yes. And apparently, so does your father. Speaking of whom..." Her cheeks turned rosy. "I think I'll go tidy up and brush my hair. When the coffee's ready, dear, would you take it out to the gentlemen?"

"Yes, Mama." And judging from the look in her mother's eyes, Mama hoped Lizzie and Josiah would sit and talk for quite a while. But if they didn't, that Mama was only too eager to be the one to sit with her love and talk into the evening out on the porch.

Whoever ended up on the porch, Lizzie's heart was already burning with God's command to forgive.

he setting sun cast golds and pinks and lavenders across the western sky. Crickets chirped unseen as though chorusing their appreciation of its beauty. Josiah and Mr. Morgan had sat in quiet for a few minutes, the rhythmic *whoosh* of the rockers almost lulling Josiah into a sense of calm. Of peace. The smell and whinnies of the horses in the corral were the icing of everything Josiah had dreamed of in a ranch. But he wasn't here to dream.

He stopped rocking.

He was here to speak man-to-man with the person his own father hated the most, had stolen the most from.

"Mr. Morgan, I came to your ranch to check on your daughter first and foremost. To make sure she was safe. But there's another reason I'm here—and why I couldn't come sooner." By all rights, without the full payment, he shouldn't be here even now.

Even though Mr. Morgan kept rocking without a word, Josiah had to finish what he came to say. "My father cheated many people. I found names and amounts of some of them and have been repaying them little by little. But you are the one he stole the most from and was still scheming to ruin you up to the day he was arrested." Josiah cleared his throat while Mr. Morgan still rocked.

"I vowed I would pay you back but not little by little like the others. All at once." Josiah reached into his pocket and withdrew the bulging envelope inside. "I can't undo everything my father did to you, but I now have almost the entire original three hundred dollars I discovered he'd cheated from you through the years." He took a breath, bracing against the hardest part, of admitting his failure.

"However, I just discovered there's yet more. Someone I trust asked around and found a few people who said they specifically bought elsewhere based on rumors, undoubtedly from my father, about the Double E. I don't have an exact amount yet, but when I do, I'll repay it. But today, I can pay this." He extended the envelope to Lizzie's father. "Two hundred eighty dollars. Unfortunately, the remaining twenty and any additional amounts will have to be in installments, but today I give this to you in good faith."

Mr. Morgan stopped rocking. But didn't reach for the envelope. "Son."

Oh...what would it have been like to have been a Morgan instead of a Calloway? But his father was his father, and he was bound to honor that. "Please take it. It belongs to you. If you feel that you're owed more, I'll make sure—"

"Josiah. Stop." Still, Mr. Morgan didn't reach for it. "Tell me this. Why do you feel you must atone for your father's wrongs?"

"Why? Because if I want to turn the name of Calloway into being an honorable name, paying his debts is the only way."

"Is it?" Mr. Morgan countered. "When I look at you, Josiah, I don't see the son of Benton Calloway, the scoundrel and thief. I see Josiah Calloway, a man who watched out for my daughter in Boise when I wasn't there to protect her. A man who is willing to sacrifice. A man who helps others even at his own inconvenience. A hard-working man. And I hope a man who loves and serves God."

"I do, sir."

"Then I see you as a man of honor."

"Sir?"

Mr. Morgan resumed rocking. "Yes. A true man of honor."

"But—" Josiah extended the envelope farther toward him.

This time, he reached for it. "You don't owe me, Josiah. And I only wish I'd known sooner that you were trying to repay some account. But I'll take this in the vein it's being offered—as from a man of honor who is doing what he embraces as right."

"Thank you, sir. I'll give you payments for the rest as regularly as I can."

"No. This cancels any debt. No more is owed. Where customers decide to buy either their horses or their saddles from is their own decision. Not your responsibility. Do you understand?"

No, he didn't. How could this man erase such a debt?

"It's forgiven, Josiah." Mr. Morgan halted his rocker once more, stood, and pulled Josiah up and into an embrace. "You're a man I'd be proud to call 'son.'"

Son. The word spoken from Caleb Morgan's lips sounded nothing like the contemptible ring his own father—who now disowned him—gave it.

Son. One who was accepted. Loved. Trusted.

"Thank you, Mr. Morgan." Josiah wiped his eyes. He may have just handed over almost three hundred dollars of hard-earned money, but the gift Caleb Morgan had given him in return was worth that plus so much more.

"And now, son, I think I'll go inside and let you and Lizzie enjoy the coffee and sunset out here together. And"—Josiah caught a hint of a chuckle—"it's getting late to take you into town to catch the train back to Boise. So you can stay out in the bunkhouse for the night." He released Josiah from the hug, slapped him on the back, and winked at Lizzie now standing in the doorway with a tray of coffee in her hands.

CHAPTER 22

*L*izzie stood frozen in the doorway until Sammy bumped the door into her.

"Come on, Lizzie. I can't keep holding the door open if you ain't going through it!"

"Shh." What had happened out here that Papa had enveloped Josiah in a hug—a hug exactly like he often gave her brothers?

"Lizzie girl." Papa smiled at her. "I'm going inside. Since you're here with the coffee, why don't the two of you enjoy it together out here?" He stepped toward Sammy and ruffled his hair. "Let's go in."

"Good. Lizzie's just standing here making me keep holding the door for her."

"That's good practice for being a gentleman. Let's go find your ma."

And suddenly Lizzie—apparently with the blessing of both of her parents—was alone on the porch with Josiah.

"Lizzie—"

"Josiah—"

Josiah took the tray from her and set it down. "Let's sit and talk."

Lizzie took Mama's rocker and sat, Kep settling at her feet.

"Where'd he get his name?" Josiah asked, sinking into Papa's rocker.

"He's Kep Two, named after the original Double E dog."

Kep lifted his head at his name.

"Where the name came from, though, I don't know." Lizzie ran her fingers through his fur, glad for something to do with her hands.

"Josiah—I was so wrong. I do trust you. I know now that you're honorable and would never hurt me."

"Never, Lizzie. I hope you believe me. I'll always choose you."

Oh, those words. Words spoken *to* her this time. "Please, Josiah, will you forgive me?"

"Of course. But..." He looked like a lost little boy for a moment rather than the strong man he was. "Lizzie, how do you forgive? How were you able to forgive me?"

"It's not something that comes easily, Josiah. In truth, I just now did." She rocked a moment. "My mother told me a story about unforgiveness and forgiveness. About how she and Papa forgave your father years ago, before they married. And how it became a foundation for their marriage. And how they will do so again this time."

She nodded at his surprised look. "Mama shared a Bible verse. 'And be ye kind one to another, tenderhearted, forgiving one another, even as God for Christ's sake hath forgiven you.' So we're to forgive as God forgives us. And how great is His forgiveness? Papa made us learn this verse. 'As far as the east is from the west, so far hath He removed our transgressions from us.' That's how we're to forgive. Though I'm just now learning how to do that."

"Lizzie." Josiah reached for her hand. "If you and your

parents can forgive my father for what he's done to you and to them..." He drew in a deep breath, released it. "Before you and God, that's what I want to do right now too. Forgive. As I've been forgiven, I forgive my father, Benton Calloway."

Lizzie clasped her other hand over their joined hands. "Amen."

"Lizzie, from the moment I saw you at the train depot with a bitterbrush bloom stuck in your hat, my heart connected with you. I have found you to be a gift in my life. Beautiful in your heart—and, if I may say so...um...all of you." His face was red as he met her eyes. "So I would like to ask you something. Would you consent if I asked your father if I might court you?"

Consent? She'd jump up and kiss Josiah if she didn't suspect her brothers were peeking from behind the door. Or that she should wait for Papa's blessing. "Oh, yes!" She tightened her hold on Josiah's hand. "You can ask Papa right now if you want to." Then she laughed, embarrassed at her eagerness.

"Oh, my sweet Lizzie." Josiah touched her cheek. "In a minute. I just want to sit here with you for a bit, being thankful for my bitterbrush gal."

They sat with hands clasped as the sun sank into the horizon.

Josiah's gaze drifted to the horses in the corral. "Did I tell you when I dreamed of owning a ranch I pictured it just like this?"

"Caldwell is the perfect place for a ranch. You could—"

"No, Lizzie. That dream is gone, what with my leg..."

"Whatever you do, wherever you go, that's where I want to be too." Grunts from the pig pen interrupted the peacefulness of the evening. "Even if you wanted a pig." Her words were in jest, to make a point that he meant everything to her.

But he didn't laugh. "Would you?"

"What?"

"Could you really be happy if I wanted pigs?"

Lizzie looked over at the creatures snuffling and rolling in their pen. Dirty, snorting, nipping animals. Was he testing her sincerity? Did she really mean it? She hated those pigs.

Josiah turned his head their way, too, as if considering them. "I've been reading up on pigs. Raising them is farm work, and they provide a decent living. I'm thinking maybe that's the sort of ranch I could still have."

A ranch was one thing. But pigs? His brown eyes, alight with the possibility of his dream, confirmed he was serious. And he was waiting for her answer.

"Pigs." She held in a deep sigh, picturing the life he was setting before her. Could she?

Then he smiled, right into her eyes. The love reflected there wound its way to the depths of her heart, and she had her answer.

"Yes, Josiah, I'd be happy even on a pig farm with you. Anywhere with you. Maybe you could buy a piece of the Double E and have your pigs exactly where you imagined your ranch."

"Oh, Lizzie. I'd be happy wherever you are too. But if you really think— Do you really mean it?" His eyes held such hope, such love.

She nodded. "The Double E was named for my great-grandparents, Elizabeth and Elliott. We could call our place the J and L."

"Or the Pig Sty."

Lizzie laughed. "I don't think so. We'll think about the name for the farm."

Josiah squeezed Lizzie's hands. "I don't care what we call it —as long as *your* name is Lizzie Calloway."

She nestled her head on his shoulder. "Yes. That's the perfect name for me."

"And if your father says yes, would you come back to Boise with me? Now that my father's debts are paid, I can start saving to buy land and build a house and invest in some pigs."

"Of course—" She sat up straight. "What did you say? Your father's debts are paid?" What about the large, unpaid amount he owed her parents? Knowing Papa, though, he would have forgiven Josiah the debt, so...

"Yes. I was waiting until I had the entire amount to pay the last person, your father. But then—"

"Wait. He took it? I don't understand—that's not like him."

"He didn't want to, but yes, he took it. Your father and I have an understanding about the entire debt."

"Then since you two are on such good terms, go in and ask him." Lizzie smiled, both excited and nervous for Josiah to ask Papa if Josiah could court her—and for Papa's answer.

A few moments after Josiah went inside, Mama came out and sat in the empty rocker. "Josiah seems like a good man." Her eyes twinkled as she reached over and patted Lizzie's hand. "Like your papa."

"Oh, Mama, he is. There's so much I want to tell you about him." Lizzie looked toward the door. If only Papa and Josiah were standing just the other side of it so she could hear Papa's answer. Surely, he could tell what a wonderful man Josiah was—

"He'll say yes." Mama laughed. "Don't worry."

"Then what's taking them so long?"

"Oh, Lizzie. This is a first for your father, having to think about giving his daughter to someone. I'm sure he'll find Josiah very worthy."

"Well, I wish they'd hurry up." She couldn't wait to be in Josiah's arms again, to shout to the world that he was courting her. Though her brothers would probably take care of that part. And if they did, she didn't mind in the least.

"So while we have a moment alone," Mama said, "I wonder how Callie, Benton's wife, is. Did Josiah mention his mother?"

"You knew her?"

"Yes. I met her when I first moved here. At one time, she thought Benton would get the Double E, and she wanted to make sure she was part of it. Though when that didn't work out, she still married him. I guess she really did love him. When the Calloways moved away, no one seemed to have heard from her. It must have been a hard life for her."

"From what little Josiah said about her, she did have a hard life. She's gone now, though. His father left him and his mother for months at a time, and they struggled to survive. But he said she was a kind, godly, strong, hard-working woman."

"That I'm glad to hear. I'm sorry things didn't turn out for her as she'd hoped. Just to be on the arm of a handsome man with prospects of money isn't a good reason to marry someone. But it sounds as though she changed through her struggles and hardships. And taught Josiah well."

And then the door opened and Josiah stepped out, his eyes, his smile proclaiming Papa's answer.

Lizzie jumped up.

Mama winked at Lizzie. "I'll just excuse myself and see if I'm needed inside." With that, she left the two of them alone on the porch.

Lizzie ran the few steps to the door straight into his arms.

Safe. Loved. Secure. That was what being with him was. And with his lips so close to hers—

"Your father gave his blessing."

Before she could utter a sound, his lips met hers, and he pulled her closer to his heart.

And his kiss, both gentle and bold, told her more than words could. With Josiah, she was home. Chosen.

She ignored the boyish snickers coming from the doorway and her mother's scolding whisper and quiet click of the door.

From now on, she had her own sunsets to look forward to with the man she loved.

CHAPTER 23

Now that Josiah and Lizzie had been back in Boise for two weeks, he was taking this Saturday morning to walk with her to visit Conor and Molly O'Shannon.

"Are you doing all right?" He studied her eyes, her expression for any sign of apprehension, since this was Lizzie's first time to come this way after the attack by his father.

"I'm fine. Really."

Still, he held her hand tight all the way from the boardinghouse, where Mrs. McPhearson had given Lizzie both her old room and job back. Except now Lizzie was helping Mrs. McPhearson full time with the cooking and housekeeping.

Josiah had moved to a small room over the main accounting office, where he had taken on more responsibilities for his boss, resulting in another raise in pay. Nightly, he was back at Mrs. McPhearson's supper table in exchange for doing dishes, repairs, and sitting on the back porch afterward with Lizzie—a stipulation Lizzie insisted she didn't mind in the least.

As they neared the O'Shannons' house, Josiah gripped her hand tighter, hoping to convey trust and courage to her. "I'd like to stop at the stable first. Would you mind coming in with me?"

Now fear flickered through her dark eyes, and he pulled her to a stop. "We can skip it if you'd like, but I'll be right by you, sweet Lizzie."

She took a deep breath as if fortifying herself. "I can do it. I'll just think of the stable as where you rescued me." She smiled up at him, the love and trust in her eyes making him love her more each day. "Plus, I would like to thank Rebel. He helped rescue us too."

"That he did."

They walked inside, and Conor stopped pitching hay into Mud Puddle's stall. "Welcome. Are you here to—" Josiah discreetly shook his head behind Lizzie's back, and Conor winked.

"Go ahead and say hello to Rebel now that we're here." Josiah let her lead the way and set her own pace, in case she had second thoughts.

But Lizzie walked up to the big horse and rubbed his head. "Hello, boy. Remember me?" Rebel made a soft noise and moved his head like a nod. "Oh, look. It's as though he knows what I'm saying. You're a smart one, aren't you, fella? I wish I could visit you every week."

"Well"—Conor leaned on his pitchfork—"you'd best be getting on to doing it, then. He won't be here a whole lot longer."

Lizzie's eyes widened. "What? Why?"

"Well, it seems I'm selling him."

"Selling him? Can't you keep him?" She put her hands near Rebel's ears as though she didn't want him to hear his fate. "Just because he's not a riding horse, and automobiles have taken over—"

"Lizzie." Josiah put his arm around her. "I bought him. He's the first animal for our farm."

She opened her mouth, as if too many thoughts were spinning and she couldn't get even one out. "I thought it was a pig farm. That maybe we'd have some chickens too."

"But we'll still need a good horse. Or two."

"Oh, Rebel. You'll be the perfect wagon horse for our farm, won't you?" She stroked his forehead again.

"Perhaps he will, but you'll need a riding horse—"

"He's not a riding horse. You know that."

"Not yet, but I have the best trainer in Idaho lined up for him—the Angel from the East."

"Mama? Oh, Josiah." Lizzie threw her arms around his neck, and Josiah gladly reciprocated, encircling his arms around her waist.

"Yep." Conor chuckled as he watched them as if quite entertained. "Guess if anyone can train him under the saddle, it's Eliza Morgan."

Lizzie kissed Josiah on the cheek, then turned back to Rebel. "Do you hear that? You're going to be ours."

"You might have to change his name, though," Conor said. "'Rebel' may not suit a docile saddle horse."

"Bitterbrush would be a good name." Josiah winked at Lizzie. "But that can be for our next horse. I think Rebel should keep his name—as a reminder that even if we've been called by the wrong name in the past, the name can come to mean who we are now."

Like the name Josiah Calloway, once a name of shame, it was now a name of integrity. He now bore a place in the hearts of the Morgan family and the name he'd longed for.

Son.

"He'll be your horse, so what do you think, Lizzie?"

"I like that. 'Rebel' he'll stay, my love."

And that was yet another name he was looking forward to hearing often, to living up to.

"Then so be it, my beautiful, courageous, wise, and forgiving Lizzie Morgan."

And that earned him another kiss, even with Conor O'Shannon looking on. But this one landed not on his cheek but on his lips. Where he silently told his Lizzie Morgan exactly what she meant to him.

EPILOGUE

Late September 1920

Evening porch life as Mrs. Josiah Calloway was everything, plus more, that Lizzie had ever dreamed of. Their small starter cabin and pens for their first pigs were on a piece of the vast Double E, not far from the main house. But this was their own land and home, deeded as a wedding gift from Mama and Papa. The new Calloway Ranch.

Josiah waved from down by the livestock he went to check on one last time each night. "I'll be right up, my darling."

Lizzie held his cup of coffee and plate of apple pie aloft. "I'll be waiting."

The supper dishes were done, and when Josiah got to the porch, they'd have the whole evening to sit in the rockers Gus had constructed for them. Just like Mama and Papa would be doing over on their porch. And like Great-grandmother and Great-grandfather had done before them. A family tradition she intended to pass on as well.

Josiah reached the steps, and Lizzie set his coffee and plate on the railing, as she did nightly. Right before Josiah swept her into his arms and kissed her as if he hadn't seen her all day.

"Ah, my sweet Lizzie." He put his hands on her cheeks, grinned, and kissed her again.

Her heart full, she led him to his rocking chair and handed him his cup of coffee and pie, then took her chair. "You know, we'll have a story of adventure to tell our own children someday."

"Are you sure you want to tell them everything?"

"Yes. So they'll know the legacy of the bitterbrush out back of the main house. Maybe we could plant a whole row of them on our side border. What do you think?"

He reached over and tucked a strand of her hair back, caressing her cheek in the process. "I'm for that. Your great-grandmother was a wise woman."

"Wise and godly, just like Mama."

"And like you'll be to our children as well."

Lizzie took his hand and held it as they settled into the quiet of the evening, the sunset blanketing the western sky with pinks and golds and purples as far as she could see. A reminder of God's extravagant blessings and forgiveness.

As far as the west.

THE END

~

*T*urn the page for a sneak peek of *Gathered from the North*, the next book in the Blooms of the Bitterbrush series!

Don't miss the next book in the Blooms of the Bitterbrush series!

Gathered From the North

BOISE, IDAHO
JANUARY 1945

All Beth Calloway had to do was smile. Stretch out her hands, pretend she was happy to hold a baby.

"Thank you for filling in." The Boise Foundling Home director placed a crying infant into Beth's arms. Mrs. Martin's silver-streaked dark bun and black suit matched the solemn occasion. "All of the paperwork is complete, and the Donaldsons will be right out to take Annabelle home. Summon me if you have any questions."

"Yes, Mrs. Martin."

The director turned and headed down the hall, the click of her sturdy-heeled pumps underscoring her departure.

Beth stared at the babe she held. If the Donaldsons had come on time this Monday morning, she'd be at her desk typing, as she was supposed to be doing, not having to hold Annabelle. But now it was feeding time, and all the nurses were busy with the other babies.

Oh, please, can't just one nurse walk by and take her?

Annabelle was so light, so fragile. What if Beth dropped her? She was the last person who should be holding this little one. She touched the infant's face, screwed up in a howl.

"Shh." Beth tightened her hold on the child and shifted from one foot to the other, rocking, the way she'd seen the nurses do. "It'll be all right, Annabelle. You'll have a home now. A mother and father to love and care for you." Beth trailed a finger along Annabelle's cheek. "Always obey them. Make them proud of you." She adjusted the baby. "Do you like music?" She hummed a few measures of a song her mother had sung to her and her siblings, and Annabelle's cries became quieter. "You do like music, don't you? I'll sing it for you."

> *"Little one, look above*
> *to the Lord—for He is love.*
> *And as He watches over you,*
> *with tenderness, He'll gently woo."*

Annabelle stopped crying. She curled a small finger around Beth's larger one. And smiled.

"Oh, Annabelle." Beth leaned down to the baby's soft skin and kissed her cheek. "See? You'll be very happy with your family."

Soft clicking echoed through the hallway as the Donaldsons approached to claim their child. Beth turned to greet them. All she had to do was loosen her grip on their baby, hand her over to her new parents. But Beth drew Annabelle closer, letting the smell of freshly washed baby fill her soul. She'd forgotten the feel of a baby, as she hadn't held one since her sister, Susannah. And that was three years ago since...

"There she is, Edward." Mrs. Donaldson stepped alongside Beth and leaned over, cooing into her baby's face. "You're beautiful, just like your name means—Belle."

Beth touched Annabelle's hair. Would the peach fuzz grow into honeyed ringlets the color of Mrs. Donaldson's? Or turn dark and thick like Mr. Donaldson's?

"Is she all ready for us?" Mrs. Donaldson spread her arms the perfect width to accept Annabelle.

"Yes, she is." Beth trailed her hand along the baby's cheek. Even through typewriter-roughened fingers, she could feel the softness of newborn life. Transferring Annabelle into her mother's care would make one more crib available for another orphan at the Boise Foundling Home. She'd seen how the nurses did it effortlessly. But this was the first occasion she, the secretary, was the one to cradle a smiling bundle and place joy into hearts that would give her a home.

Annabelle was beautiful in the frilly pink store-bought dress the Donaldsons had an employee drop off yesterday to take her home in today. A dress all her own. And the purple velvet collar on the tiny winter coat made her look like royalty.

Her smile in place, Beth handed the little princess to Mrs. Donaldson. "God bless you with this addition to your family."

Mr. Donaldson beamed. "Thank you so much. You've no idea what having Annabelle means to us. Do you have any further instructions for us?" He glanced at the paper Beth had typed up that morning.

Beth reached over and retied the strings of Annabelle's hat. "You have her eating and sleeping schedules, a list of what to feed her. So just love her. Call us if you have any further questions. And be sure to bring her by to visit us sometime." The parting speech she'd heard Mrs. Martin say countless times tumbled out.

Mr. Donaldson shook hands with Beth, tucked his arm through his wife's, and ushered his family out the door. As soon as the door clicked shut, Beth's smile vanished. She stepped to the window and lifted a corner of the drape. Snowflakes smacked the sidewalk as Mr. Donaldson removed his coat and sheltered Annabelle and his wife under it as he shepherded them into their black Packard.

No one else heralded Annabelle's victory in finding a new home, not even the commanding face of Uncle Sam on the nearby recruiting poster. The only passersby who stopped to look were a lady with a long brown coat, a black scarf wound around her head, a market basket in one hand, and a little dark-haired boy, maybe four, reined in on the other. Within moments, the Donaldsons' car pulled away, taking with them a life that Beth would never have. For she was unworthy of being a mother.

"Did you get Annabelle off all right?"

Beth turned at the director's voice behind her and stepped back to her metal desk, the place she belonged.

"Yes, I did. But, please, Mrs. Martin, I'm just a typist. You know I'm not good with the babies." She'd seen that truth in her mother's eyes the last three years. Beth placed a sheet of paper into the typewriter and rolled the platen until the paper stuck out two inches, ready for her keystrokes.

"When we're shorthanded, everyone has to pitch in."

"Yes, Mrs. Martin." Beth clicked away on the keys, feeling the director's eyes on her.

"Beth."

She met her boss's gaze. "Yes?"

"Come with me into the kitchen and have some soup."

"Yes, ma'am." Had she done something wrong? As it wasn't break time for her.

Beth rose and smoothed her apple-green skirt, the one Mama had styled and added pockets to, even during war time. The one that brought pleasure with each step as the gores in the gabardine swished and swirled around her knees. Except there was no joy today as she trailed behind Mrs. Martin down the hall, following the enticing aroma of chicken broth.

As they passed the infant room, Beth shut her ears to the cries of the babies still in the foundling home. Why weren't more people like the Donaldsons lining up to claim each one of these children? By tomorrow, Annabelle's crib would be filled, and they'd be back to looking for homes for twenty-five children again. Some of these babies had been here so long that they were able to eat the chicken soup.

At the kitchen, Mrs. Martin opened the door and held it, allowing Beth to scurry through. "Pearl?"

The gray-haired cook standing over the stove swiped her forehead with her arm.

"May we have two bowls of soup, please? I'll take mine to my office. Beth, you stay and eat here. Enjoy a few minutes of an extra break."

"Yes, ma'am. Thank you." Beth sat at the small table. So maybe she wasn't in trouble, after all?

Cook Pearl ladled the bowls and handed one to Mrs. Martin, who left with a nod to Beth.

"Here you go, Beth." Pearl slid the other bowl to Beth with a smile. "Are you staying after work for Chester's birthday party? Already two. I made a cake for him and the staff. Though it's quite light on the sugar, he still deserves a celebration of his birth."

Oh, the sweet boy certainly did. He was the oldest of the children, but she couldn't get attached to any of them.

"No. I'd best be heading home after work." She gestured toward the window. "All this snow, you know."

"It's sure a doozy of a storm out there." Pearl nodded. "But if you change your mind…"

"Thank you."

Sweet Pearl always included Beth in invitations to gatherings and celebrations but seemed to accept Beth's answer was always going to be no. How could it be anything otherwise, given her history? And there was no point in getting too attached to anyone.

∽

Timothy McPhearson shivered in the wind as he leaned against the rail of the troop transport ship as it lumbered into New York Harbor. Home. Except his future was as empty as the vast ocean now separating him from the fighting in Germany. He tuned out the incessant laughter and talk from other returning soldiers crowding around the railing, all most likely with someone waiting to welcome them home.

Once the ship docked, a private sidled into the now-empty spot beside Timothy, scanning the crowd waving onshore. "You got a girl out there waiting?"

"Me? No." With her arm raised in the midmorning sun, the Statue of Liberty had been the only one welcoming him home.

"I sure hope mine is. When I find her—there she is—Viola!" The man waved his arms furiously, then slapped Timothy on the back. "I hope you find someone like her one day."

Unlikely. But he wished all the best for this guy and the shoving soldiers making their way to their screaming gals.

When the gangway lowered, he slung his duffel bag over his shoulder and joined the other soldiers as they disembarked the ship returning from Germany, some with visible wounds, others with unseen ones. He had both.

People clustered in groups, girls craning their heads,

jumping and yelling when they spotted their sweethearts or brothers. Mothers exuberantly greeted their sons.

He dodged couples kissing just to get to the street. Once he made his way to the apartment of Mr. and Mrs. Jackson, friends of his parents, he'd greet them, then be on his way. More of an aunt and uncle to him, they'd welcomed him into their home after the tenement he lived in had burned, taking his parents and most of the other fifth-floor tenants with it. They'd been his anchor until he was old enough to join the army. So of course, he had to stop and visit before heading to Grandmother's house in Boise. She and Great-aunt Cora up in Sandpoint were the only family he had now.

As soon as he knocked on their door, Auntie Georgette and Uncle Eugene flung it open, and he was engulfed in the Jacksons' arms.

"Timothy. What a joy to see you." Auntie Georgette's hugs were as sweet as his own mother's had been. "Your letter said you'd just be passing through, but we have an early lunch prepared for you. At least stay that long with us?"

"Of course. Thank you so much."

"Then you're heading out to be with your grandmother?"

"Yes. This afternoon, leaving from Grand Central." Hopefully, his letter to Grandmother would arrive before he did.

"Then sit, sit." She ushered him to the table already laden with food. "I'm sure Bea is anxious for your arrival. I imagine she has certainly missed your family living out there for a few years before moving back here to aid your other grandmother when her health declined."

"Both of my grandfathers were gone before I was born, so Mama and Papa made sure their mothers were cared for as they aged."

Auntie Georgette patted Timothy on the shoulder. "Your folks were good people. We miss them, as I know you do."

His throat clogged, so he simply nodded.

SNEAK PEEK: GATHERED FROM THE NORTH

"Let's ask the Lord's blessing on our meal and Timothy's travels, then we can eat as he catches us up." Uncle Eugene reached out, and Auntie Georgette and Timothy completed his circle of prayer as they joined hands.

After the amen, Auntie Georgette passed a platter of sandwiches. "I'm sure there are many things you don't wish to speak of, but can you tell us about your discharge? Medical, was it?"

His discharge. Not exactly medical, with the stigma of *Combat Fatigue* inked across his record. Now he was deemed unfit to even scrub the floor of an overseas hospital. Sent home to—what? Recover?

But battle fatigue had nothing to do with his actions when he'd sat up in that hospital bed and heard the truth—or lack of it—from the private in the next bed. His shaking hands, tears so close to spilling out, "overreacting," and his attack on PFC Roland Johnston, trying to choke the answers out of him, weren't symptoms of combat fatigue or anything else the army wanted to call it.

They were the actions of a man wanting the truth. And he'd get it from the soldier he'd vowed to track down after this war was over—Roland Johnston, the man who was there when Timothy's best friend, Stanley Tomaszewski, was killed. The man who knew what had happened in that moment Stanley was shot.

"My buddy Stanley and I were advance scouts on a mission. There was gunfire, and in the process, the door of the abandoned apartment building we were in splintered, and a piece landed in my eye. While the surgery was deemed successful, my eye just needs time to heal." Probably he should still be wearing the patch the doc had recommended. "The vision is returning, even the pain is decreasing, but the surgeon said the main thing to watch out for is irritants, especially smoke."

"Then you will follow his advice, yes?" Auntie Georgette gave him a firm nod.

"Yes, I will."

They chatted a while, then Timothy stood. "I need to head on over to Grand Central to catch my train. It sure was good seeing you both."

Auntie Georgette wiped tears from her eyes, then clasped Timothy into a hug. "We're so glad you stopped to see us. May God's grace walk with you."

"Thank you, Auntie."

She loosened her grip but reached for his hands. "Do you remember those words?"

"That's what Mama used to say."

"She did. That was her prayer for everyone she met, but especially for you. Never forget them."

"I promise, I won't."

He exchanged an embrace with Uncle Eugene, then headed to Grand Central to catch the 20th Century Limited. By the time he reached Boise, he hoped to have a plan in place to track down Roland Johnston. And this time, combat fatigue or not, he aimed to get the truth—one way or another.

Did you enjoy this book? We hope so!
Would you take a quick minute to leave a review where you purchased the book?
It doesn't have to be long. Just a sentence or two telling what you liked about the story!

Receive a FREE ebook and get updates when new Wild Heart books release: https://wildheartbooks.org/newsletter.

AUTHOR'S NOTE

Dear Reader,

Thank you for continuing this generational journey in the Blooms of the Bitterbrush series. I hope that Lizzie and Josiah's story has encouraged or touched you in some way as they struggled with forgiveness.

I invite you to join in the continuing legacy of the family in *Gathered from the North*, where you'll meet Lizzie's daughter, Beth, and Mrs. McPhearson's grandson, Timothy. And, of course, Elizabeth Roberts's legacy of the bitterbrush plant still stands as a reminder of God's goodness and faithfulness through the generations.

May you, too, cling to His faithfulness.

Barbara

ACKNOWLEDGMENTS

Many thanks go to those who have had a hand in this story and who have prayed. To each one, thank you.

I'd also like to extend a special thank you to Denise Farnsworth for her wonderful editing and questions.

And to Danielle Rafoss—thank you so very much for setting up my website and Facebook author page—and for your tenacity in solving the technical problems!

For each one who had a part in the book along the way—the many who offered encouragement, prayers, research help, and marketing aid—from my heart—thank you!

Want more?

If you love historical romance, check out the other Wild Heart books!

The Rancher's Unexpected Bride

In the rugged Montana Territory, a Boston socialite's bid for freedom collides with a rancher's quest for a family.

According to Boston's elite society, Ella Mountbatten has it all: status, prestige, and a bright future. What they don't know is that her life as a socialite has become a gilded cage of abuse and oppression under the control of her cruel fiancé and domineering parents. Desperate to escape, Ella flees Boston and seeks refuge in the small town of Harmony Springs, Montana

Territory, where her former friend now resides as the sheriff. But with her family determined to drag her back to Boston, Ella's hard-won freedom—and her very life—hang precariously in the balance.

Rancher, Cody Brooks, is ill-equipped to be the guardian of three orphaned children. But that's the situation he's in after the death of his best friend. Now, what he needs is a wife to help provide love and stability to his makeshift family. So when a runaway heiress arrives in need of protection, it seems a marriage of convenience may be the answer to both their prayers.

But with danger closing in from Boston and the challenges of building a new life together, Cody and Ella must confront their deepest fears and desires. Can their marriage of convenience blossom into true love, or will the shadows of Ella's past tear apart the fragile hope they've found in Harmony Springs?

The Bandit's Redemption

A holdup gone wrong, a reluctant outlaw, and the captive she's sworn to guard.

Life in the American West hasn't been easy for French refugee Lorraine Durand. She has precious few connections and longs to return to her native land. So when the man who rescued her from a Parisian uprising following the Franco-Prussian War persuades her to help him with a deadly holdup, she reluctantly agrees. Despite his promises otherwise, the gang kidnaps a man, forcing Lorraine to grapple with the fallout of her choices even as she is drawn to the captive she's meant to guard.

Jesse Alexander must survive. If not for himself, then for the troubled sister he left behind in Los Angeles. At the mercy of his captors, he carefully works to earn Lorraine's trust, hoping he can easily subdue her when the time comes. But as they navigate the treacherous wilderness and he searches for his opportunity to escape, he realizes there may be more to her than he first believed.

∽

Murmur in the Mud Caves by Kathleen Denly

He came to cook for ranch hands, not three single women.

Gideon Swift, a visually impaired Civil War Veteran, responds to an ad for a ranch cook in the Southern California desert mountains. He wants nothing more than to forget his past and stay in the kitchen where he can do no harm. But when he arrives to find his employer murdered, the ranch turned to ashes, and three young women struggling to survive in the unforgiving Borrego Desert, he must decide whether his presence protects them or places them in greater danger.

Bridget "Biddie" Davidson finally receives word from her older sister who disappeared with their brother and pa eighteen years prior, but the news is not good. Determined to help her family, Biddie sets out for a remote desert ranch with her adopted father and best friend. Nothing she finds there is as she expected, including the man who came to cook for the shambles of a ranch.

When tragedy strikes, the danger threatens not only her plans to help her sister, but her own dreams for the future—with the man who's stolen her heart.